The Third Key of Kalijor by: Paul Lell
© 2011 Paul Lell
Cover art by: David Magoun (Full Spectrum Arts & Services)
© 2011 David Magoun
Editing/Proofreading: Christina Lell, Paul Lell, Josh Pressnell,
Diana Pressnell, David Magoun, and Michael Ethridge
ISBN 978-0-578-08155-7

For more information,
 See the author's website at
www.kalijor.com
or the artist's website at
www.fullspectrumarts.com

Dedicated to my friends, my family, and my fans (the simple thought that I actually have fans is more than a little humbling). I can only do what I do, because you are all here to support me.

Special Thanks: To David and Taeva. The two of you, and your support groups, keep the energy high, the motivation strong, and the job worth doing.

-1-

A hail of bullets slipped past Riana's lithe form as she dove behind the metallic cargo crate, rolling into a crouching position with her bull-pup machine gun held at the ready and her back to the crate. Glancing at the translucent casing of the magazine on top of her weapon, the computers in her brain told her she had twenty one rounds left to expend.

"How're we doing?" she said calmly into her comm link.

"Everything is moving along swimmingly." Willhelmina's voice replied silkily. "Another five minutes should do it."

"Five minutes. Right. No problem, take your time," Riana's voice dripped sarcasm as she looked around to see what she could use to keep her attackers occupied for a while longer. Finally, she planted her heavy boots on the floor, set her shoulders against the pressurized shipping crate and pushed with her legs.

It took a moment, but eventually the bottom edge of the crate came up off the floor and she redoubled her efforts, extending her legs and bringing her cybernetic strength fully to bear. Bullets continued to ricochet off the crate and the nearby wall until the ten-ton box finally toppled over.

Instantly, the room was filled with the sound of a metal-on-metal crash, followed by the groaning of the floor and its support structure being bent and distended by the sudden impact of the immense weight. The room shook and light fixtures broke away from the ceiling, causing the lighting to change and throw strange, jagged shadows across the crowded space. Several smaller crates in the area also toppled over, only adding to the cacophony, but the constant gunfire came to an abrupt stop as the armor-clad soldiers scattered.

Whipping around with the butt of her weapon pressed snugly into her shoulder, Riana picked out a couple of the soldiers and squeezed off a short burst at each, the bull-pup machine gun pressing into her shoulder with each burst. The brief hail of armor-piercing slugs tore up her selected targets, driving them violently to the ground where they twitched for a moment before shuddering to stillness.

Satisfied that she had succeeded in keeping them occupied for a few more minutes, she stripped a concussion grenade from her combat webbing and tossed it into the center of the room before dashing out of the blast radius and crouching behind another crate. Absently, she brushed a lock of royal purple hair out of her face as she stripped the spent magazine from the top of her rifle, slipping it into an empty pouch and extracting another.

The loud thump of the explosion washed over the room, knocking out the rest of the light fixtures in the area and bathing the scene of the battle with deep, foreboding shadows. The sound of boots scurrying and shuffling around came to her long, pointed ears as she casually set the fresh magazine on top of her weapon and slapped it down on top of the receiver, locking it into place.

Looking over her shoulder into the shadows, she shifted her vision into the ultraviolet spectrum. Tapping her headset, she activated the UV light that was mounted next to the camera at her temple, causing the room to fall into stark relief as she scanned around for signs of her opponents.

Catching sight of someone dashing out of the center of the blast radius, she took aim and cut loose a short burst. Her weapon belched fire as she cut the soldier down and then rolled back behind the crate as return fire homed in on her muzzle flash. Spinning toward the other edge of the crate, she peeked around the container, leveling her rifle and squeezing off another short burst. Her target fell to the ground clutching his stomach.

Her long, tapered ears dropped down low as she focused on the sound of footsteps creeping up behind her, getting a fix on the person's location. When she heard the click of a trigger being pulled, she uncoiled her legs from beneath her, launching herself into the air as a stream of projectiles passed through the space where she had just been crouched. Throwing her legs over her head, she wheeled around in mid-air, grabbing the surprised soldier by the shoulder straps of his combat webbing. As her feet came back to the ground, she bent over forward, hauling the man off his feet and launching him bodily out from behind the crate. The panicked soldier crashed like a discarded rag doll into a pile of smaller containers twenty feet away, sending the metal boxes scattering in every direction. He then slumped down to the ground, motionless.

The clamor of the event distracted the rest of them further, allowing Riana to pick off two more as she rolled behind another crate and quickly checked her magazine again.

"Are we done yet?" she asked calmly into her comm link as she looked carefully around the edge of her cover.

"Two more minutes," Willhelmina's voice panted back. It sounded like she was in the middle of running a marathon.

"Having trouble?" Riana smiled as she taunted her sister.

"No," Willhelmina replied breathily. "No trouble. Just ten or twelve armed people who don't seem to want me leaving with this thing."

Riana's smile faded a bit as the thought of her best friend, her sister, being chased down by an armed lynch mob raced through her head. "Where are you? I can…"

Willhelmina cut her off, knowing full well what she was thinking of doing. "Stick to the plan Ree. I'm fine. I'll be ready in two minutes."

"Fine," Riana growled into the comm link. "Two minutes. Mark." She tapped the small computer on her wrist and a two minute count-down began on its tiny holographic display. A few seconds ticked off before the display went dark in order to keep her position secure. She didn't need the wrist computer. Her brain was more than half computer as it was. But something about using the device, just like everyone else, helped her feel in some way... normal.

"Mark." Willhelmina echoed through the comm link.

Poking her head out from behind cover again, Riana's ears twitched and she yanked herself back behind the crate as a storm of bullets converged on her position.

"Took them long enough," she mumbled to herself as she detached a smooth metal disk from the combat webbing at her hip and attached it to the crate with a dull 'thunk' noise. Springing lightly up on top of the ten foot high crate, she picked off two more of the soldiers, who were taken completely by surprise at her shift to higher ground. She then dove across twenty feet of open air onto another stack of crates, slipping quietly behind some smaller boxes.

Removing an identical metal disk from her other hip, she attached it to one of the small crates, then stripped off another grenade and tossed it back toward the soldiers as she leapt across another huge gap. Several sprays of gun fire followed her as she arced through the air, and she felt several projectiles tear through the shimmering fabric of her long, fitted duster. The flowing garment did its job, obscuring her form and causing the bullets to miss the reactive armor covering her body like a second skin.

Skidding to a stop behind cover, she braced her sensitive ears, clenching her jaw just as the concussion grenade exploded with a loud thump that rattled the entire room again. This time, she removed a slightly smaller metal disk from the outside of one of her knees and attached it to one of the crates she was using for cover, then jumped down to the floor and made her way to the other side of the room.

The group of soldiers was obviously falling apart. She passed within a foot of a pair of them and they didn't so much as twitch at her passing, focusing instead on the area in the center of the warehouse where all of the action had been thus far. She could have easily dispatched them both, and all of their comrades as well, given enough time, but she hated the thought of killing people unnecessarily. She preferred to just do her job and go home.

As she approached the door to the room, she clicked the disk off of the outside of her other knee and attached it to a nearby crate. Tapping her wrist computer, she conjured up the holographic display and its steady countdown. One minute and thirty seconds remained. She sighed heavily as she eyed the door, then focused her attention back toward the soldiers in the center of the room. Concentrating on the sounds in the room she could hear four… no, five of them moving around the area, searching for her and trying not to cut one another down in the process. Apparently, she had them pretty riled up.

Glancing at her computer display again, it read one minute and four seconds. She eyed it as it counted down and when it hit fifty nine seconds she turned her head to the side and shouted into the room, "You have sixty seconds to get out of here, otherwise you will be leaving in a refuse bin when they clean up the mess."

Then, she dashed for the door and slid calmly out into the adjoining hallway. She let her bull-pup fall back to its resting place between her right arm and body, allowing it to be concealed by the shimmering fabric of her jacket.

She didn't look much like the normal employees in the area, but she knew she stood a better chance of moving unhindered if she didn't appear to be bristling with weaponry so she tugged the duster closed and moved off into the corridor. As she rounded the fourth corner between the storage room and the airlock where the Kestrel was docked, she glanced down at her wrist in time to see the counter reach zero. She braced herself as a massive explosion rocked the entire station, before dashing, full speed, toward the airlock.

-2-

The Kestrel hurtled away from the small space station at maximum throttle. The ion drives screamed in protest as Riana leaned on the throttle, trying to coax more out of the straining engines than they seemed wiling to give.

"You're going to break something, Ree," Willhelmina commented as she stepped into the cockpit from the staging area. She had dashed into the ship from the wounded station and Riana had cycled the airlock closed and bolted away from the facility as soon as she'd confirmed that Willhelmina was aboard.

Willhelmina had quickly pulled off her weapons and stowed them in the staging area and was now sliding into her seat. Her long, raven hair was pulled into a tight braid that hung to the middle of her back and her bright, green eyes inspected Riana suspiciously. Her athletic form fit the contours of the acceleration seat perfectly as she pulled the harness closed across her body.

"I want to put as much distance between us and them as I can. There's been enough death and destruction for the day." Riana replied with a sour look on her face. Her own dark purple hair was pulled back into a ponytail that dangled down to the small of her back and her normally bright, violet eyes were dark and brooding. Her long, tapered, elven ears were swept back from her head, displaying a level of annoyance that seemed to be increasingly, and disturbingly, normal these days.

Willhelmina continued to watch Riana for a moment, then sighed heavily as she produced a small data crystal from one of her belt pouches. She looked at it for a moment before slipping it into the protective metallic carrying case and snapping the container shut, sealing the thing inside.

"What's bugging you, Ree?" she asked as she smoothed some errant strands of her long, raven hair out of her face and secured it to the mass behind her head.

"Nothing." Riana lied, keeping her violet eyes focused on the control panel to try and conceal the deception. But her long, tapered ears splayed out from her head, revealing her distaste for the situation and foiling her attempt at avoiding the conversation.

Willhelmina nodded at her friend. "Right. Nothing." Her emerald eyes glared at Riana knowingly. Even without her elven ears to betray her emotions, Willhelmina had spent far too many years with her purple-haired friend to be fooled.

"I just keep wondering why we are doing this Kat. We aren't couriers. We are some kind of special operations death squad or something. Running around and scooping up Xavier's treasures and laying waste to anyone who gets in the way."

Willhelmina sighed again as she poked idly at a few controls on the panel in front of her. "Ree this disc contains all of the source code for Kalijor. If anyone was to get hold of this they would be able to use it to figure out how Kalijor works and exploit any weaknesses in the system."

Riana backed off the throttle a touch and instantly the engines sounded less like they were winding up to an explosion. Jabbing her index finger at the autopilot button, she spun her chair around to face her sister. "I understand that Kat, but it still doesn't feel right. I mean how many people have to die? Will he ever be satisfied?"

Willhelmina turned to face Riana, folding her arms under her breasts and screwing up her face. "Ree, he may be cold, but he is not evil. He is trying to protect Kalijor, which is something I would think you, of all people, could appreciate."

"I'm not sure of anything any more Kat. All I really know is that we are buzzing around the solar system at Xavier's whim, breaking into places we shouldn't be, to get things he says he has lost. I mean, he looses more stuff than anyone I have ever met before in my life! And why is it that every time we find whatever it is, it is inevitably surrounded by legions of armed soldiers?"

"This is a cut-throat business Ree. And Solidarity has a corner on the market. They have for over one-hundred years now, and the competition gets tired of playing second fiddle."

Riana raised an eyebrow at Willhelmina. "How can the Conglomerate allow this sort of activity? Shouldn't they be protecting Kalijor since it is used as the medium for most electronic meetings and transfers? I would think it would be in their best interests to keep it functioning properly."

Willhelmina shook her head, relaxing her arms a bit. "No, they don't care. Even though Solidarity Online is ruling the field, there are others playing the game. The Conglomerate can use any of them just as easily, so they don't really care who is running it."

"So they are going to let us kill each other over it regardless," Riana huffed, folding her own arms across her chest and slumping down into the acceleration seat a bit.

"They have a Darwinist philosophy about it, Ree. The system that is best fit to fill the void will be the one to survive. While some of what we do may be distasteful, it is necessary to keep Kalijor running, and we need to keep Kalijor running in order to keep Ezrina alive and figure out what is going on in there."

Riana narrowed her eyes as she stared at some point on the wall over Willhelmina's right shoulder. Her ears drooped down low in disgust at the situation. "Maybe. But I don't have to like it," she finally acquiesced as she turned back toward the controls and sat up in her chair.

"Twenty hours to The Tyconderoga. You want to have a bite to eat?" She spun her chair fully around and stood up as she spoke, moving into the staging area and finally setting about stowing her own artillery in the various racks and bins.

"Sure," Willhelmina said as she unbuckled herself from her seat and moved into the area, squeezing between Riana and the bulkhead, on her way toward the tiny galley. Pulling a compartment open, she peered inside at the rows of foil-wrapped packages stacked up neatly in the various compartments, all labeled nicely so that they were easily identifiable by contents. "So, what'll it be?"

Riana leaned over, peering past Willhelmina's shoulder at the myriad of packets as she continued to unbuckle her combat webbing. "Um… Banana and beef," she said as she straightened up again and stepped out of the combat webbing. She then set about inspecting the various straps and buckles for signs of wear or damage as Willhelmina stared at her incredulously. After a few silent seconds she looked up into her friend's disbelieving face. "What?"

"I didn't think anyone actually ate that stuff," Willhelmina finally said, still staring at Riana oddly.

"I like it," Riana said dismissively as she stowed her webbing on the hanger and turned back toward the kitchenette in time to receive the small foil packet. Tearing the top of the packet off with her teeth, Riana spit the waste into a receptacle in the wall and squeezed the base of the packet. A candy-bar sized chunk of dehydrated foodstuff slid up out of the packet and she bit off a chunk, chewing it thoughtfully as she stared at the weapon rack.

"Something else on your mind?" Willhelmina asked as she opened her own packet.

"I was thinking about catching the next Resonance show. She's supposed to be on Earth Station next week," Riana said around a mouth-full of banana-flavored dehydrated beef.

"You think she'll actually be there? Or will she be broadcasting there from somewhere else?" Willhelmina eyed her food suspiciously before taking another bite.

"She'll be there," Riana said definitively, nodding to her dinner as if to reinforce her hope.

"And the visit wouldn't have anything to do with a certain Captain would it?" Willhelmina grinned knowingly at her sister.

"Maybe…" Riana cast her gaze on the floor, ears splaying out and flushing red. "We haven't had a chance to get together in a couple of months now. I miss him."

"I bet you do!" Willhelmina grinned knowingly.

"It's not like that Kat." Riana looked at her sister out the tops of her eyes.

"Well if it isn't, then it should be." Willhelmina grinned even wider as she returned to her meal.

-3-

It felt strange to be almost completely unarmed. Riana wandered through one of the massive promenades in Xaman-Otoch, the North Pole section of the Earth Ring Station, as she made her way toward Vincent's apartment. Willhelmina had decided to go back to Tranquility on the moon rather than come with Riana. She wanted to see if she could reestablish some of her childhood friendships since Xavier had been kind enough to grant them both a week's leave from duties. Riana had offered to fly her sister to Tranquility but Willhelmina had insisted that she use public transportation so that Riana could go straight to Earth Station. She had told her to maximize her time off since she had yet to really explore the world on her own.

She had stopped more than twenty times now in various shops and stores along the way from the Kestrel's hangar on the ring. It seemed that the pay for being a courier for Solidarity Online was definitely something out of the ordinary.

She hadn't really been watching her account but over the course of a couple of years she had managed to accumulate millions of credits, and this was the first opportunity she had actually had to spend any of it.

Thus far, she had acquired several new outfits, numerous pairs of shoes, various accessories in the form of necklaces, bracelets, anklets, and a myriad of decorative hair clips and fasteners. She hadn't had so much fun shopping for clothes since her last big spree in the Rathalon Bazaar years ago, and worlds away, and her only wish was that her sister could be there to help her through the selection process.

Throughout the experience, she had to keep shifting her monowire sword around as she changed garments in order to keep the shopkeepers from noticing it. She wasn't sure if it was the sort of thing that would cause her trouble or not but she saw no reason to take chances with it. Her day would have been much smoother if she had left it onboard the Kestrel, but the last time she had come to Earth Station she had ended up being chased halfway around this promenade by a mass of armored soldiers with automatic weapons. She was not about to be caught unarmed on the off chance that someone recognized her.

Slowly, due to the numerous stops as opposed to any real traffic issues or obstructions, she made her way out of the promenade and into the housing area where Vincent lived. She hadn't called him before coming to the station. Rather, she had used her connections through SO to verify that his ship, the Neophyte Serendipity, was still secured in its berth and he had not left the station through any monitored points. This meant that she could be about ninety percent sure of the fact that he was here somewhere. At this point, she had but to find him.

Her last stop had been at a small grocery store where she picked up some fresh produce and some other essentials that she intended to use to reproduce one of the more interesting meals she had eaten while aboard The Tyconderoga. She had never actually prepared the dish before, but she had tasted the flavor and researched the preparation of several varieties of the dish on the net. The computer imbedded in her skull insured that she recalled every step, ingredient, and flavor perfectly and she had no doubt at all that she would be able to replicate the dish.

Moments later she arrived at Vincent's door, laden with the fruits of her afternoon shopping extravaganza. With no effort at all, she raised an arm-full of fully loaded bags and pressed the call button on Vincent's door. The tone rang out clearly inside the apartment and almost immediately afterward she heard the sound of two people approaching the other side of the door.

The panel slid quietly into the wall and Riana's heart leapt at the sight of Vincent standing in front of her. His long blond hair was pulled back into a lose tail at the nape of his neck and his tall, athletic body filled the doorway as he took an instant to recognize the person standing on the other side.

"Riana!" he shouted exuberantly, throwing his arms out wide and stepping into the hallway to embrace her.

She wrapped her arms around him and squeezed him as tightly as she thought his body could handle, leaning into him heavily, and still managing to keep hold of all her shopping. When she placed her chin on his shoulder, she saw the other person standing behind him. She was a gorgeous, statuesque blonde woman, wearing a smart, classy outfit that revealed most of her lower legs, her arms up to the shoulders and just enough of her chest to provide a tantalizing view of her impressive cleavage. She stood there with one arm around her waist and the other holding the collar of her jacket that was tossed casually over her shoulder.

Riana's heart sank. In a flash, she went from being elated to feeling like a bug crushed under someone's heel. She shrunk out of Vincent's embrace, ears drooping down low and shoulders sagging.

"Well I had better get going, Vin. I'll see you next time I get leave," the mystery woman said as she moved past Vincent, kissing him on the cheek as she slid by and then striding confidently down the hallway, calling over her shoulder, "Have fun hon."

Riana narrowed her eyes at the woman's back, her ears pointing back in annoyance and briefly, she considered what might happen if she were to lob one of the fresh melons she had purchased at the back of the woman's head. Her line of thought was interrupted by Vincent's voice.

"Ree? Are you alright?"Turning back toward him, her inexplicable malice toward the other woman softened a bit as she saw his concerned expression.

"Uh." She glanced back down the hall in time to see the other woman turn a corner and disappear from sight. Turning back toward Vincent once more, she smiled somewhat weakly. "Yeah. I'll be okay."

Vincent made a strange face at her, then stepped aside and, placing one hand on her shoulder, made a grandiose movement with his other, inviting her into his home. "Please, come in. It's certainly a surprise to see you here. A very welcome surprise I might add."

She made her way into his living room and set her bags down on the coffee table. Turning around to face him, her ears and shoulders drooping almost comically. Finally her emotions got the better of her. "Vin, I'll understand if you don't... I mean, if you and I..."

Vincent looked at her quizzically for a moment before understanding finally spread across his face. "What? Her? Oh lord. Riana that was a client. She needs some cargo hauled out to Titan next week and was just here making arrangements for the pick-up and payment. You didn't think that she and I..."

"No!" Riana almost shouted, suddenly feeling like she should be crawling under the couch. "That is I... Well I know I stopped by unannounced and all, but I thought... you know... I mean I know we aren't like, married or anything, but I did think that we had something, and when I saw her I..."

Vincent cut her off with a wide grin on his face, "You thought she and I were what? Hooking up? Riana I would never do that to you."

"Well I wouldn't blame you, it isn't as if I'm a regular girl." She plopped down on the couch, which groaned loudly in protest of her deceptively heavy, cybernetic frame. Her dark purple hair cascaded around her shoulders, framing her face against the white wall behind her.

Vincent's face clouded for a moment before turning into a warm smile. Slowly he moved to the couch and sat down next to her, taking her hand in his and squeezing it tightly. "Riana, I would never do anything to hurt you. I know we haven't had as much time together as we would like, but I have not been with anyone else since we first met in Kalijor, and I would not," he paused for a moment to emphasize his point, "be, with anyone else as long as we are seeing each other."

Riana squeezed his hand in response and smiled weakly. "Thank you. I'm sorry I just…"

Vincent stopped her by shaking his head. "Don't apologize Riana. These feelings are normal. Your origins may be a bit irregular, but your reaction is as human as it could possibly be."

Riana leaned into him, wrapping her arms around him once more. "Thank you Vincent."

"Think nothing of it. Now, to what do I owe the pleasure of this surprise visit?"

Her mood brightened instantly as she sat up straight, beaming at him happily. "I got some time off to come and see my… that is, to see Resonance. I thought I could come see you while I was here. I went shopping and found all of this great stuff, and I even bought some things to make dinner with."

She was up rummaging through her bags happily, offering him brief glimpses of several different articles of clothing and other trinkets. Finally she held up a dead chicken by its legs and grinned broadly at Vincent. "That is, if you aren't doing anything. I don't want to intrude. I mean, I kind of do want to intrude, but not really if you have something else going on. Is there a place nearby that I can stay for the week?"

Vincent laughed as she continued rambling on and rummaging through her bags. Finally, he stood up, took the chicken from her, and made his way to the kitchen with it. Setting it gently in the sink, he turned back to her. "It's okay Riana. You can stay here with me, and I am excited that you are here. You are welcome in my home any time."

He made his way back to her as he spoke, wrapping his arms around her waist and pulling her athletic form up against his. Looking down into her violet eyes as he moved closer and closer to her lips, he spoke softly. "Of course, I will be a perfect gentleman. I have a spare bedroom you can use."

Riana's eyes glinted as he drew closer to her. She felt a strange, tingling rush run through her body as his breath washed across her lips. "And who said I want to room with a gentleman?"

-4-

"So, you've never prepared that dish before?" Vincent asked as they moved across the promenade hand-in-hand.

Riana shook her head. "No. In fact I haven't cooked anything else before, except for meal packs and cans of stew. Not in this world anyway."

"Huh." Vincent looked at her in amazement for a moment, then shrugged and pointed toward the door they were heading for. "This is our stop here."

Riana followed his gesture toward the open door, squeezing past the small stream of people moving in and out of the fitness center, which bore a large sign proclaiming that no better sparring rings could be found anywhere nearby. She still wasn't sure why so many people in this world were so obsessed with fighting.

"Well it was phenomenal."

"What?" Riana spun around to look at him, startled out of her musing.

He looked at her with a smile. "Your cooking. It was phenomenal."

"Oh. Thank you." She watched him with interest for a moment before he pointed behind her. "What?"

"We're blocking the doorway," he grinned.

"Oh. Sorry." Her ears swept back and flushed as she turned around and moved through the doorway into the structure.

The inside of the building was strangely familiar to her. It was a large gymnasium with a swimming pool, a myriad of weight training stations and equipment, numerous stationary bikes, and other motion machines. Several small sparring rings, about half of which were occupied by pairs of people, were surrounded by small crowds of cheering fans. Suddenly she felt as though she were back aboard The Tyconderoga again.

"Refresh my memory Vin. Why are we here again?" She readjusted the duffle bag on her shoulder as they stepped into the interior of the gym.

"Because I need a workout, and I would never miss an opportunity to see you in something skin-tight."

She looked at him with feigned indignation. "I would have thought you'd gotten enough of a workout last night. And how is skin-tight better than... you know... skin?"

He grinned at her again as he pulled her up against him, wrapping his free arm around her waist. "Now you know as well as I that that is a loaded question Miss Thorindal. I will not be so easily defeated."

She narrowed her eyes at him, ears sweeping back sharply away from her head. "Alright then mister. I guess I'll just have to see to it that you get the workout of your life." She placed her open palm on his chest, almost seductively, then pushed him away and spun around on her heels, headed for the women's locker room.

A few minutes later, they were facing one another in the center of one of the previously vacant rings. Each of them had their hair pulled back into a tail at the back of their heads. They bowed to one another and then Vincent stepped back into a fighting stance. Riana stood there with her arms at her sides, watching him attentively.

"You really should get ready, I won't hesitate just because I like you." He flexed his fingers a few times before curling his hands into fists.

"Don't worry about me buster. You've got an ass kicking headed your way."

"Fair enough. Although I have never been one to take advantage of a lady." He quickly stepped in and launched a probing attack, which she calmly sidestepped, backing away from him deftly.

"Nice move," he quipped, spinning around with a back fist aimed at her jaw. She ducked under his attack and stepped into his abdomen with her shoulder, lifting him bodily off the ground. Snatching his ankles out of the air and yanking on them, he spun in mid-air, then she drove him into the floor with a loud thud.

Standing up straight again, she stepped away from him as he kipped back up to his feet. "Wow," he said.

Riana nodded at him, still standing in her neutral stance.

Vincent stepped in with a series of kicks aimed at her head and chest. As she stepped to the side, he readjusted his kicking sequence and narrowly missed her temple, but his foot was deflected by a deft swat from her left hand. Trying to retract his leg, he realized that she still had a grip on his ankle.

Before she could lock his leg he jumped into the air, swinging his free leg around in a wide arc, aiming his instep toward her temple. Riana ducked her head under the attack, twisting his other leg around and driving him into the ground again. This time he wasted no time. Launching himself up at her, feet first, the moment his shoulders hit the mat, his body moved toward her with an impressive amount of force and despite the suddenness of the movement, she managed to step to one side and drive an elbow into his side.

He hit the floor with a thud and rolled away from her, spinning up to his feet and facing her again. She stood passively a few feet away, watching him calmly.

"Wow," he said again, a tone of awe in his voice. "How long have you been doing this?"

"Officially?" A small smile began to creep across her lips. "Nearly two years."

"Have you been classified yet?"

"Almost immediately. Remember, I'm an experiment," there was venom in her voice now, her ears swept back and her eyes narrowed.

"Sorry, I was just curious," there was a genuine note of apology in his voice.

"It's alright. I know you didn't mean anything by it. My instructor says I have a particular gift for the arts. He has registered me as a class 2 hand to hand combatant."

"Class 2. That's about what I would have guessed. You're very good," he replied with a smile.

"Thank you. I work very hard at it."

"It shows. I'm more of a guns guy myself. I try and keep this stuff on ice as a last resort option. I've never really been fantastic at it.

Riana grinned at him. "You don't give yourself nearly enough credit. You would be a really good match for Kat."

"But not for you, huh?" he smiled.

"I'm sorry." Riana frowned, afraid she had said something wrong. "I have a tendency to say things that people don't like to hear."

"Don't worry about it. It's actually kind of refreshing. Most people will tell you what they think you want to hear."

They continued to circle around one another as they spoke, occasionally engaging back and forth with a few kicks or punches. After a few minutes, Vincent stepped in with what looked like a punch, but when Riana made to step aside, he shifted his weight and wrapped his arm around her waist, twisting his stance and driving her to the mat with a loud thunk. Instantly he was on top of her, pinning her feet and thighs to the mat with his own and then pinning her arms at the elbows.

She made movements as though she were struggling against him but did not manage to pull free. He grinned widely at her. "Got you right where I want you."

He leaned down toward her and placed a few gentle kisses on her lips. She responded in kind, answering his kisses with her own. When he stopped she grinned at him.

"What is that for?" he asked.

"Because you are confused, you don't have me where you want me. You have me where I ~want~ to be."

"It looks a little different from my perspective." He grinned wider.

Suddenly Riana rolled over, slamming him into the mat and effectively incapacitating him with only three of her limbs. With her free hand she tweaked his nose back and forth as she spoke to him. "Do not underestimate me, Mr. Torres. I will not be toyed with."

He moved back and forth beneath her, as much as his position would allow, but it wasn't much to speak of. He knew she had him. "So it would seem," he finally confessed, his muscles going slack beneath her.

"Now that's more like it," she cooed as she leaned down further, pressing her body against his. As she was about to kiss him, she saw something out of the corner of her eye that made her look up. At the door of the gym was a familiar figure. A tall, thin man with wispy silver-grey hair, wearing grimy denim overalls over a dirty white T-shirt. His back was to her so she couldn't see his face and he quickly disappeared through the door, preventing a positive identification.

In a flash Riana was on her feet, vaulting over the ropes of the ring they were in. In three steps, she was at the door of the gym pressing her way through the crowd. When she finally forced her way through to the promenade outside, she spun around looking for the person, but could not find any sign of him.

When Vincent finally caught up to her, he was winded and looked extremely concerned. "What's the matter?"

Riana kept looking around frantically, trying to find some sign of the person. "What?" she asked absently.

He stepped in front of her and grabbed her shoulders, squeezing them gently and looking into her eyes. Finally, she stopped looking from place to place and focused her eyes on his. "I said, are you alright?"

"Yes. I'm sorry. I thought I saw... someone..." Her shoulders and ears both sagged.

"I am guessing this wasn't a long lost relative..."

"No," she said simply, "He isn't."

"You're kidding! Gregory Shantal?!" Vincent looked at her as though he expected her to call out 'April Fool's' at any moment.

"Yes. Gregory Shantal," Riana echoed as she poked through the produce on the stand.

"The Gregory Shantal? The mercenary that's, like, a hundred years in the business?" Vincent's tone was disbelieving as she handed him a bunch of fresh carrots.

"You make it sound as though he is some sort of legend." She eyed him suspiciously for a moment before grabbing a basket full of purple onions. "You sound like the president of his fan club or something."

"Well," Vincent paused a moment as he pointed to one of the onions. "Check that one, it looks really good." He continued, fiddling with the carrots, "Anyway, he sort of is a legend I guess. I mean, you don't go a hundred years in the mercenary business without people talking, you know?"

Riana picked up the onion and smelled it. Frowning at it, she set it back in the basket saying, "It's past ripe." As she selected another, she responded to his implied question. "I suppose you're right, but I'm telling you he's an ass. Just the sight of him makes me want to hurt him, badly. He's an egotist, megalomaniacal, and has a terrible inferiority complex." She set the onion in the basket that Vincent was toting around. "This one's perfect."

"I don't doubt any of that to be honest with you, but most people have never seen this guy, let alone seen him fight. And here you are telling me that you beat him pretty soundly."

"Sure, the first and last times we met. But that second bout was pretty damn embarrassing."

"Three times?!" He nearly dropped the basket.

Riana looked at him like he was some sort of insect she was about to swat.

"I'm sorry, Ree, it's just… cool, I guess."

"Not from where I'm standing it isn't. Where are the shallots?" She turned around to scan the rest of the produce.

"What the hell is a shallot? And what are you making anyway?"

"This is a shallot." She beamed as she picked up the vegetable and waved it under his nose. "And I am making that duck dish I had when we went out to eat the last time I was here." She set a bundle of shallots in the basket along with the rest of the produce.

"That was months ago. Where did you find the recipe?"

"I haven't found the recipe. I just remember what it tasted like." She was browsing through the fresh herbs and spices now, sniffing at each container carefully before either returning it to its shelf or depositing it in the basket.

"You remember how it tasted? Should we get some take-out or something on the way home in case it doesn't turn out?"

Riana glared at him icily for a moment before returning to her inspection of the herb racks. "Did you like the chicken I made last night?"

"You already know the chicken was incredible," he admitted with an approving nod.

"Well, I tasted it once in the restaurant on The Tyconderoga. Xavier's gourmet chef made it for us a year or so ago, before Kat and I accepted this courier job."

"Really?" He didn't stand a chance of restraining his amazement. "How did you do that?"

Riana shrugged absently as she moved them toward the meats department. "I'm not sure really. I just remember the flavor and aroma, and I just add all of this stuff up until it's the same."

Vincent followed her with a strange look on his face. When they arrived at the meat counter he raised an eyebrow at her. "How long have you been studying martial arts?"

"A couple of years," she shrugged again.

"No really. How long?" He stopped and looked at her seriously.

Riana stopped and turned around to look at him, her ears cocked back severely. "I said a couple of years Vin, what are you doing?"

Vincent smiled warmly at her. "Just bear with me Ree. You know, don't you? You know exactly how long you have been studying..."

She sighed heavily, her shoulders drooping slightly. "What do you want from me Vin? You want me to tell you exactly how long?"

He nodded confidently, "Yes."

"Fine," she said, standing up straight and squaring her shoulders toward him. "One year, eleven months, three weeks, five days, seventeen hours, thirty three minutes, and fifty two seconds. If you count whole days since I began. If you'd like to know actual time spent practicing and learning..." She stopped speaking when she saw his face.

His mouth had fallen open, "Okay..." He seemed at a loss for words.

Riana stared at him for a long moment, neither of them talking while the crowd moved around them, as if they were a fixture in the store. "I thought you knew that I knew," she said at last.

"I knew you knew. I just didn't realize how much you knew. Riana, how do you know that?"

She sighed again, ears drooping low. "I told you, I don't know. I just do. I remember everything. Every single detail of my life, in full, living color, all the tiny little minutia, all time-stamped, indexed and filed away. Sights, smells, sounds, feelings. Every single little thing that I am ever exposed to is permanently etched into my memory. I remember all of it, down to the tiniest details."

Vincent stared at her for a moment. She looked back at him with a look somewhere between hopeful, expectant, and angry fixed on her face. Finally, he smiled again, picked a carrot up out of the basket and showed it to her. "And you can tell how fresh all these vegetables are just by smelling them?"

Riana sighed in exasperation, shifting her hips and crossing her arms. "Yes."

Vincent grinned widely then as he took a bite out of the carrot and chewed it thoughtfully for a moment. When he looked at her again, his blue eyes smiled brightly. "Cool. I'm tired of this market getting all my money and giving me half-dead produce in return." He watched her with an impish grin, chewing on the carrot for a long moment before she ultimately broke down and started laughing loudly.

"Ok then. How about duck? Can you tell how fresh the duck is?" He moved up to her and stood beside her as he eyed the meat counter suspiciously, all the while chewing on the carrot.

"Yes," she said as she turned around and began poking through the selections there.

As they made their way across the promenade with their shopping bags a few minutes later, Vincent still munching on the carrot, they chatted idly. "So, do you use the navi-comp in your ship?"

She looked at him strangely for an instant then blushed a bit, ears drooping. "No. Not since I finished my first flight to the moon."

"Are you okay dealing with random objects and drift?"

"Yeah, it's actually pretty easy. Once you know the item's mass, it's a pretty quick calculation." Her head turned as a new smell greeted her nose, followed by the laughter of children. "Oh! What are those?"

"Easy?" Vincent stared off into space for a moment as Riana dashed toward a shop selling food that looked like colorful balls on top of cone-shaped handles. After a second, he moved after her saying, "Riana, that's ice cream. Don't tell me you've never had ice cream…"

"I haven't. What is it? It's really colorful." She was now leaning into the glass that covered the various tubs of ice cream flavors.

Everyone else in the shop was staring at her like she was out of her mind, a few of them even going so far as to point and giggle.

"It's mostly cream and sugar," Vincent said as he moved up behind her and placed his hand on her shoulder. "Plus some flavors. Pick something out."

She eyed the selection for a moment and then grinned from ear to ear as she pointed toward one of the tubs. "Banana!" She beamed happily.

Vincent nodded to the smiling person behind the counter and they quickly scooped some of the yellow ice cream into a cone and handed it to Riana, who accepted it tentatively. She eyed it for a moment, and sniffed at it before carefully licking the treat. As she tasted the ice cream her eyes went wide and her ears splayed out in contentment. "Mmmm," she cooed as she licked it again, while he offered payment to the clerk.

Vincent chuckled as he steered her out of the shop. "So you are doing spatial course corrections in your head, and think doing so is easy, but have never had ice cream before."

She looked up at him, ears laid back from her head. "Is that a bad thing?" She worried aloud.

He chuckled, taking her hand in his as they moved back toward his home. "No, it isn't bad at all. It just isn't every day that a guy meets a girl that is an exceptional martial artist, cook, pilot, navigator, and gorgeous to boot, but can still be pleasantly surprised…"

She squeezed his hand a bit as they walked and enthusiastically licked her ice cream with a mischievous grin on her face. "That isn't all I can do."

"Really? What else can you do?"

"Let's hurry up and get home so I can show you."

-6-

They stepped into the private box at the stadium and the door quietly slid shut behind them. Riana looked around with wide eyes, marveling at the plush seats and décor in the small room. Against the back wall was a table with various beverages, fruits, candies, sandwiches, and assorted other treats.

She had been surprised when she ordered the tickets on the computer terminal. She was looking for seats as close as she could get to the 'stage' in the center of the venue, but instead, the machine had spit out box seat tickets with no explanation at all. When she had contacted the venue, they told her that she had received the tickets she ordered and there was no error in the system.

Vincent had suggested he buy another set of tickets just in case, but Riana stopped him with a gasp. When he asked what was wrong, she smiled and hugged him excitedly, a huge, happy grin spread across her face. After she calmed down, she informed him that when she looked at the tickets in the ultraviolet spectrum of light, another trick he was very surprised to hear about, there were some additional words printed on them.

Dearest daughter. Please enjoy the show; I look forward to seeing you there.

-Resonance-

Riana had been so excited about the evening that it took her hours to get ready. She said she wanted to look perfect for the evening and despite the volume of things she had purchased over the course of the week, she insisted on going shopping again for a new outfit.

She ended up with her hair flowing loosely down her back, a few braids interspersed throughout its volume. A slim, tight top underneath a fancy, cropped jacket and a mid-thigh, pleated skirt over a pair of fancy, knee-high boots. The fabrics were all made of the most amazing, soft, smooth material she had ever worn before and the colors were vibrant, shimmering dark reds, deep blues and royal purples with black accents.

She also found some jewelry to wear, a couple bracelets and a simple necklace. She had even thought about having her ears pierced but decided against it since she wasn't sure anyone would have equipment that was actually capable of piercing her skin.

Vincent had gone all out as well, especially once he saw how excited she actually was about the event. He ended up wearing a pair of tight leather pants and form-fitting shirt under a fancy leather jacket, mostly in black, although the shirt was a dark, shimmering titanium color that set his blue eyes ablaze.

As she finished her assessment of the private room, her eyes came to a stop on Vincent's and she smiled like a giddy child on her birthday morning.

Suddenly, she dove across the short distance between them and wrapped herself around him in an almost crushing embrace. "This is so incredible! Thank you for coming with me!" she gushed as he tried to keep his feet under him.

"It's my pleasure Ree. This whole week has been fabulous. I couldn't imagine a better way to finish it off."

The lights in the booth and the amphitheater outside began to dim, and the pair moved to their seats to watch the concert. As they sat down, Riana scooted up against Vincent and leaned into him, twining her fingers through his and resting her head against his shoulder.

The holographic elf started with a moving ballad, floating around the vast open area of the venue and teasing her fans with subtle eye movements and turns of her body. All the while, she wove together a complicated story about a young elf growing up away from her parents and coming into her own with the help of her friends and her sister. The dangers they faced together, and how they prevailed in the end, with love conquering all.

The next few numbers were new songs, with driving beats and pulsing rhythms that had Riana and Vincent up out of their chairs and dancing around their private room together, gyrating their bodies as the melody swept them away.

For nearly three hours, they danced, moved, and sang along with the songs they knew. Every word of every song was sung in elvish, as usual, and when it was finally over, one hundred-fifty thousand people screamed out in a standing ovation. Vincent was sweating profusely, but the huge grin on his face let Riana know he would gladly do it all over again. Riana, on the other hand, was ready for another three hours. Her senses were alive and she was beaming as she continued to dance around the room, picking at the refreshments on the table.

As the lights came up in the coliseum and people began moving toward their homes, restaurants or wherever they would head next, Riana danced her way around to the front of the room, stopping suddenly in the middle of a pirouette with an audible gasp.

Vincent looked up just in time to see Riana throw her arms out and embrace another elf that had just appeared in the room.

"Mom!!" she gushed as she embraced the woman.

Vincent looked on in interest as the new elf smiled warmly and disengaged herself from the beaming, purple-haired, bundle of excitement and smiled. The elf bore the same features as Resonance, but lacked the glowing aura and flashy clothing. Instead, she looked more earthy, wearing a simple, knee-length dress that clung to her curves flatteringly, but wasn't overly revealing or sexy.

"Hello Riana, I am glad you could make it to the show." Her voice was a bit lower than Riana's and more controlled, but it was immediately apparent that they were related.

"Thank you for the great seats mom! The show was amazing. How have you been?"

The other elf frowned a bit at that question. "Things are not going well. We have much to discuss I am afraid." Then she cast an eye toward Vincent who had moved up behind Riana. "Who is this?"

Riana glanced over her shoulder and then her ears splayed out in embarrassment. "Oh! Oh, I'm sorry! Mom this is Vincent. Vincent this is my mother, Ezrina!" She wrapped an arm around Vincent's back as she spoke, leaning into him and smiling at her mother.

"I see," Ezrina replied, eying him critically. "I've seen you before…"

Vincent looked confused, but offered his hand to Ezrina in greeting. "It is very nice to meet you Mrs. Thorindal. I'm not sure how we could have met before." He screwed up his face as his hand passed right through hers.

"No, I am sure of it. You have a character in Kalijor?" Ezrina seemed to not even notice the hand issue.

"Yes ma'am. I play a Weapon Master by the name of Jumah. Riana and I spent quite a lot of time together in Kalijor last year when she was looking for her sister." He took his hand back and inspected it with a raised eyebrow.

"Werecheetah…" Ezrina said thoughtfully, almost to herself. "This may be of use to us."

"Mom, what's going on?" Riana asked with a worried look on her face.

Ezrina looked up at them, her own ears cocking back in annoyance as she folded her arms across her chest. "The third key is in the open. Malice is moving to take it. You and your sister are in terrible danger."

Riana's mood changed instantly. She sank into a chair and dropped her chin into her hands, ears laid back flat. She massaged her temples vigorously as she waited for her mother to continue.

Vincent sat down next to her and folded his hands in his lap, also waiting for the narrative to continue.

Ezrina began to pace the room, wrapping her arms around herself and staring at the floor as she moved. After several long moments, she finally began to speak. "Several adventurers heard of a treasure that could be found in the mines of Talanor, guarded by a powerful, ancient golem. They mounted an expedition and when they returned they were in possession of the key. Malice heard about it and now he is gathering his own fighting force to take the key from them. The adventurers are currently holed up in the Great Arena in the Plane of Serenity and Malice's forces are marching on their location as we speak."

Riana sighed heavily as she looked up at her mother. "Mom, how does this put Kat and I in any sort of danger?"

Ezrina stopped her pacing and bent slightly, taking her daughter's face in her hand and caressing it lightly as she peered into her violet eyes. "Riana, if Malice gets the key he will be in a position to obtain one of the artifacts. You, yourself, possess one of the artifacts and know its power. If he gets hold of one, it will only be a matter of time before he comes for yours. Not to mention the potential havoc he will be able to cause by merely possessing the artifact itself."

"So we're in danger because of me. There's a surprise." Riana ran her fingers across her scalp, sighing heavily.

"Xavier is going to order you into Kalijor to retrieve the key for him, but he must not have it."

"Mom, what the hell is so important about these artifacts? Why is it that we are constantly in danger over these virtual trinkets?" She had reached the end of her rope with this subject. It seemed as though every time she started to get comfortable in her new life, these artifacts cropped up again and tipped her world on its edge.

"You possess one of the artifacts Riana. Do you not understand its power?" Ezrina had moved to the window and was looking out into the now-empty stadium.

"No, mother, I don't understand it, and thus far no one has been willing to even begin to explain it to me. Frankly, I am more than a little tired of being treated like this," Riana was on her feet now, gesturing wildly as she spoke.

It happened so quickly that she didn't have a chance to defend herself. Ezrina whirled around in a graceful pirouette and lashed out with her hand, slapping her daughter hard across the face. "This is not about you Riana. This is about all of us. Every man, woman, and child in two worlds. Everything hangs in the balance if the wrong people possess the artifacts."

Vincent came up out of his chair, hands ready for a fight as the force of the blow rang through the room. Ezrina cast him an angry glare, daring him to challenge her authority. He paused, remembering his hand passing through hers, and instead turned his attention to Riana.

Riana shrank back from the assault, dropping heavily back into her chair. She nursed her face gently where an angry red handprint was forming. "I... I'm sorry mom. I just don't understand all of this."

"I know your frustration, Riana, but you must open yourself to the situation. The answers are there for your understanding. You have but to see them. Do not allow your feelings to stand in the way of your understanding."

"I don't understand that, mom. Why won't someone just tell me what is going on? Why does all of this have to be so damn cryptic?!" She balled up her fists as she spoke, spitting every word as if it were a foul-tasting morsel of food in her mouth.

"No one is being cryptic Riana. You simply refuse to see what is right in front of your face. Until you open yourself to the reality of the situation, you will be nothing more than an unwilling participant. You must embrace your place in these events. Only then will you truly understand." She knelt down in front of Riana and took her hands in her own, squeezing them lovingly as she looked into her daughter's eyes again. "I am sorry that this is so difficult for you, but it is of your own making. You are a piece in the game, whether you wish to participate or not, and right now it is time for you to make a move."

Riana sighed again as she looked into her mother's golden eyes. "Alright. So we have to get the key from these adventurers, keep Malice from getting it, and keep Xavier from getting it as well."

"Yes."

"And do you understand at all the kind of hell I am going to have to go through in dealing with Xavier if I try and keep the key from him? He's still mad about the artifact."

"I understand, Riana. I am truly sorry. If you think for an instant that this is the life I would have chosen for you, then you are very wrong."

Riana looked at her mother again, shook her head, and stood up, beginning her own pacing circuit around the room. "We need to let Kat know and get to somewhere we can login," she finally said, turning to face Vincent who was still standing quietly near the chairs, observing the proceedings. "I can't ask you to do this with us."

He smiled warmly and shrugged slightly. "You'll never have to. We can login from my place. I have two EI headsets."

Riana grinned, ears perking up a bit. "All I need is an ODN port." Then she turned to face her mother who was standing near the window again, smiling softly as she watched them. "Alright mom, we need a little bit to get to Vin's house. Is there any way you can get in touch with Kat?"

"I already have. She is waiting for you in Rathalon, at home."

"Alright. Let's go then." She moved to her mother and embraced her once more.

As they embraced, Ezrina leaned in and whispered into Riana's ear. "I love you Riana."

"I love you too, mom," Riana replied.

As they began to separate Ezrina whispered again, barely audible this time, "He's a good soul Riana. Good job."

Slowly, they pulled apart, holding one another's hands for a long moment before finally pulling fully away. Riana moved toward Vincent, who wrapped a protective arm around her waist. He offered the other to Ezrina, who made as if to take it in her own, but again they passed right through one another.

"It was nice meeting you, Mrs. Thorindal. Thank you for the concert." He said after retracting his hand and looking at it again, confused.

"And you as well. Thank you for your help and please watch over one another."

"We will," they said in unison as they exited the small room together.

After the door closed behind them, Ezrina smiled to herself for a moment before silently blinking out of existence.

-8-

The crisp, clean air of Kalijor caressed her like an old friend's welcoming embrace. She stretched her arms up as far as they would go, working her fingers in and out of fists as she closed her eyes and simply listened to the sounds of daily life in Rathalon.

"Heyas gorgeous," Jumah's voice purred from behind her as he slipped his arms around her waist and pulled her into a loving embrace against his bare chest.

She dropped her arms down behind her and laced her fingers behind his head, pulling him in closer to her as she laid her own head back against his shoulder. "Hello there. Long time no see," she lilted.

"Indeed. You smell wonderful," he purred as he inhaled deeply, still holding her to him.

"Why thank you. But you know we have to put this off until after the war right?" She sounded upset at the prospect.

"Yes, but that won't stop me thinking about you the whole time." He smiled warmly as she twisted around in his grasp to face him.

"Well, you had better be keeping your mind on the job mister. Otherwise there may not be an afterwards for us," her voice washed over him like silk as she closed the distance between them and kissed him hungrily.

Breaking off the kiss, she stepped back from him, eyes roving over his statuesque form. "Alright. Let's go get Kat and save the worlds already. I want to get on to other activities as soon as possible." She grinned wickedly at him as she took up his hand and they began moving toward her home.

"So what are you saying? That my mom is some kind of freak?" Riana admonished Jumah as they headed up the stairs to her home a few minutes later.

"No. I am not calling your mother a freak, Riana. I just think it's a little odd that you two were able to touch each other and my hand passed right through hers twice." He shook his head slightly as they crested the top of the staircase and approached the door.

"Well I have no idea what to make of it. This is all new to me." She waved her hand at the stone door to her home and it silently slid away into the wall, revealing the slightly dusty interior.

Stepping through the door, she invited Jumah in with a nod of her head as she continued, "Anyway, it isn't as though my life has ever exactly qualified as normal. I'm not sure why anyone would expect it to start being that way now."

"I suppose that is a fair statement," Jumah acquiesced before nodding slightly in the direction of one of the bedrooms with a grin on his face.

Riana followed his look, her ears perked up. A rustling noise greeted her keen elven hearing and she smiled as well. "So, can I get you anything? Wine? Water? Something to eat? A bowl of berries and fruit perhaps?"

Jumah dusted off the top of a stool with one hand as he repositioned it with the other, then slipped onto it, facing the kitchen area across the raised breakfast bar and smiled at Riana. "A glass of water would be great. You know, you really should get in here and dust every so often." He ignored the casual reference to the werecheetah's romantic tradition of feeding berries and fruit to their loved ones for hours, or even days, during courting.

Riana withdrew a glass from the cupboard and rinsed it off in the sink before filling it up and setting it on the bar in front of him. "Here's your water wise-ass. You know, what with saving the world and working and all, I just haven't had a lot of time to come home and take care of the domestic stuff."

He smiled as he sipped at the water. "Now I know what to get you for your birthday."

"And what would that be?" she asked over her own glass.

"Cleaning service." he grinned.

A retort stopped on Riana's lips as Katrina came skittering out of her bedroom, hastily fastening her robes about herself and primping her hair. She looked up at Riana and Jumah and together all three of them feigned surprise.

"Ree!!" Katrina squealed as she bounded into the kitchen happily and embraced her sister.

"Kat! How's your week been?" Riana returned the embrace enthusiastically.

Katrina let her go and went after a couple of her own glasses, cleaning them off and filling them up. "It's been great. I hooked up with some old friends, saw a couple shows, and did some shopping. How about you?" She sipped at one of the glasses and held the other at the ready as she looked at her sister.

"Oh, we had a great time. Lots of shopping. I cooked quite a bit. That was pretty cool."

"Wow. Cooking. I didn't know you could cook, sis."

"She's quite good at it actually," Jumah chimed in. "She could easily run a successful restaurant."

Riana blushed at the compliment and Katrina raised an eyebrow at her curiously. Finally another form emerged from Katrina's room and moved toward the group in the kitchen. He stepped up next to Katrina and accepted the offered glass of water as he looked at the others and smiled at them, his bald pate and well trimmed mustache and goatee framing his grey eyes.

"Exodus!" Riana greeted him warmly, moving around her sister and offering him a warm hug.

40

"Hello friend," Jumah echoed, offering him a smile and a nod.

"Hello you two. It's nice to see you again."

"I logged in as soon as Resonance contacted me and Exodus was on so I brought him up to speed. He agreed to help us out again." Katrina explained, then with a slight blush and a dip of the ears she added, "And we hadn't seen each other for a while…"

"We're glad for the assistance. Thank you very much," Riana said as she released him and moved toward a stool next to Jumah.

"So. What's the plan?" Jumah asked.

"Well. Mom said the battle was going to happen at the arena in the Plane of Serenity," Riana began. "Exodus, can you teleport there?"

"I can," he replied.

"Alright. Here's what I am thinking. Mom said the people that have the key are already at the arena. Malice and whatever forces he has assembled are en route to there now. If you and Kat 'port there, you can talk with them and see if you can get the key before he arrives. At the very least, see if they are willing to accept our help in dealing with him. Jumah and I will head there on foot. With Xanthe, we should be able to overtake Malice and his cronies so we can get an idea of what we are dealing with."

Katrina shook her head vigorously. "Ree what if they see you? You two won't be able to handle them on your own."

"There'll be three of us Kat. We'll be fine, trust me. Once we figure out what we are up against, we will pass them up and meet the rest of you at the arena."

"I don't like it Ree," Katrina continued to protest.

"We'll be fine, really," Jumah finally chimed in with a confident tone.

Katrina looked back and forth between the pair a few times before finally setting her glass down and sighing heavily. "Alright. But if you let anything happen to her, I'll…" Words seemed to come up short for her.

Jumah smiled warmly and wrapped an arm around Riana's shoulder, pulling her in close to him. "I promise no harm will come to her."

"Ree, what do we do about these adventurers? We can't let them keep the key even if we do manage to keep it from Malice," Katrina frowned.

"I know, Kat. We'll have to work that out once we finish with Malice. I honestly don't know what we will do…"

-9-

After they had hammered out the details, they all spent a few minutes preparing themselves. Finally, Katrina and Exodus stood together and, with a word of power and a gesture from Exodus, they vanished with a quiet popping noise leaving Riana and Jumah alone.

Looking at one another, they linked hands and moved out into the city, Riana calling out in her mind to Xanthe. She felt the wash of love and happiness run through her as their minds touched and by the time they had stepped through the west gate he was standing a few paces away from the guards, all of whom were nervously eyeing him, weapons at the ready in case he made a sudden movement in their direction.

"Heya Xanthe!" Riana cooed as she strode up to the large, draconian creature. Wrapping her arms around the long, sleek neck of the finely scaled, silver-white animal, she smiled as he nuzzled her with his dragon-like head. A loud cooing noise that almost sounded like the purring of a large cat issued forth from somewhere deep in his chest while his long, whip-like tail slashed back and forth through the air, its bladed, bone tip slashing the top of the tall grass.

"Hello there, friend. Are you ready for a run?" Riana whispered as she looked deeply into his large, cobalt-blue eyes.

He enthusiastically nodded his head, then squatted down low and presented the foreleg nearest to Riana so that she could use it as a step and swing up onto his back. Once she was seated and had her feet in the stirrups, he stood up straight and offered Jumah a serious look.

"It's alright, friend. I think I'll stay on foot. We're going to need all the speed we can muster on this trip." He said as he scratched Xanthe behind his eye ridge.

"C'mon you two, let's get out of sight of the guards."

Moments later, they moved around a gentle bend in the road and a stand of trees obscured them from the sight of the guards. Jumah stopped and looked around intently, focusing all of his senses on the task of detecting anyone near by.

"I don't hear anyone," Riana offered, her ears twitching with concentration.

"Noorrrr doooo I," came a growling response.

Spinning her head around, Riana saw that Jumah had already transformed. Where he had been standing, a large cheetah now stood with Jumah's swords strapped across its back and his bracers wrapped tightly around its lower forelegs.

The cheetah looked up at her and offered a toothy grin, his blue eyes still shining brightly at her.

"That was fast," she said with a note of awe in her voice.

"Yerssss…" he growled. His face making strange shapes as the quasi-word issued forth from him.

"Plays hell with your speech uh?" She grinned at him.

He offered her what she was sure qualified as a reproachful look. "Yerssss…"

She smiled widely. "You think Xanthe can outrun you?"

Xanthe instinctively coiled his muscles beneath her, ready to leap into action.

"Noooorrr…" Jumah replied in his husky, rumbling growl.

"Okay. Well somewhere between here and the arena are Malice and his gang. Let's see who finds them first." Her ears cocked back and she leaned forward into Xanthe's neck. By the time the powerful animal leapt into action, Jumah was already out of sight, a trail of dust settling in his wake.

-10-

Long after they had broken out of the sparse tree coverage near Rathalon, Riana was surprised when Jumah suddenly loped up beside them, coming from behind. He moved along at a casual pace, no sign of exertion even after an hour of running. Watching as his body coiled up with each move forward, folding nearly in half and then springing open again to launch him ahead. Riana admired his grace as he matched Xanthe's speed and glanced up at her with his crystal clear, blue eyes. His growling voice rolled across the distance between them, but she could still hear it despite the speed they were moving. "Beaarrr rrriiighhhht. Mmmaliiccccee aaaheeaaaddd."

For the briefest of moments, Riana actually considered barreling ahead into Malice and his companions. She still owed him for what he had done to Katrina and she wasn't one to let an unsettled debt stand for too long. As she was about to press Xanthe on toward the group, she felt her friend's mind pressing comfortably against her own. Xanthe knew her thoughts and was trying to impress upon her how impulsive she was about to be, not to mention his complete lack of desire to be killed in combat if it was anything less than absolutely necessary.

"Rrrrreeeeee…" Jumah's low, rumbling voice shook her out of her reverie. Jerking her head around toward the large cheetah loping along next to her, she blinked a couple of times before guiding

Xanthe off to the right a bit. Jumah's gaze followed her for several long moments as they sped across the endless green expanse of the Plain of Serenity, but no more words were spoken between them. Nearly an hour later, when he signaled to her that they could veer back toward the Great Arena once more. A few soft words indicated that he had gotten a solid accounting of the mercenaries with Malice, via scent and sound, as they had moved around them. For her part, Riana had used what magic she had for the purposes of investigation to add some information about weapons and armor.

Several hours later, they entered the northwestern corner of the Forest of Brume. This was the leading edge of the massive forest and, as such, the trees were much smaller and spread further apart. They had not yet grown large and strong enough to coat the ground in the dense white mist that brume trees were famous for, although each tree did have a small swirling vortex of the white mist floating around its trunk and roots, each one looking like a miniature tornado cloud revolving quietly in place, in a strange, surreal sort of slow motion.

They weren't in the forest for more than half an hour before they came upon a massive clearing. A blanket of lush, green, well manicured grass, stretched from the forest's edge, ending in a jagged rock wall some three-hundred feet high. The wall of rock was in a roughly oval shape. It was easily two-thousand feet long and over one-thousand feet wide at its extreme points. It sat in the center of the clearing, which was carpeted in a blanket of lush, green grass that ran right up to the impressive stone wall of the arena.

Following the base of the structure for several long minutes, they finally came to one of the four entrances. An immense gate led into a large hallway cut through the stone of the wall. The tunnel was ornately carved from the worn-smooth floor to the apex of its high arch, and could easily permit fifteen ogres standing shoulder to shoulder to pass through unhindered.

As they entered the dark, relative seclusion of the entryway, Jumah stopped abruptly and closed his eyes for a moment before his body began twisting and writhing in strange ways. As Riana watched, his legs thickened and his muscles crawled around beneath his skin seemingly of their own accord, rearranging themselves into an almost completely different configuration. The short, golden fur

47

with its pattern of black spots seemed to be sucked back beneath his skin as his mouth opened in what looked like a silent roar or scream of intense pain. She bit down on her lip, almost sick, as a series of popping and cracking noises accompanied his short cheetah's jaw pulling back into his head and his sharp canine teeth shrinking back out of sight.

In all, the process probably took no more than a couple of seconds, but to Riana's stunned mind it seemed to go on for an eternity. Finally, he stood up straight, adjusting the various leather straps and strategically placed metal plates around his body to insure a secure fit.

In response to her gaping look, he simply smiled and patted Xanthe's neck reassuringly. "No," he finally said, "it doesn't hurt."

She blinked at him, not sure what to say, but knowing that question had been foremost on her mind somehow didn't seem to alleviate her concerns any. "If you say so. Because I'm here to tell you, it looks as though it hurts like hell."

"It isn't something I like other people to see, but I figure you'd see it sooner or later." He grinned roguishly at her, eyes twinkling in the darkness of the tunnel.

Riana pulled herself together and swung down from Xanthe's back, patting him on his thick shoulder before moving down the dark corridor. The trio walked in silence for a while before Riana finally spoke.

"So, what's it like? I mean, if it doesn't hurt, what does it feel like?"

Jumah thought about it for a long moment before finally, grinning happily. "Obviously, you remember the ritual my people have, about fruit and berries."

Riana thought about it for a moment, trying to decide if now was the time to rail him for ignoring her earlier tease. When he had told her about the tradition, his lips had been pressed against her sensitive ear-lobes, and her body shivered in remembrance of the heat of his breath against her skin. "Yes," she finally whispered, her ears splaying out widely and flushing red with the intensity of the memory.

"Well," he said brightly, either unaware of her state, or enjoying it just a little too much for her taste. "When we get around to doing that, by the time it's all said and done..." he mused thoughtfully, "you'll have a subtle idea of what it feels like to shape-shift."

"So it's... pleasurable?" she sounded incredulous.

"Well it isn't something we normally think about or focus on, but if we do it slowly, forcing ourselves to feel the change, then yes, it can be extremely pleasurable. Although I am told that it isn't necessarily the same for all Lycanthropes."

"I never imagined..." she whispered again.

Before the conversation could go any further, they stepped out of the wide tunnel into the brightness of the Great Arena and found themselves immediately surrounded. A massive reptilian wearing heavy plate armor hefted a tall naginata threateningly in his right hand. The impressive claymore slung across his back was nothing to scoff at either. An elf that was a few inches shorter than Riana, wearing a fine suit of studded leather armor and wielding a slender scimitar in her right hand looked over at another, much shorter, elf. This elf was wearing full plate armor, like their larger companion, but she was absolutely bristling with weapons strapped across her back, to her waist, her thighs, her upper arms and brandishing a naked blade in each hand.

The group looked as though they meant to do the travelers serious harm and both Riana and Jumah drew their blades. Riana's violet eyes flashed brightly in sync with one of the mystical tattoos on her body as she conjured a ball of fire in her left hand, setting herself in a solid stance, preparing for battle. But Xanthe gave her pause, staying her hand with his overall air of happiness and, indeed, eagerness.

Following the Equun-Draco's line of attention, Riana's eyes came to rest on a pair of robed figures standing on the other side of Jumah. As they stepped closer, Riana noted that each was carrying a simple stave. The taller figure's staff was carved from what had to be brume tree wood as it had a swirling white mist surrounding it and the shorter figure's was a simple metal rod carved with a chaotic pattern of dwarven runes. Recognition struck a chord in Riana's mind and she stood up straight as the two robed figures pulled their hoods down, revealing themselves to the group.

49

"Heyo!" Katrina chirped happily as her platinum hair cascaded out from under the hood and her long, tapered ears perked up cheerfully. A radiant smile spread across her face as she took in her friends and she lunged forward to embrace Riana in a sisterly hug.

Jumah scanned the group and, seeing most of them putting their weapons to ease, he sheathed his twin blades and turned to face Exodus. A smile broke across Jumah's face as he took Exodus' hand in greeting. "Hello again, friend. I trust your trip met with success?"

"Indeed it has," Exodus replied with a smile on his face. "If only it could have been under less dire circumstances. It seems our friends here are more than willing to help us out with the matter at hand."

"Excellent!" Jumah grinned as they broke free of one another, turning to face the rest of the small group. "And who are our friends here?"

As if that were some sort of key phrase, Katrina suddenly let go of Riana and turned to face the others, now standing around watching or ignoring the reunion. The short elf seemed completely bored with the entire situation, her swords had been added to the impressive collection on her body and she plopped down, cross-legged on the dirt floor of the arena with a loud clang and proceeded to clean her fingernails with a wicked-looking dagger. Fiery red hair fell in a curtain around her features, obscuring her face from view.

The taller elf was smiling warmly at the group, her ears reflecting genuine interest and happiness around her tightly braided brown hair and bright hazel eyes. One of her delicate hands was squeezing the free hand of the tall Reptilian who still held the naginata at the ready and looked around alertly, completely ignoring the reunion altogether.

"These are the adventurers who managed to acquire the third key," Katrina explained. Pointing to them each in turn, she announced them to the newcomers.

"This," she pointed to the warmly smiling elf, "is Desse, and her life-mate Xembak." She pointed at the Reptilian who twisted his head around, regarding Riana and Jumah with his large, piercing blue eyes for a moment before nodding his head and returning to his vigilance. Desse, on the other hand, curtsied politely and spoke in a soft, singsong voice, "It is a pleasure to meet you all, I am happy that life has seen fit to intertwine our threads. Please do not take my life-mate's response as discourteous, he is simply doing what he does."

Riana bowed to the pair, smiling as Katrina continued, pointing to the porcupine sitting on the ground picking at her fingernails idly with the bizarrely-shaped knife. "And this is Firiel, their companion."

At the sound of her name, Firiel stood up and the knife seemed to instantly disappear of its own accord. She brushed her fiery red locks behind her ears, revealing a pair of acid-green eyes, bright as one might see on a poisonous tree frog. A spark ran down Riana's spine at the sight of those eyes, those piercing green eyes, but she couldn't figure out why they set her on edge. Gracefully, and with speed belying her apparent load, she moved up on Riana and extended her hand in greeting, never once breaking eye contact. "How do you do?"

"Fine, thank you," Riana replied, a bit standoffish. "Yourself?"

Firiel shook Riana's hand, nearly crushing it with her unexpected strength, then took her hand back and offered it to Jumah, all the while keeping her eyes on Riana. "Oh, I'm doing alright. Although I am a bit bored."

"Oh, I imagine we will have plenty to do here before too long. If you intend to stand with us, that is," Jumah said as he shook her hand, casting Riana a quizzical eye.

"I'm sorry," Riana finally cracked. "I feel as though I know you from somewhere. Have we met before?"

Firiel just smiled as she released Jumah's hand and stepped closer to Riana, so close now that their bodies were nearly touching fully from head to toe. The fact that Firiel was nearly two heads shorter than Riana didn't seem to make any difference at all to the smaller elf.

"Oh, I'm sure you'd remember me if we had. And of course we intend to stand with you. I haven't had a good fight in days and I am itching for some action." She grinned wickedly as she turned away from Riana and stalked off a few paces before finding a good stretch of wall to lean up against. The nasty looking blade suddenly reappeared from its hiding place on her body and she began picking at her nails again.

"I swear I recognize her from somewhere," Riana breathed to Jumah as Katrina moved to fill in the gap between her and the other two adventurers. Riana focused her mind as she looked intently, first at Desse and then Xembak. Her mind raced as her vision warped and bent, as if she was racing through a long tunnel at incredible speed. She could feel the strange power of the circlet permanently affixed to her forehead working to trace back to the people behind the avatars she was seeing. With Desse, the journey ended in a game pod with a young woman sitting in its womb-like embrace, and EI harness fit snugly to her head. With Xembak, her vision eventually came to rest on a young man, sitting in an uncomfortable chair in a cramped little room with an ODN cable connected to an implant at the base of his skull.

Next she turned her altered vision on Firiel and the color of her aura informed Riana that she was not being controlled by a live person. Her tunnel vision sprang forward and in an instant she was looking at one of the familiar computer servers on the game deck of The Tyconderoga.

"She's an NPC…" she whispered to herself.

"Who is?" Katrina asked, leaning over towards Riana.

"That Firiel woman."

"My apologies for interrupting, and eavesdropping, but she can't be," Desse breathed. "We've been adventuring together for over a year now."

"Well I don't know what to tell you other than she's an NPC." Riana reiterated, still staring at Firiel who was doing an amazing job of completely ignoring the group.

"She couldn't possibly be an NPC," Desse repeated. "I have seen her log out on more than one occasion, and she is far too clever to be computer controlled."

"You think so do you?" Riana suddenly grew irritated, her ears cocking back angrily. "And just what would you know about the things these computers are capable of?!"

"I… Uh…" Desse was clearly taken aback by Riana's sudden change of attitude. In a flash, a wall of scales and armor appeared between Riana and Desse. Xembak narrowed his slitted, reptilian eyes at Riana as he held out a hand toward her, nearly touching her, but careful not to look too menacing.

"This conversation is counterproductive, we need to be planning for the coming battle," he said simply, although his perfect pronunciation and enunciation took Riana by surprise. Most reptilians tended to slur their S's when they spoke, but Xembak sounded as eloquent as any human one might meet in the streets of Rathalon.

"Right," she finally agreed, nodding her head at the lizard. He dropped his hand and stepped aside, allowing the women to see one another again.

Desse seemed completely serene as she smiled sweetly. "He is right of course. My apologies Riana."

"So anyway, they say they found the key deep in the mines under Talanor..," Katrina began suddenly, trying to restart the proceedings as she pulled a small leather-wrapped object from a fold in her robes and handed it to her sister.

Riana accepted the parcel, rolling it open in the palm of her outstretched hand. As the leather cover fell away it revealed a pale yellow crystal that fit snugly in the palm of her hand. It was a beautiful, flawless gem with an ancient elven rune suspended within its heart. The rune was instantly recognizable as the elven word for Secrecy.

-11-

The comrades stood in a line facing the entrance to the Great Arena, each with their weapon of choice held firmly in hand as they watched the silhouetted figures make their way from the darkness of the tunnel into the well-lit, open interior of the coliseum.

Riana's eyes flashed brightly as Malice slid his blackened blade from the scabbard on his back, grinning evilly at her before sweeping his malevolent gaze across the rest of the group. His armor seemed to absorb all light, making it nearly impossible to discern any details on the surface of the inky black metal and forcing the eye of the beholder to take a second look in order to separate his form from the darkness of the tunnel behind him.

On either side of him stood the mercenaries Jumah had detected on the path from Rathalon. On Malice's right stood a young woman with vibrant blond hair that was restrained in a tight braid that fell nearly to her ankles and wearing a loose fitting silk Gi covering her body. She stood confidently with her arms folded across her chest and a look of boredom on her chiseled face. To her right stood a Felinoid that was decked out in shiny silver platemail with a large metal maul dangling lightly from his right hand. The thick muscles rippling beneath the surface of his mottled fur made the weapon look like a toy in his hands as he swung it idly back and forth. On Malice's left stood an ogre, easily twice his size, who bore a long wooden staff topped with several fetishes. Loose-fitting leather armor that seemed as though he had pieced it together from several suits that had been meant for someone half his size covered much of his body, but what was exposed was thickly blanketed in tribal tattoos from the top of his bald head down to his bare toes.

The final individual, standing in the ogre's shadow, was a tiny little goblin who wore an expensive looking chain shirt over his clammy green skin. A bandolier of daggers was slung over each of his shoulders and he picked idly at his claws, much like Firiel, with one of the pointy implements as the groups faced off with one another.

"I see you scraped the bottom of the barrel for our little soiree ladies," Malice sneered, eliciting a few chuckles and evil grins from his friends.

"We don't have to do this Malice," Riana replied, trying to keep her voice calm and collected.

"You're right. Hand over the key and we will let you all walk out of here. Without your weapons and armor of course." He rapped the flat of his inky black blade against his gauntleted hand.

"Get over yourself," Katrina snarled at him.

At that, Malice's group broke out into open laughter. It seemed they weren't too particular as to who was being insulted.

"Far be it from me to start a fight when it is anything less than absolutely necessary..." he began to say.

"That's a laugh," Riana and Katrina cut him off in unison.

"You'll have to pry it from our dead hands," Riana offered defiantly, ears laid back from her head and eyes narrowed. This elicited a giggle from Katrina that made her look around, bewildered. "What?!" She hissed at her sister.

"Nothing Ree. Let's just get this over with."

The twins and their friends turned collectively to face Malice and his companions. There was a brief moment of calm as the anticipation of the coming battle rolled across the occupants of the arena. Then, in a wave of noise and chaos, all hell broke loose.

-12-

Riana's eyes flashed brightly, one of her tattoos glowing into vivid color as an arc of lightning raced down her arm and leapt across the distance between her and Malice who batted the blast aside with his magical sword. Katrina and Exodus both began chanting words of power, drawing mystic symbols in the air with their hands and producing a series of fireballs and lightning bolts that shot towards their opponents.

Desse closed her eyes, mumbling quietly for a moment before raising her arms above her head. A tangle of roots and vines grew up out of the packed earth floor of the arena and began twisting and winding their way around their enemy's feet. Next to her, Xembak tightened his grip on his polearm and leapt at the Ogre with a loud hiss rolling through the air behind him.

The fire-haired woman called Firiel drew a wicked looking, curved sword from her back and unhooked a jagged-bladed axe from her belt. Holding the sword in her right hand and the axe in her left, she bellowed a fearsome battle cry and charged toward the unarmed woman.

Malice's cohorts were quick to take action of their own. The Ogre and the platemail-clad Felinoid began chanting their own magical words causing a series of shimmering barriers to blink into life around each of Malice's warriors. The unarmed woman calmly stepped into a solid stance and advanced to meet Firiel's charge while the Goblin dashed to the side, stripping daggers from the pouches on his bandoliers and flinging them like darts at Desse who stepped away just in time.

Malice stalked toward Riana with a look of pure hatred on his face. "You had one chance elf, and you just wasted it." He raised his sword over his head and brought it down toward her head with such speed that it moved like a blur through the air.

Riana moved to the side and raised Elkorine to deflect the blow. When the two weapons collided, blue-white lightning filled the air around them. "Your breath is wasted on me Malice." She spun around and launched a powerful reverse kick into his kidneys that made him stagger with its force.

Recovering quickly, he brought his sword back up, trying to catch her in the side, but she quickly pirouetted around the blade, bringing her left hand around. In an instant of concentration, she conjured up a ball of crackling electricity that surrounded her fist just as it slammed into the side of his head. The air between them exploded with lightning and the force of the attack sent Malice sprawling to the ground with a gasp.

Katrina continued conjuring fireballs, lightning bolts, and blasts of magical energy that she flung at the opposing forces, showering them with deadly attacks that forced them to break their ranks in order to avoid the maelstrom. Having their feet tangled up in the rapidly growing plant life caused them to stumble and stall in their movements. A few errant knives, flung from the goblin's clawed hands headed her way but were quickly knocked aside by a shimmering wall of force that appeared in front of her.

"Careful, you, this isn't a one-on-one fight," Exodus smiled at her as the force wall vanished in a flash.

"Thanks for that," Katrina replied after another fireball appeared in her hand. She smiled back at him before flinging the deadly sphere at the little goblin. The goblin cursed at her in its native tongue, sounding like a series of growls and chirps, as it threw itself to the ground to avoid the blast.

A few mystic words from the Ogre caused a wave of mystical blue energy to wash over the entangling plants, which quickly wilted away into dust. The instant the plants were gone, the enemy group broke up, each of them trying to pair off against their chosen partner.

As the Ogre finished dispelling the entangling plants, Xembak slammed into him with his armored shoulder. Despite the fact that he was easily a foot shorter than the Ogre, he caused the other to stagger back, giving him a window to slash across the larger's stomach. The Ogre, after recovering his balance, planted his fetish staff in the ground to intercept the reptilian's blade. Responding quickly to the blocked attack, Xembak spun around, slamming his thick tail into the Ogre's knees and causing him to stagger backward again.

Meanwhile, Firiel was slashing wildly at her opponent, who seemed to be effortlessly blocking and avoiding her attacks. She kept her blades moving quickly but her unarmed opponent seemed extremely adept at keeping herself inside the warrior's stance. For her part, Firiel also seemed to be able to ward off the other woman's attacks using the pommel of her sword and the haft of her axe, but the two seemed to be at a standstill, moving back and forth, around and around one another, their limbs and blades forming a blur in the scant space between them.

The Felinoid shook himself free of the withering plants just in time to catch Jumah's leap kick square in his chest plate. The force of the blow knocked him off his feet but even as he fell, he flung his heavy weapon at the nimble werecheetah. Jumah spun himself around in mid air, trying to avoid the hammer but it clipped him in the ribs, ricocheting off of his body and sending him off in another direction.

Rolling over backward, the Felinoid came back to his feet and quickly conjured a magical hammer to replace his discarded weapon. Jumah managed to recover from the hammer-blow mid air and land gracefully on his feet, facing his opponent with swords in hand. Not waiting for another counter attack, Jumah charged the cleric down, moving at impossible speeds as he closed the distance between them.

"Your team is fighting well," Malice drawled at Riana as the pair exchanged sword strikes with a metallic clang and a shower of blue lightning bolts.

"If I thought you were capable of even the most basic unselfish thoughts, I might take that as a compliment," Riana growled, her ears laid straight back from her head in annoyance as she ducked under a widely arcing sword swing.

"Oh, it was meant as a compliment. However, since you seem bent on seeing nothing but the worst in me, I see no reason why I should disappoint you." With that, he batted away the stab she leveled toward his head and dropped to one knee, driving the point of his sword into the floor of the arena.

As the blade pierced the earthen floor, the entire structure began to rumble and shake violently. The sapphire on the pommel of Malice's weapon flashed and glowed brightly, sending pulses of bright blue light washing through the arena. The wave of light seemed to invigorate all of Malice's companions, causing them to stand up taller, looking stronger and more confident.

Firiel began giving up ground to her opponent as she found herself suddenly showered with a barrage of punches and kicks that her obvious skill with the blades could not repel. It was all she could do to escape being pummeled by the woman, who kept pressing in on her with murderous intent in her eyes.

Xembak ducked under the Ogre's staff as it swished through the air over his head and brought his naginata in beneath the shaman's guard only to have his weapon slam into a shimmering wall of magical force. He spun himself around, moving to hook the haft of his weapon behind the Ogre's calf and trip him up, but the Ogre seemed to read him like a book, stepping over the attack and slamming his huge foot down on Xembak's back. The Reptilian sprawled forward under the force of the blow, tucking his shoulder under him and rolling back to his feet again.

Jumah closed to within a foot of the Felinoid cleric before stepping to the side and slashing out with one of his weapons. Much to his surprise, the sword impacted something that sounded nothing like the soft tissue he was aiming for. Before he could even try to figure out what had happened, he felt a solid object connect with his right calf, lifting it up off the ground and sending it in a wide vertical arc in front of him. He rolled over backward, tucking himself into a ball and kicking his legs over his shoulders, the momentum of his fall carrying him heels over head and back to his feet again. The two of them faced off, Jumah holding his twin swords at the ready and the cleric wielding the glowing, translucent hammer formed of pure magical energy.

Desse found herself under assault by a torrent of throwing daggers. It was all she could do to keep her defensive shield in place under the constant barrage, which meant there was no chance of her going back on the offensive. Instead, she grunted her displeasure at the situation, while trying her hardest to keep herself covered and watch her teammates for any signs that they might need healing.

Katrina and Exodus were the only two people that seemed unaffected by the wave of blue energy, although it became more difficult for either of them to safely target their opponents since most of them were now much closer to their allies. It was clear that the tide had turned when Xembak took a major hit to his mid section from the Ogre's staff. The blow knocked the Reptilian to the ground and was followed up by a blast of lightning that caused his body to convulse painfully.

Seeing her life-mate fall, Desse screamed out to him. The lapse in her concentration resulted in one of the Goblin's throwing daggers getting past her shields and sinking deeply into her side. She screamed out in pain and staggered forward, clutching at the handle of the weapon protruding from her ribs. Several more knives, sinking into her right shoulder, left thigh, and just below her navel, followed the first hit. She sank to her knees, wincing in pain as the knife in her thigh sliced more muscle tissue.

"Desse!" Katrina shouted as she rushed toward the fallen elf, hurling bolts of lightning and magical bolts at the Goblin as she moved.

"Get away from him, ogre!" Exodus parodied Katrina's actions as he advanced.

The human woman smiled slightly as she took a step closer to Firiel, standing almost chest to chest, then shifted herself around to the left. A moment later, Firiel was on the ground with her right arm twisted around painfully and trapped in the other woman's embrace. She smiled down at the elf, kicking aside the axe that Firiel tried to slash at her with and stepping firmly on her other wrist, pinning her to the ground.

Jumah charged in toward the cleric, swords at the ready. Pouring the speed on, he knew he was moving faster than most people could even hope to see. The cleric panicked and fired off several magical bolts in his direction, which Jumah batted away with his own magical blades. He dodged to the side and slashed out with his right arm. The sword bit into the cleric's flesh between plates in his armor and caused him to yelp in pain and jump back from the attack. This caused him to fall on Jumah's out-stretched blades as he appeared suddenly on the Felinoid's opposite side.

The cleric made a sickening noise and dropped to his knees as Jumah wrenched his swords free and turned to face the human woman standing over Firiel.

"You see? You don't have what it takes to stop me," Malice growled as he stood up, dislodging his sword from the ground and swinging it over his head in a downward arc toward Riana's head. "You will all die here, and I will have the stone!"

Riana sidestepped the attack, slashing out with Elkorine. The magical blade of her sword opened Malice's armor with little effort, biting into his flesh and leaving a narrow slash across his side. She moved back into a neutral stance, holding Elkorine at the ready and making sure he could see his blood dripping from its tip as she waited silently for his next move.

Malice touched the wound with his left hand, bringing his bloody fingers to his lips and tasting the blood. He grinned from ear to ear as he raised his sword up again. This time he came at her with speed that she had never seen before. He moved like she had seen Jumah move on so many occasions, so quickly that there was almost nothing to see between where he started moving and where he stopped.

The black sword rained down blows on her like a hailstorm, coming so quickly that she could not defend against them with her sword skills alone. Instead, she somehow managed to block several of his attacks with her sword and erect magical shields in the path of the other attacks. She was fast enough to keep his blade from her flesh but the effort was swiftly draining her both physically and mentally. She knew she had to do something quickly or he would press an attack through her overtaxed defenses and it would all be over.

With a flash of desperation, she stepped toward him instead of away the next time he advanced, pressing herself up against his armored chest, cheek to metal. It took him a a few heartbeats to figure out what she had done, but in that span she pressed Elkorine's tip up to his chest and, finding a joint in his plate mail, slammed her weight into the weapon, driving it through the armor as if it were paper.

Malice shrieked as the thin, grey blade ran him through. He nearly dropped his own sword as he staggered back away from his assailant who kept her grip on her weapon, drawing it painfully back out of his body as he retreated. A look of abject terror washed over his countenance as his hand went to the fresh wound and came away again, this time drenched in his life's blood.

"Care to revise your call on the battle yet?" Riana asked with a smirk as she shook his blood from her sword and stared at him.

A loud grunt from Firiel's direction drew Riana's attention away from Malice in time to see the human woman twist the elf's arm around, producing a series of sickening popping sounds. Riana winced in sympathetic pain for the other woman but when she saw Jumah finish off the Felinoid and move toward the pair she knew Firiel was in good hands.

"Bad idea letting your concentration wander," Malice hissed at her as she felt his body slam into her midsection.

A searing pain flared up in her stomach and back as his weight bowled them both over. He landed fully on her and the burning sensation in her gut flared outward from the center as he leaned heavily on his sword to support his weight. He used the weapon as leverage to get himself standing again and it was a long moment before Riana realized what had happened.

He grinned down at her sadistically, leaning heavily on his sword's pommel with his right hand and holding her belt and pouches in his left. When she tried to get up off the ground and snatch them back, a searing pain ripped through her body, racing up and down her spine like lightning bolts. Reaching down to put pressure on the source of the pain she was horrified when her hands came into contact with the blade of Malice's sword.

"That's right youngling. Feel it. Taste the bitterness. Know that you have lost!" he yelled at her.

Riana lifted her head, ignoring the searing pain the action caused, to look down her body to where the inky black blade rose up out of her abdomen. She couldn't tell where the blade stopped and her skin began and it took a moment to realize why. Finally it dawned on her that the blackness of the blade was seeping into her skin surrounding the wound.

He sneered down at her as the realization washed over her, slowly seeping through the pain, "That's right. Death may be temporary in Kalijor, but I'm going to make sure you remember this for a long time to come." Then he made a motion with his other hand to draw her attention back to her belt, its various pouches dangling loosely in the air. "And I'm taking a souvenir for myself as well."

With that he wrenched the blade out of her stomach with a violent twist that caused her vision to tunnel. Unconsciousness began to creep in on her. She felt her body shifted and jostled and, after a moment, partially lifted up into the air. A warm feeling began to spread through her stomach and her mind and vision began to clear as the pain slowly receded. She felt a firm, warm embrace around her body and the cool, earthen floor of the arena was replaced with the warmth of someone's legs.

Her vision slowly returned and she looked up to see a form leaning over her, holding her to them. As the tunnel vision and blurriness began to fade she could begin to make out Jumah's strong features, a look of some great concern showing on his face. "Hey," she croaked, smiling up at him.

"Hey," he smiled back at her, his features quickly migrating back toward his usual, happy demeanor. "We thought we'd lost you for a minute there."

"You should know I'm made of sterner stuff than that," she replied, her ears perking up a bit.

"Yeah, well I'm afraid it isn't all good news," he said, looking toward her waist.

She looked down to see Desse, bleeding from numerous wounds of her own, holding her hands over the wound in her stomach. Her eyes were pressed tightly closed and a warm glow was emanating from her clasped hands. The healing energy coursed through Riana's body and the wound had almost completely closed, but there remained a thick black line. It looked like a scar, jagged and rough around the edges, and indeed it rose up from her flat abdomen like a berm of earth, but the flesh was black in color, just like Malice's sword.

Surrounding her were the faces of her other companions, all of them looking down on her with concern in their eyes. Everyone except Firiel who stood off to one side, her right arm hanging limply at her side, bent in all the wrong places as if it had several extra joints in it. The look on her face was one of calm indifference, showing no signs of pain or discomfort at her own twisted limb. However, when their eyes did meet for a moment, Firiel narrowed hers accusingly at Riana, her own ears laying back away from her head in annoyance.

That was when Riana remembered it, like a bolt, from the clear, blue sky. "He took it!" She started to sit up which caused a stabbing pain to shoot through her stomach, which elicited a frustrated sigh from Desse and caused Jumah to squeeze her to him a little tighter in an attempt to keep her still.

"We know Ree," Katrina's voice came back soothingly. "We saw him standing over you with your belt in his hand. As soon as we started moving toward you, he pulled his sword out of you and sounded some kind of retreat. They all just vanished in some kind of flash."

"It was like no teleport spell I've ever seen before," Exodus added.

"The magic seems to be originating within the dark one's sword," Xembak offered as he moved up behind Desse, resting his hands on her shoulders. Lowering his voice a bit he added, "I think it is time for you to focus your healing energies on yourself dear heart, lest we loose you, and thus, the rest of the wounded afterward."

Desse stood up and looked toward Firiel with a look that seemed full of a need to alleviate the other woman's pain. "But Firiel…"

"I'm fine for a while," Firiel said curtly, her useless right arm twitching spasmodically at her side as she spoke. "Take care of yourself, then we can handle this."

"But it looks horrible!" Desse protested as Xembak pulled at her arm, trying to get her to move off with him.

"It isn't going to kill me," Firiel said simply, narrowing her eyes at Riana. "I just wish it had been for some purpose."

Riana lowered her eyes to the ground in shame. If she hadn't hesitated, she could have finished him off. Somehow she didn't think that telling Firiel that it was concern for her that allowed Malice to gain the edge and eventually escape with the key would help. She didn't come off as a particularly caring individual and that was completely disregarding the fact that she wasn't even a player to begin with.

"We'll get it back," she finally muttered, pressing herself further in against Jumah's chest for some reassurance as the group began to make plans for what would happen next.

-13-

It took another hour to get the group patched up. Desse's wounds closed up quickly and the color rushed back into her skin shortly after that. Firiel's arm made several horrifying cracking sounds as the bones were magically set and the wounds healed. Throughout the entire process she didn't so much as twitch a muscle, her face remaining calm and passive, although she did offer Riana the occasional angry glare.

Despite her best efforts, Riana could not figure out who, or what, Firiel actually was. The circlet permanently attached to her head allowed her to see the real-world location of the person or software behind any character in Kalijor. When she looked at Katrina and focused on her intently, she could see a shimmering image of her friend, in her game pod with the EI harness resting snugly on her head.

Looking at Exodus produced a very similar image of Jax in his game pod (this made her giggle as Jax and Kat had always been at odds whenever they met, and Kat had no idea that Exodus was really him), and Jumah produced an image of Vincent laying on his couch. Desse and Xembak had both traced back to real people as well.

However, when she looked at Firiel in the same way, the only thing she was able to see was a deep, blue aura surrounding the elf, presenting a sort of negative image of her within the blue silhouette. She could see none of the regular yellows/golds or reds that she had come to associate with NPC's and player's respectively. Instead there was just empty space, surrounded by the dark blue, cloud-like aura. And tracing her back to her real-world source, revealed only the same bank of computers on The Tyconderoga's game deck as before.

The effect was extremely disconcerting, especially when she let her concentration slip and the elf snapped back into sharp focus with a look of annoyance on her face, always directed at Riana.

Finally, the group decided that they needed more information before making any steps toward recovering the key. They agreed to log out, do research, and get back together in Rathalon in two days, Kalijor time. That gave them less than seven hours to find out anything they could about Malice, the key, the possible location of the next artifact and, in Riana's case, as much as she could discover about Firiel.

Vincent's bedroom ceiling faded into her view as she logged out of the game. She took a moment to collect her senses, then disconnected the ODN line from her right wrist and shook her head in disbelief as she watched the tattooed skin on her inner wrist quickly seal itself, covering the data port up completely.

A moment later she was out in the living room, stretching languidly, much like a cat waking up from a long nap in the sun. Vincent was just getting up off the couch, setting his EI harness gently on the coffee table. He looked up at her with a mirthful smile that warmed her soul with its genuine, welcoming embrace.

"Well that could have gone better," he said conversationally as he stood up and stretched his own muscles.

"You think?" She replied sarcastically, turning into the kitchen, opening the refrigeration unit and bending over to pick an apple from the bowl of fresh fruit they had bought at the market.

"Um..." Vincent stammered from the other room.

"Um what?" Riana asked, standing up and taking a bite from the crisp red apple as she flicked the door of the refrigeration unit closed and spun around to face him quizzically.

The look on his face had changed to one of near terror and he stared at her as if she were some complete stranger in his house, eating his food. "Is it normal for battle scars to follow you out of the game?"

Riana stared at him vacantly for a long moment, the bite of apple in her mouth forgotten as she gaped back at him. Finally she managed a tentative, "Excuse me?"

Vincent stood up and moved slowly toward her, pointing at her midsection. "You have a mark right where Malice stabbed you." His voice was still uncertain, as if he didn't believe his own words even as he spoke them.

"I what?!" The forgotten piece of apple in her mouth chose that moment to slide toward her throat, causing her to nearly choke on it. She spent the next few moments coughing and sputtering as Vincent moved up to her and lifted the hem of her shirt, revealing her midriff.

"That is so bizarre," he commented as he poked her stomach with his index finger.

Riana finally managed to recover from the apple's assassination attempt and looked down at her stomach, grabbing the hem of her shirt and pulling it tight against her stomach so she could see past it. Sure enough there it was. An ugly, jagged-edged, black line, running diagonally across her stomach. The mark was raised like a fresh scar, four inches long, and perfectly bisected her navel.

"Crap!" Was the only thing she could think to say.

-14-

"The only thing I can find on the key is that the protection of the elves was once considered to be akin to some form of divine intervention. Apparently they were pretty good at keeping people safe once they accepted them as charges." Vincent ran his fingers through his long, blond hair and leaned back into a stretch in his chair as he spoke to her. When she failed to respond, he looked in her direction to see what was going on.

Riana was sitting on the couch, the hem of her shirt rolled up to the middle of her abdomen. She clutched the bottom of the shirt in one hand and poked the thick black scar on her stomach with the other. She didn't even seem to realize that Vincent had been speaking to her in the first place, let alone the fact that he had since stopped and was now staring at her.

"Riana?" He quirked an eyebrow in her direction as she continued to drag her fingers over the scar with a look on her face that hung somewhere between abject terror and total submission to an unfavorable thought. She still gave no sign of having heard him.

"You know, I thought we might take the traction drive out of the Kestrel and hot-rod the Neophyte Serendipity with it tonight after dinner." He knew that suggesting any sort of changes to her ship would normally elicit a string of suggestions as to what he could go do with himself. Instead, she proceeded to press her fingers into the mysterious mark as if she were attempting to feel her kidneys.

Finally he gave up trying to get her attention and stood up. He retrieved a beverage from his refrigeration unit and opened it up, taking a long drink from the container as he made his way across the living room and sat down next to her with a louder than necessary sigh.

She still failed to look away from her stomach, although this time she actually spoke to him. "I guess I should have expected as much. I mean the tattoos probably should have been a hint. I can't believe there's one on my back too!"

"Ree." Vincent put his hand on her knee gently, squeezing her leg with affection. "I know that sucks. But it doesn't seem to be causing you any real discomfort or issues, and we are running out of time to check things out before we have to meet the others in Rathalon…" he trailed off, hoping she would pick up where he left off.

"No discomfort? What do you mean no discomfort? I am in the middle of some sort of a break-down here!" She looked up at him, her violet eyes wide like they were about to break into tears at any moment, but they wouldn't come

"Are you in pain?" He suddenly looked aghast, leaning forward, ready to rush her off to a medical facility.

"No," she sniffled, rubbing the heel of her hand over her navel as she looked at him.

He visibly relaxed, but his eyes remained concerned. "What is it Ree?"

"I don't know. I just… I keep thinking I am going to find some measure of happiness and then something like this happens to remind me how much of a pawn I am in this whole situation."

He wouldn't have believed she wasn't streaming tears if he hadn't been looking right at her as she spoke. Her voice conveyed the emotion as well as any amount of tears ever could have. "I'm so sorry Ree, I keep forgetting…"

"And I just bought a bunch of new clothes that show off my midriff too!" She hollered at her belly angrily.

Vincent just stared at her dumbly. "Um…" The look on his face was priceless.

"What?" she shot at him, narrowing her eyes venomously.

"Nothing!" There was a defensive tone in his voice. "It's just that…"

"What?!" Now she was loosing her patience and he could have sworn her violet eyes flashed just like they did in Kalijor before she cast a spell, usually the sort of spell that caused people or objects to explode.

"I've just… never heard you say anything so… girly… before." He grinned a bit as her jaw dropped, instantly banishing her anger and replacing it with astonishment.

"Really?" she sounded taken aback by the comment.

"Well… I mean this is really the first chance you've had, what with your work and all but, yeah. Really."

She rubbed her fingers across the black scar on her stomach, now covered by her released shirt hem, as she eyed him for a moment. Then her look changed to one of hunger. "Let's take an hour to ourselves before we get into this research."

His eyes glazed over for a moment before he caught himself and said, "As much as I love the sound of that, we really need to get this done, Ree. I promise we'll get some more time before your vacation is over, though." He kissed her gently then, never breaking eye contact.

Riana put on her very best pouty face, tipping her head down and looking up at him from under her bangs. She actually managed to get him thinking about taking a break, but in the end he stood up and shook his head at her. "You are too much, you know that? I think I might actually be falling for you."

She grinned nefariously at him as she stood up. Turning to face him, she leaned in close enough that their noses were touching. "All part of my villainous plan!" Then she backed away with his drink in her hand and moved over to the computer terminal while draining the container.

"What is it else? A madness most discreet, a choking gall and a preserving sweet," he said under his breath as he moved up behind her.

"That was beautiful!" she gushed as she seated herself in the chair and brought the terminal to life with a few taps. The computer lit up the corner of the room with several holographic displays hanging in mid air and a holographic keyboard appeared under each of her hands as she held them out.

"I wish I could take credit for it," he responded as he began massaging her shoulders and looking at her screens. "I can't for the life of me figure out how you can use four screens and two interfaces at the same time."

"I'm still not used to the ODN interface. This is the next best thing," she replied simply. "That feels great, thank you."

"You're welcome. What do you mean you're not used to the ODN interface?"

She scrolled through numerous pages of information on each of the four hovering screens as she answered him. "I mean my ODN jack."

"The one you use for Kalijor?"

"Yes. Did I hear you say that you found a reference to the protection of the elves?"

"So you were listening after all," he smirked.

"I'm always listening."

"So you can interface with a regular computer terminal through your ODN jack? I thought that was just a replacement for an EI harness."

"Is this the reference you found?" She pointed to one of her displays.

Vincent squinted at the display for a moment before indicating that it was. Riana reached out and grabbed the display with her left hand and dragged it through the air to her left, leaving it hanging in air by itself. She conjured up another display, where the relocated one had been previously, and resumed paging through information as she replied to him conversationally. "It's some kind of computer interface. I'm not exactly sure how it works but I can use it to log in to Kalijor, control computer terminals, all kinds of stuff. I unlocked a door once. Oh! And I hacked a secured network once as well."

He stopped rubbing her shoulders and leaned in over her to point at one of her screens. Tapping a spot caused it to enlarge to fill the screen, revealing an image of the elven glyph within the stolen key. "What's this?"

Riana eyed the glyph for a moment before returning the screen to its previous zoom level and examining the context. "It seems to be a reference to an elven temple where those under the protection of the elves could be secreted away." With a wave of her hand the three other displays scattered to the right, hanging in mid air in a ramshackle pattern.

Grabbing the corners of the display with their nugget of treasure on it, she stretched the screen out to fill the space previously occupied by the group of them. "Let me see if I can track down a name."

Vincent touched one of the other displays, straightening it out and conjuring up an interface of his own. He pulled up the information she had found and began going over it in more detail. "It says something about a great elven king, but it doesn't mention a name. How long has it been since there was an elven king?"

"A real king? That's been since before the war."

"The Elf-Dwarf war?" He looked at her as she turned toward him with a look of disgust on her face. "What?!"

"No such thing," she said simply, turning back to her screen.

"No such thing as an elven king?" he asked, confused by her reaction.

"Not that," she replied before reaching to her right and grabbing one of her other screens. She dragged it in front of her, positioning it in front of the larger one and began working on it furiously, pages and pages of information flying across it in seconds.

"What? The war?" He continued staring at her.

"Yeah. Never happened."

"You're telling me there was no great war?" he sounded like she had just told him that people had been living on the Earth's surface for the last five hundred years.

"That's right. It was a cover-up."

"Where did you hear that?" The levity in his voice said he thought she was playing a joke on him.

"Well it isn't conjecture if that's what you are getting at. Let's just say that I have been doing a lot of reading in my spare time. Practicing my hacking skills on the company computers and such. And while I have yet to confirm my suspicions, I think I know someone who was there."

"There? You mean you know someone who witnessed the Great War?"

"No."

"I didn't think so," he smiled.

"I'm telling you that I know someone who witnessed the events that the Great War was invented to cover-up." The information on her smaller screen was scrolling by so quickly that Vincent couldn't even make out the individual characters.

"And who is this person?" he still sounded as though he was being made fun of.

"I don't get the impression that they are particularly interested in having their name spread around. Not to mention the fact that I have yet to confirm my suspicions."

He thought for a moment, staring idly at his own screen as he considered her words. "Okay. So what was being covered up?"

She smirked at him. She knew he would come around in good time. "The deaths of a king."

"Deaths? Plural?" He turned to look at her again. "Which king?"

"This one!" she said matter-of-factly as the blur of text on her screen came to a sudden stop and she pointed at the glowing rectangle triumphantly.

Vincent examined the screen with interest. "King Tinaan... Doesn't ring any bells."

"Nor should it. No one alive today has heard of him outside of a select few people." She flicked her finger across the screen, scrolling the information back and forth.

"And yet here his name is on the net," Vincent replied with a chuckle.

"Yeah, well this is just a site with some conjecture about how things may have been. To be honest it looks a little bit like privileged Solidarity Online information. I should probably report the site to security."

"Fair enough. So does it say anything other than his name?"

"Actually it mentions a temple known as Aranar, which translates as 'divine protection'." She raised her eyebrow as she stretched the screen out, enlarging the text even more. "Although there is, of course, no mention at all of where said temple might actually be located."

"Nothing could ever be that easy," Vincent confirmed, looking over her shoulder at the text.

"It gives me a headache," Riana said as she reached to her right and grabbed the fourth screen, dragging it back over in front of her and whipping through some pages.

"I'm sorry, did you want me to get you something?" Vincent sounded concerned and took a step toward the kitchen.

"No, not this. I meant using my ODN port to interface with computers other than the Kalijor servers. I always get a raging headache whenever I do that. Besides, your best headache cure isn't in your medicine cabinet." She grinned at him as she watched him shift uncomfortably for a moment.

"Um… Does it say anything at all about where it might be?" He dodged her appreciative look with little in the way of grace.

She grinned at him as she turned back to the terminal. "Not really, although I think we could probably tap my source in Kalijor for some more information."

"You don't think they will mind being outed?"

"I think, knowing you, that it won't be a problem. Besides, we're talking about the fate of Kalijor here, right?"

"I suppose so," he agreed, sitting down beside her. "Do you ever get the feeling that this whole thing is just a little bigger than us?"

She turned toward him, offering a serious expression. She took his hand in hers and squeezed it comfortingly, although to look at her face it seemed to be more for her own comfort than his. "Only every waking moment of my life."

He squeezed her hand in return and smiled at her reassuringly. "I think we'll manage alright. I just thought it seemed a little contrived is all. For you to always be in the wrong place at the wrong time."

"That seems to be the story of my life. Anyway, I want to see what I can find out about Firiel before we go back to Rathalon." She turned back to the terminal and with a broad, sweeping motion of her hand through the air, all of the various screens vanished, returning the terminal to the four screens she had originally started with. "Although I think I may need to call in a favor on this one."

She quickly navigated through the network, hopping from system to system with a speed that made Vincent's head spin. "Have you ever thought about changing professions? You'd make an excellent Digerati."

She chuckled at his words, never breaking her stride. "Thought about it, sure. But I can't leave SO until I get all of this settled. That and I don't think I like computers much."

Vincent laughed openly at her words. "You know, it shows. I don't think I've ever seen anyone move through the net like that before."

Riana rolled her violet eyes, returning her attention to what she was doing. In moments, she was having a conversation with Jax, who was at his terminal on the game deck of The Tyconderoga.

RSThorindal> Hey Jax. Was wondering if you could do me a favor?

JArianas> Sure! What's up?

RSThorindal> I need to know whatever you can tell me about the Firiel avatar.

JArianas> Still concerned about her, huh? Okay, let me see what I can find.

RSThorindal> Yeah. I'm telling you, she isn't a player. But she doesn't read as an NPC either. Thanks, Jax.

JArianas> No worries. Anything for a friend of Kat. This will take me a few minutes. Will you be there for a bit?

RSThorindal> Oh, I think I can find some way to occupy my time…

Riana's lips curled into a devilish grin as she replied. Turning to Vincent who was dealing with some paperwork that looked to do with customs, she tackled him to the floor so suddenly that he never even knew what hit him.

-15-

The sky in Rathalon was as blue as any blue could be. The weather was warm and calm and the streets were filled with their usual throngs of travelers, shoppers, merchants, residents, and adventurers. Riana and Jumah threaded their way through the crowded streets toward the tavern they had all agreed to meet at. The pair's short journey had quickly turned into a race where Jumah pressed his speed to his advantage, slipping around people and through empty alleys, and even over rooftops. To make up for her lack of lycanthropic speed, Riana invoked her magic, repeatedly teleporting herself to empty spots in the crowds and on rooftops.

Their separate techniques seemed to produce similar results as they both arrived on the porch of the tavern at nearly the same instant. Jumah came to a sudden stop on the porch, standing coolly as if he had been there for an hour, and Riana appeared with a slight 'popping' noise as she displaced a volume of air with her appearance.

They grinned at one another, grasped hands and pressed their way through the open, double doors, into the tavern's common room. The space was packed with every manner of creature, from orcs and ogres to goblins and elves.

Threading their way across the room, they ordered and picked up a couple of drinks before scanning the room for signs of their companions.

"There they are," Riana pointed to the back corner of the room where Xembak stood stock still next to Desse, who was seated at the table with a glass of wine in front of her. She smiled sweetly at them as they began moving toward the table.

"Welcome, friends," Desse said softly as they approached, although her voice was easily heard despite the din of the other patrons.

"Hello again," Riana replied brightly, casting her gaze around the room in search of any other members of their group. "Where is Firiel?"

Desse smiled as she spoke, "She said she had some errands to run around town before we left for wherever we are bound."

"So where are we bound?" Xembak asked.

"We're not sure yet," Jumah replied.

"But we have a good idea of where to find out," Riana added.

"Then we should make haste. When will your sister and Exodus arrive?" Xembak spoke with his perfect enunciation.

"They should be along any time, really. But I'm not sure if the person who may have the answers wants the whole world to know who they are," Riana replied.

"I see," Desse said in her same, sweet tone. "Where shall we reconvene then?"

"Let's meet in the Cohai portal chamber tomorrow morning around sunrise," Riana suggested. "If we get going now we stand a better chance of catching them before then," she finished, looking directly at Jumah.

"Alright," he nodded.

"Very well. We will inform your sister when she arrives and meet you both in Cohai tomorrow," Desse smiled. "Good luck to you in your investigation."

Riana nodded, pushed herself up from the table and bowed slightly to Xembak, who inclined his head in her direction. She grabbed Jumah's hand and dragged him out of the building behind her.

"I can only assume that you have a good reason for not telling them about Firiel," he said as they stepped down the few stairs from the porch into the street.

"They seem to trust her. Just because she isn't real doesn't mean that she is evil or anything." She shouldered her way through the crowded street, pressing toward the nearby portal building. "Besides which, what am I going to say? Oh by the way, your friend there isn't a real person, or an NPC. In fact she doesn't exist anywhere in the system, or out, as near as we can tell." She shrugged her shoulders. "We need more information before we do anything about her."

"Ok, I admit that we don't know much at this point, but don't you think it's a little strange that she doesn't exist, and yet there she is, pounding on the bad guys alongside us?" Jumah countered.

She turned to face him with a look of confusion, her purple eyebrows raised in his direction. "You ~were~ there at the concert with me right? You know, the one where my mother appeared as a hologram and told us about the key and the bad guys? Because I could have sworn you were there for that."

"Point taken. I guess I'm just not used to all this strangeness yet."

"Tell me about it," she said as they slipped through the heavy, paneled stone doors of the portal building. Moments later, there was a flash of light as they stepped into the Cohai portal and the small, torch-lit Cohai portal chamber greeted them. Riana rang the heavy, bronze bell that was hanging inside a small recess in the wall near the locked, reinforced wooden door that separated the portal chamber from the rest of the Cohai Observatory. Returning to where Jumah had laid out a blanket on the floor, she sat down next to him, leaning against the wall and prepared for the long wait before the doorbell would be answered.

"So, when this is all taken care of," he asked as he wrapped his arm around her shoulders, "do you think there will still be any time left in your vacation?"

"Somehow that doesn't seem terribly likely," she frowned as she spoke.

"You know. I've done work for SO before. Maybe I could swing another charter from them. That way we could work together from time to time." He squeezed her to him as he spoke.

"That could be interesting. I don't want to abandon Kat, though. She can get a little crazy sometimes." She leaned her head into the crook of his neck.

"A little crazy? You mean like getting all shot up and chased through the Ring Station by Aegis Online's private army? Or maybe something like appearing suddenly, unannounced and bloody, at a near-stranger's door? That kind of crazy?" There was humor evident in his voice as he spoke, but his words still stung.

"Did I ever apologize? For dragging you into all of that mess?" The events of that day played themselves out in her head. How an assignment to retrieve some code from AO had brought them into Gregory Shantal's trap. She had covered Kat's escape by calling out Shantal, then lopping off his hand and making a run for it. During the escape, she'd been shot up pretty badly and stumbled to Vincent's home because it was the only place she could remember the address for in her wounded state.

He cocked his head thoughtfully for a moment before responding, "You know, I don't think you did."

She pressed her lips together into a smile and snuggled in against him. "I will."

He sniggered at her, deciding not to rib her any more. The mood had changed a bit and he thought it would be nice to just sit and hold one another for a while. The irony was that as soon as he had made up his mind, the door leading into the Cohai Observatory groaned open on its wrought hinges.

In the doorway stood the prettiest troll that anyone had ever seen, which is to say that he was a long way from winning any beauty pageants, but at the same time, was not in danger of killing anyone from the mere sight of him. He filled the large opening almost completely with his misshapen form and the near-symmetry of his face was not nearly as disconcerting to look at as that of a gorgon's.

"Master Gornin!" Riana squealed as she leapt to her feet and dashed across the room to greet him with a warm embrace. The troll didn't protest the action, although he didn't seem terribly involved in it either.

"Welcome, Riana. It has been a while since you have stopped by. What can I do for you this fine morning?" His low voice was like a boulder being dragged across a field of gravel, almost soothing but at the same time, bordering on painful.

"We need help with something. I hope you don't mind, but I've told Jumah some of the things that you shared with Kat and I." Riana finally took a moment to show her respects by bowing to the old troll. He immediately returned her bow, seeming much more comfortable with this action.

"Of course not. Jumah has long been a pupil of mine and I understand his involvement in current events." He bowed to Jumah as the lycanthrope walked up to them, still securing his traveling things as he moved.

Coming to a stop near them, he returned the bow and smiled. "It is good to see you again, Sensei."

The two exchanged a firm handshake before Gornin invited them inside the observatory. Closing the heavy door behind them, he led the pair through the narrow, winding stone passageways of the ancient keep. Eventually they arrived in a medium sized, open room that looked to be equipped for sparring practice and meditation, with several thin cushions surrounding the large open area in the center of the room. Again, he closed the door behind them, bolting it tightly with a resounding clang of metal on stone.

Finally, he moved to the center of the room and knelt down, motioning with his hand that they should follow suit. Riana and Jumah quickly knelt side by side, each facing Gornin as he inspected them critically. His deep, blue eyes finally coming to rest on the thin, metal band encircling Riana's head, nearly concealed by her long, purple locks.

"You know that I do not approve of you seeking the keys, nor the relics that they seal away." His gravelly voice held no malice, or even disappointment, but it was still a statement of sufficient magnitude to cause Riana to look away in shame.

"I'm sorry, Master Gornin. They had Kat tied up in some oubliette and I didn't know…"

"I understand your reasoning, Riana. My lack of approval does not constitute any form of admonishment on my part. It seems that despite my best efforts to steer things differently, the prophesy is at hand."

Riana groaned. She tried to contain it, but the inevitability of his words just seemed comical to her after everything else she had seen and done recently.

Both Gornin and Jumah were staring at her by the time she realized that her groan had actually turned into stifled giggling. She quickly stopped herself before clearing her throat. "Um… I'm sorry. I just… find that statement to be the most cliché, ridiculous thing I've heard recently, and that is saying quite a lot at this point in my life."

Gornin raised an eyebrow at her and Jumah actually offered a chuckle. "I know that your life circumstances can make things seem fairly contrived from time to time Riana, however I think it is important that you meet these tasks with a certain level of decorum."

Riana looked at the troll very seriously for a moment before nodding and offering her apologies. "I'm sorry, Master Gornin, it's just that the more of these situations I encounter, the less real it all seems to me. How often can one person find themselves wrapped up in something like this? I mean, a prophecy? Wasn't it bad enough that a computer program accidentally gained sentience and was shuffled into a real body? But no! It didn't stop there! No sir! That person then has to become tangled up in some millennia old struggle for ancient, virtual I might add, artifacts that can somehow change the course of history!"

"Riana…" Gornin began, but was cut off again by Riana's ongoing tirade.

"But wait, there's more!! Not only am I the lucky recipient of all of the aforementioned prizes, but to sweeten the pot, I am also the daughter of some magical lesbian relationship that was torn apart by unrequited love from another, virtual, woman! And to make matters worse, that woman was trying to destroy the world with her evil offspring. Oh and did I mention that one of my mothers is now prowling around the real world as a wildly popular, holographic singer? Because that would seem to be relevant information under the circumstances." She hardly seemed to be breathing, she was talking so fast.

"Riana..." Jumah began, resting his right hand on her left shoulder.

It was his turn to be cut off as she continued on, shrugging off his touch. "And now I am about to find out that I am the centerpiece of some millennia old prophecy that no doubt will have me chasing all across Kalijor for the good of all creation. And never mind the fact that I may actually have decided on a course for my own life. That, of course, has no bearing whatsoever on the shape of events to come. No, I'll be roped in no matter what I say because not only am I 'the chosen one...'" she traced quotation marks through the air on either side of her head as she spoke. "But I am also somehow wired to feel morally responsible for all of this garbage."

When she stopped speaking, both Gornin and Jumah just sat there and stared at her for a few moments before either of them responded. Finally, after it seemed that the silence had gone on long enough to indicate that she was actually finished, Master Gornin cleared his throat and began to speak again, "I am sorry for your trials, Riana."

Instantly, a look of shame washed over her. She turned crimson from head to toe and looked away from both of them, hiding her face from them. "I'm sorry. That was uncalled for."

"You are right to be upset. Your life has been difficult and complicated in the last few years. However, there is one thing that I try to impart upon my students above all else. As much as we are capable of becoming who we want to be, there is always that bit of who we were born to be. Sometimes in life, reconciling these facets of ourselves can be the most trying of lessons. Many people are never able to live in peace because of this simple truth."

"Things are a little weird in your world, Ree, but together we can make things work out," Jumah added in.

Riana looked back at them, tears pooling in the corners of her eyes. "I'm sorry, that was very selfish of me. I just hate that nobody ever asks me. It's always assumed that I am all about this stuff, but no one ever just asks. And I really, really hate the fact that this is the only place I can shed my tears!"

Jumah moved up next to her and wrapped an arm around her shoulders, squeezing her to him comfortingly. "We'll work it out Ree."

She wiped the tears from her eyes and sniffled a bit as she leaned into him. "I'm sorry," she repeated again.

"You will find, Riana, that the things in life over which we have the least amount of control are usually the same things that we value most after they are said and done." Gornin's words did little to comfort her, but she seemed to understand his meaning, nodding in agreement.

"I know your time is limited, so I will make this as short as possible," the troll began. "It was shortly after the Lich King was destroyed that the prophecy was penned by one of Kalijor's most respected scholars. He claimed that the words came to him in a dream so vivid that when he awoke from it, the transcription was already writ in his best hand. All five artifacts had been sealed away and their respective keys scattered across Kalijor, but his dream made a very clear declaration that one day they would be needed again and that a child born of two worlds would be the one to collect them." He nodded solemnly at Riana as he spoke, "His words foretold of some very unspecific events that would endanger two worlds and all of the people in them."

"Unspecific?" Riana eyed him suspiciously, "Doesn't that sort of open a prophecy up to more than one interpretation?"

Gornin nodded his head solemnly. "It does, indeed. Which is why I have never personally placed much faith in this particular prophecy. However, several events that were very specific within the writings have come to pass and I have come to believe that there may be more to this scholar's musings than I had previously thought."

"What sorts of events?" Riana asked.

"Specifically, the finding of the keys and the first of the artifacts. I am sorry to say that from the moment I first met you, I suspected that you may be more deeply involved in world events, but my opinion of the prophecy kept me from acting upon those suspicions."

"Now that events are in motion and the validity of the prophecy is less in doubt, I feel it is time to share this with you. First, the prophecy states that a child born of two worlds will collect the keys and use the artifacts to protect both worlds against destruction."

"What sort of destruction?" Riana asked.

"The specific method of destruction is not mentioned. However, it does say that whatever it is will affect both worlds at the same time, so it is something we haven't seen before."

"But mom and I move in and out of both worlds all the time. Are we the first ones to do that in all this time?"

"Both you and Ezrina do spend time in both worlds. Neither of you exists physically in both worlds, however. Ezrina is insubstantial in your world…"

"Except when she's slapping me," Riana added, rubbing her cheek with her fingertips in remembrance.

"… and once you left Kalijor the first time, your avatar here became much the same as any other player's, merely a representation of you, rather than actually being you." Gornin artfully ignored her comment about her mother slapping her.

"So whatever is going to cause all of this trouble is able to physically exist in both worlds at the same time?" She raised an eyebrow at the troll.

"Is that really possible?" Jumah added in.

"To quote one of your own philosophers, 'There are more things in heaven and earth than are dreamt of in your philosophy'," Gornin said. "But to be perfectly honest, I have never seen anything to support the idea that someone, or something, can exist in both our worlds at once. Not physically."

"Okay. Well so far I don't really see anything in this prophecy of yours to indicate me. Born of two worlds could be talking about someone with mixed parentage, or a hundred other things," Riana sounded happy as she tried to debunk the troll's words.

"While that is true, the prophecy is specific about the order of the keys appearance, as well as the relics themselves, and at this point your actions are following the scholar's predictions exactly.

Even to the extent that you found the first key but have not yet used it."

Riana grimaced, more at the thought of whose hands the first key was in than at her having been further implicated in this tale. "Alright. So let's say I'm the person in this prophecy. That means everything works out alright and eventually this will all come to an end right?"

Gornin offered her a look somewhere between sympathy and admonishment. "It is never a good idea for a person to know too much about their own fate, Riana. Suffice to say that these sorts of events tend to come to a final conclusion, yes."

Riana glared at him for a moment, ready to attack with her usual venom. However, Jumah's light touch on her arm changed her mind. "Whatever," she finally replied, "We need information on the location of the next artifact. We found the key and we think we've tracked the location of the artifact to an ancient elven temple of protection called Aranar. I thought it might be on the dark side of Kalijor, somewhere in or around the ancient elven city, from before the war with the Lich King."

Gornin's face went almost pale for a moment, making his normal grey-green color look even sicklier. He was quiet for a long moment before finally clearing his throat to speak to them. "Aranar is indeed the location you seek and you are correct to assume that it is located in what was once the elven empire, but this is going to be even more troublesome than you may think."

"More troublesome than locating and entering a long-forgotten elven temple that doesn't officially exist? Oh, and it also happens to be on the dark side 'somewhere'." Her disgruntled attitude was fast resurfacing in the conversation.

"Yes," Gornin replied calmly. " Firstly, because the ancient elven empire is now at the bottom of what is known as the Dead Sea. It was swallowed up by the waters after the Lich King appeared. When he moved his seat of power to that abominable castle, Kalijor seemed to act quickly, subsuming his former kingdom in a torrent of tainted waters. Secondly, the guardian of that artifact is likely to be one of the most dangerous creatures you have ever encountered."

"Worse than a Death Dragon?" Riana's voice betrayed her disbelief.

"Yes, worse than a Death Dragon, Riana. Even a creature as deadly as a that has sense enough to avoid such a toxic cesspool as the Dead Sea. No, the guardian there will be something far worse, something that not only causes death, but revels in it, is fed by it."

"That's a comforting thought, Master Gornin. Thank you for that." She screwed up her eyes at him, folding her arms across her chest. "So we need to figure out a way to get beneath the Dead Sea and try to figure out what could be living down there." She looked at Jumah, half hoping he would have her answers at the ready.

Instead he offered, "That and we need to figure out where Malice is so we can retrieve the key from him."

"You had to throw that out there, didn't you?" Riana jabbed him in the ribs.

"When searching for a rat it is usually best to begin with their food," Gornin interjected. Riana swiveled her head around to look at him, squinting her violet eyes down into slits as she considered his parable.

"The Crossed Swords," she finally said, opening her eyes wide and cuffing Jumah on the shoulder, "Almost every dealing we have had with him has been there. Even when he kidnapped Kat, he did it there!"

"Sounds as good a place as any to begin looking for him," Jumah nodded.

"Right. Let's get after it then," Riana said as she hopped to her feet.

Jumah looked in Gornin's direction and, receiving no objections, sprang to his feet as well. "Alright, the others should be arriving soon, if they haven't already."

As they headed for the chamber door, Gornin called after them, "Riana, it is important that you not only understand who you are, but accept it. Without that acceptance, your life will always be more difficult than you can imagine."

Riana let go of the door handle, her shoulders slumped, and she turned slowly to face the troll. "Master Gornin, what does that mean?"

He shrugged uneven, lumpy shoulders at her. "To use another human phrase, 'It is what it is.' My point is that until you accept yourself, you will always find the road ahead to be an insurmountable path. Only you can change this."

"By understanding who I am," she repeated.

"Yes, but understanding is merely the first step. Accepting it is the journey."

She dropped her eyes to the floor and shook her head. "And what is the destination? Where am I headed?"

Gornin smiled his toothy, crooked smile then. "I think you will find that once you begin your journey, reaching the destination tends to loose its importance." He bowed deeply to them, "I wish you a good journey, and look forward to our next meeting." Then he turned and disappeared through another door in the side of the room.

"Well, I would like to say that this entire exchange has been depressingly typical, cryptic, and frustrating," Riana said as she turned and pulled the door open.

Jumah followed her out into the hallway, resting his hand on her shoulder. "Never let it be said that he leaves you without something to ponder on the way home."

"Now, if only I were going home," she stabbed.

"Is it really so bad? I know events tend to pile up around you, Ree, but you have your family and your friends with you. There are much worse ways to be swept up in things."

She knew his words were meant to be encouraging and supportive, but they didn't do anything to untie the knot of anger in her stomach. Again and again she was forced into these incredible circumstances. She was expected to play along, to be a good elf and make the world right again. In truth, she probably would do it without a second thought no matter what. After all, here she was at it again. But she just couldn't get over the fact that, despite all of that, she had never once been asked what her feelings in all of this were, even now.

By the time they had made their way back to the Cohai portal chamber, the rest of the group was there waiting for them. Desse stood serenely in the center of the room, barely leaning against a support column, while Xembak stood next to her, his scaly arms folded across his chest and his naginata slung across his back with his claymore. The pair were at ease, although it was almost difficult to tell when taking in Xembak's ever-alert state.

Katrina and Exodus sat against the far wall and Kat was giggling about something as she prodded playfully at Exodus' side. For his part, Exodus was trying very hard to not appear as though he might be having some form of fun, although he was failing entirely to pull it off.

Then there was Firiel. The strange, fire-haired elf was leaning back against a pillar that stood as far away from the rest of the group as she could get. Her body was stiff as a board, with only her shoulder blades touching the pillar and the heels of her booted feet touching the floor, and yet she still managed to look horribly bored.

As Riana and Jumah entered the room, the others looked toward the door expectantly. "Hey everyone!" Riana said, making her best attempt at sounding upbeat.

"Heya sis!" Kat responded almost immediately. "Where're we headed?"

"Several places, in point of fact," Riana sighed, "C'mon. Let's head to The Crossed Swords and I'll tell you all what's going on."

-16-

The Crossed Swords. It had been over a year since Riana had been there. On her last visit she had been searching for Katrina, who had been badly beaten and then taken hostage by Malice in an attempt to get the first key. Riana was sure she liked the grungy establishment no more now than she had then, and a shudder from Katrina told her that she was none too keen on being there either. The place was not much more than a large, square pit surrounded by tables and chairs. Everything in the place was arranged in such a way as to provide the best possible view of the pit, which was where all of the fighting took place. Even now, as they walked in off the crowded street, in the middle of the afternoon, two creatures were circling round one another with weapons in hand, trying to place the final strike on one another.

The floor of the bar was filthy, strewn with small bones, the shells of nuts, fingernails, discarded food remnants, and what looked like 500 years worth of dirt and slime. Most of the big chunks had been swept to the corners and the air was thick with the stench of organic matter that was long past the point of rotting. All of the windows had been covered by boards or bricked in with stones and the room was lit, instead, by the flickering light of several, although nowhere near enough, torches that protruded from the stone walls at odd angles.

"Well, this place is just as cheerful as I remember it being," Katrina commented, only half joking.

"Well it's better here now than the last time I was here," Riana replied.

"Why's that?" Katrina raised an eyebrow, her ears perking up in curiosity as to how it could possibly be any worse.

"The last time I was here I spent the afternoon threatening people's lives if they didn't tell me everything they knew about you and Malice." Riana breathed, watching images of herself screaming at people, threatening their lives if they didn't tell her what she thought they knew. "And the time before that, I was forced to watch helplessly as Malice nearly beat you to death." She nodded reassuringly to herself. "So yeah. It's actually much nicer today."

Katrina watched her sister stroll into the bar and pick the least filthy of the larger tables to sit down at, placing herself in a position that allowed her a view of the rest of the bar's patrons. "I suppose that would make it a bit nicer," she finally replied to the rest of the group as memories of Malice's beating washed back over her. After a moment, Exodus put his hands on her shoulders and guided her to a chair near Riana.

Jumah sauntered into the place, took one broad, sweeping look around, and then made his way to the bar, looking no different than his usual, smiling, carefree self. Desse's reaction was similar to that of Jumah. She took a moment to absorb the feeling of the place, and then smiled her serene, knowing smile, and made her way to the table. Xembak followed his life-mate and remained standing behind her, his face still as impassive as ever, as he folded his arms across his chest and stared at the room, daring anyone there to make trouble.

Firiel's reaction was anything but what Riana would have expected, especially given her behavior during the battle they had so recently fought. The tiny elf made her way immediately to the bar, stepping away again with four tankards of ale, which she brought to the table, setting them down roughly enough that they shed fully a quarter of their combined volume all over the table top. She then turned her back on the action in the pit, sat down with a thud and drained one of the tankards in a single pull.

"Are you feeling alright?" Riana asked the other elf with a note of real concern.

Firiel looked up at her, ears laid back in annoyance. "I despise this place," she said simply as she picked up another tankard.

"So you are going to drink until you can't see it any longer?" Riana accused, her own ears splaying out in an open display of anger.

"You bet!" Firiel responded with enthusiasm, raising the tankard in salute to Riana and pressing it to her lips. She drained it in a single pull as well, slamming the empty vessel back to the solid wooden table with a bang just as Jumah arrived with a tray of elven wine, glasses, and some cheese. "Where the hell did you get that in a place like this?" Firiel eyed the tray suspiciously.

"The owner's son is an acquaintance of mine," Jumah replied simply, eyeing the belligerent elf.

"And you trust him to give you the good stuff because you know his kid?"

"No," Jumah smiled slyly at her, "I expect him to give me the good stuff because I saved his only child's life from a horde of giants in the Northern Wastes." He poured six glasses of the wine and began distributing them to everyone but Firiel who was now brandishing her third tankard of foamy ale. "That and I think he knows me well enough to understand that I tend to take care of those that take care of me and mine."

Firiel had pressed the third tankard to her lips as he spoke, but didn't get around to drinking any of it, listening to the meaning behind his words instead. When he finished speaking, she took the tankard away from her lips and raised it toward him in toast. "Fair enough. To you and yours then. May we all live to tell our children of these turbulent times!"

Jumah eyed her for a moment before grinning widely and raising his own glass. After a moment the rest of the group followed suit, all raising their glasses. Even Xembak took a break from his imitation of a golem to partake in the toast.

"Here here!" They all chorused before drinking from their glasses, Firiel and Jumah both draining their's in one try.

"So. What's the plan?" Exodus finally broached the subject, "As much as I like the stench here, I can think of several other locations that I would rather patronize."

Riana nodded solemnly. "Ok. We have several different needs at this point. First off, we need to get the key back from Malice. We're here because this is where he comes for his meetings and to amuse himself in his off-time. Sooner or later we will find some clue as to his whereabouts."

"Fair enough," Exodus agreed, looking around the table at the rest of the nodding faces. Even Firiel seemed to be getting into the spirit of things. "What else is on the to do list?"

Riana pressed her lips together in a hard line for a moment, toying with her wine glass idly as she thought about how to pass on the information. Finally she seemed to make up her mind and spoke again, raising her eyes to Katrina and Exodus specifically. "We need spells to keep us alive and able to fight at the bottom of the Dead Sea."

Katrina smiled widely for a moment before Riana's grave expression convinced her that this was not a joke. "You're serious?" she gaped at last.

"Unfortunately, yes. We were told that was where the temple is located, and that the guardian is likely to be something a lot worse than a Death Dragon, given the environment."

"We should also do some research on what that could be. I'd rather not go into this fight blind if there is any way to avoid it," Exodus said seriously.

"Right. So whatever it is, it can either breathe that toxic water, or doesn't need to breathe at all. Add to that the fact that it has been there for millennia and it should narrow the field quite a bit," Katrina chimed in, taking out her journal and making some notes in it.

"My thinking is that if the two of you can go handle the spell and monster research, then the rest of us can cast as wide a net as possible in order to get a line on Malice," Riana suggested.

"It would be advisable not to limit our search to Rathalon," Xembak offered, "Both Avian and Talanor have similar establishments." His hand twitched in the direction of the pit in the center of the room.

Desse nodded her agreement. "That is true, the pattern is seldom so limited in scope."

Riana thought for a moment, chewing on her lower lip as her ears twitched. "That's a good point," she conceded, "but we need some way to keep in touch, or even to rally quickly if the need arises."

"I think I can help there," Firiel chimed in, banging her fourth empty stein on the wooden table loudly.

The entire group, with the exception of Desse and Xembak, swiveled their heads toward the elf, who's ears lay back and eyes narrowed at them. "Just because I don't speak much doesn't mean I am some kind of idiot, you know," she spat at them.

It was Desse who finally broke the stunned silence with her soft smile and lilting, singsong voice. "Of course not, Firiel. They are simply unaccustomed to your thread. What do you have for us?"

Firiel eyed the group suspiciously for a long moment. Her face said that she was considering keeping her mouth closed after all. When Desse reached over and gently touched the back of her hand, Firiel hefted a large belt pouch to the table. She flipped the heavy flap over and began rummaging through the pouch, muttering under her breath about getting organized some day, before finally emerging with another, much smaller pouch. This one she opened, and then overturned onto the table. From the bag poured a large collection of identical rings, each one a dull silver color and bearing a hefty, cut blue stone atop it.

"Those look kind of like portal rings," Katrina said as she picked one up gently and examined it with a critical eye.

"No, not exactly," Exodus chimed in again, "Yes they are similar, but the magic is different somehow, where did you get these?"

Firiel smiled with a touch of pride as she leaned back in her chair and folded her arms across her chest. "I had them made the other day while we were on that research break."

"What do they do?" Jumah asked as he picked one up as well.

"That's the great part. When they are activated, in the same manner as normal portal rings, they will open a portal to the location in which they were initially worn. Simply putting it on attunes it to whatever location you are in and using it brings you straight back there again." She was positively beaming with pride as she described their function.

"That explains the weird feeling," Exodus said with a tone of triumph. "Once the attunement happens I bet they feel more like a regular portal ring."

"How much did they cost?" Riana asked with a tone of amazement in her voice.

"Don't worry about it. I'm just glad they turned out to be of use," Firiel smiled.

"How do they work through the anti-teleporting wards around the city?" Katrina asked with a hint of excitement.

"There is an exception to every rule," Firiel narrowed her eyes at the curious elf, her look screaming that she expected the subject to be dropped.

"Where should we attune them?" Jumah asked pointedly, trying to move the conversation on.

"It would have to be somewhere with enough space for all of us, plus Malice, which means there could be some fighting involved," Exodus said, looking at the rest of the group curiously.

"How about the Great Arena?" Katrina offered. "There's plenty of space there for whatever we might need to deal with."

"While that is true, the Great Arena is hardened against teleportation and portal magic, primarily to prevent people from appearing or disappearing during battles," Exodus grimaced, "It will have to be somewhere else."

"What about here?" Riana offered, "I mean, none of us really likes this place, but there is plenty of room, especially if you consider the pit."

"It does seem an appropriate location for such a conflict," Desse agreed.

"He will have the home field advantage here," Xembak added, focusing his reptilian eyes on the pit below them as if he were looking for some hidden supply of weapons or secret trap-operating levers.

"I don't think that is a real problem. Every time we have fought him in the past, he has used nothing but what he has on him. There seems to be a note of pride in his fighting skills, even if he does come off as the cheating type," Jumah replied.

"Besides, no one says we can't set up a few surprises of our own in anticipation of the main event," Katrina grinned from ear-to-ear as she spoke.

"There is that," Riana grinned back at her sister, ears perked up mischievously. "So, any objections to this location?"

"None that I can think of," Exodus replied.

"This is as good a place as any for round two," Firiel smiled.

"Sounds good to me." Jumah breathed.

Riana looked around the table at the agreeing faces and nodded back. "Alright then. We should put the rings on in the pit there, that way we can bring him in without destroying all of this fine furniture."

Katrina stifled a snort of laughter as the group stood up and made their way toward the center of the building, each holding a ring in preparation for setting their trap.

-17-

"Can I get you something to eat?" Jumah asked as he moved up behind Riana and began rubbing her shoulders.

"No, I'm alright. Thank you." Riana sighed as she attempted to relax her stiff muscles under his ministrations. "How long have we been here?"

"Nearly four days now," Jumah replied with a hint of displeasure.

"This sucks," she said, picking up her glass. She took a sip of the water that had replaced the elven wine, several days past.

"To say the least," he agreed.

"Any word from the others?"

"Katrina and Exodus say they are close to figuring out the needed spells and that they have a couple of ideas what may be down there. Last word from everyone else was similar to what we have seen here." He ticked off each snippet of news on his fingers, finally splaying his hands open wide to indicate the same nothing that they had encountered at The Crossed Swords.

"That isn't encouraging." She groaned as he hit a particularly tight muscle in her back.

"Not especially, no," he agreed. "I know that catching Malice strolling into the tavern is a little unlikely, but it seems like one of his cronies would be sent out for supplies and news sooner or later."

"Maybe sooner than you think," a scratchy, high-pitched voice dripped from behind them. "Keep your hands on the elf's shoulders and you keep yours on the table, youngling."

Jumah's hands tensed up for a moment before relaxing completely on her shoulders, which Riana knew was a sign that he was ready for a fight. "Who are you calling youngling, goblin?" she spat at the table, making no sudden moves. She still hadn't seen the creature, but she had dealt with goblins enough in the past to recognize the characteristic sound of their voice.

"I have seen enough of you to know the truth. Although, I must confess to a certain curiosity concerning your demeanor. You seem much more like an NPC than a player to me. Excepting of course your beau here." Pressure from whatever implement the goblin had against his skin caused Jumah to move in closer to Riana's back.

"I don't suppose this is the part where you tell us where your boss is so we can trounce you and then dash after him?" Jumah asked jovially.

"That wouldn't be my first choice, no," the goblin sneered. "Truth be told, I didn't even want to risk coming out here to get you, but when I am paid this well to do a job, I tend to loose most of my rebellious streak."

"Come to get us?" Riana's voice echoed Jumah's curiosity.

"Well, one of you at any rate. He was non-specific as to what I should do with you there, muscles." Jumah was pushed harder against Riana's back.

"If you take her and leave me alive, you are signing your own death warrant," Jumah stated.

"I suppose that pretty much says it all then, doesn't it?" The creature pushed the blade further into Jumah's back, causing him to grip Riana's shoulders tightly for an instant before his hands disappeared from her entirely.

"I imagine so."

The next few seconds were a blur. Jumah twisted himself away from the unseen blade, stepping to the side as Riana stabbed backward with Elkorine. The magical blade bit shallowly into the goblin's flesh before the creature managed to jump back from the blade's tip.

Unfortunately for the goblin, the movement brought him up against Jumah who had spun around behind him in the space of a heartbeat. To his credit, the goblin moved faster than most people would have been capable of, spinning to the side and moving toward the door, but even his speed was nothing compared to Jumah's supernatural reflexes.

As Riana came up out of her chair, Elkorine held firmly in her right hand and a ball of swirling, black energy forming in her left, she saw Jumah grab the goblin by his leather bandoliers and spin around, flinging the creature bodily across the tavern. There was a loud crashing noise as the goblin slammed into the rail above the pit and, before he could catch his breath, Jumah was on him again, pressing a solid side kick into the goblin's temple and sending him sprawling over the edge and into the arena.

The goblin landed with a thud and as his eyes refocused on the ceiling, now some thirty feet above him, he caught sight of an enraged Riana vaulting over the edge of the pit. As she cleared the rail he had just tumbled over, she flung the ball of crackling energy at him. He rolled to the side in enough time to avoid catching the spell in the chest, but it still hit his right hand, exploding into a shower of black lightning. He winced in pain but kept himself moving toward his feet. By the time Riana landed, Jumah was already on the ground in the pit, swords drawn and poised to strike.

"Give up your boss and this won't have to end badly for you," Riana said as she brought Elkorine up, ready for action.

"That's not going to happen, youngling witch," he sneered as he stripped two knives from his bandoliers with his left hand and flung them at her. The spent daggers were almost instantly replaced with new ones and he moved around the pit, randomly, keeping in constant motion as he flung volley after volley at the pair.

Riana's eyes flashed as she summoned a magical skin of stone that caused the knives directed at her to carve out a couple of chips before falling to the ground. Jumah put on an incredible display of agility as he dodged and wove his way around and between the throwing knives, all the while trying to position himself for an attack, but the goblin proved quite adept at confounding his opposition, refusing to stand still for an instant, or make a single predictable move.

For several long moments the pair chased their diminutive adversary around the pit, unable to land a single attack on him. Finally, Riana's eyes flashed and the room came to a standstill. She causally walked across the pit and positioned herself on the goblin's side. As the duration of her stop-time spell elapsed and the world began to surge back to life, she extended her foot slightly, hooking her ankle in front of the goblin's shin just as he started moving again.

The goblin lurched forward, his leg suddenly not where it was supposed to be. Tumbling forward with all the grace of a falling tree, he tried to absorb the impact with his arms but his wounded hand buckled on impact. Momentum carried him face first into the packed earth of the floor and his long, tapered nose made a sickening crack as it folded beneath his weight.

As Jumah descended upon the wounded goblin, a column of floating blue rings appeared in the center of the pit. Xembak stepped through, weapon at the ready, followed by Desse, then the rest of the group within a few minutes, but they were too late to prevent the creature's next move.

With a speed that belied his wounded condition the goblin dashed toward Riana, pulling a small blue crystal from a pouch on his belt as he moved. With no aplomb whatsoever, he threw the crystal against the wall behind Riana and dove head first into her mid-section. The crystal exploded into a shower of blue-white sparks that enveloped the startled Riana as she fell backward through the fireworks and vanished.

-18-

Tumbling backward onto the hard floor, Riana pulled her legs up between herself and the goblin and kicked him free of her as she continued over backward, coming to a crouching position. Elkorine at the ready and a conjured ball of fire in her left hand as she scanned the area for aggressors. What she saw was anything but expected.

Standing on the opposite side of a well-appointed sitting room was an individual that Riana could only assume was Malice. Her lack of certainty was born from the absence of his tell-tale inky black armor and his equally distinguishing sword. Rather, he stood before her wearing some of the finest, most distinguished clothing Riana had ever seen a man wear. His dark hair was clean and neatly arranged and he actually gave her a shallow bow as he dismissed the goblin, who left the room quietly through a large, ornately carved wooden door, closing it behind him.

"I'm sorry for the means of your arrival, but I could not be certain you would have accepted anything more civil under the circumstances of our past meetings," the normal hostility and, well, malice, was almost completely gone from his voice as he spoke.

Riana scanned the rest of the room for any signs of potential attack or the inevitable trap but, despite her best efforts, she could not seem to locate any such danger. Slowly she stood up and clenched her fist tightly around the roiling ball of flame in her left hand, extinguishing the eager blaze with a thought. "What is going on here, Malice?"

"We need to talk, you and I." He motioned to a comfortable looking chair near where he stood and shrugged as she raised a critical, purple eyebrow at him. "I know I could not have had the conversation we need to have in the presence of either your friends or mine, so I have invited you here to my own home in order that we might be civil for a short time."

"Invited me? You must be joking. You had your creepy little goblin attack us and accost me!" She squeezed the handle of her magical sword and it pulsed in response, eager to do her bidding.

"Again, you have my apologies. Please, come speak with me for a moment. Maybe we can figure this relationship out." He motioned toward the chair again. "Please. Sit. Let us talk."

She eyed him critically as she moved toward the indicated chair, Elkorine ready to cut down any dangers that might arise. Try as she might, she could still not identify any potential threats in the room. Excepting, of course, her apparently now-generous host.

"What do you want, Malice?" she asked after checking out the chair and gingerly seating herself on the very edge, ready to leap up in an instant.

"Your paranoia does not do you any favors, Riana. If I had wanted you attacked it would have happened before you were in my sitting room. You are in no danger from me here," he said as he sat down opposite her and reached forward to pour two steaming cups of tea from a silver pot on the table between them.

He didn't wait for her, or even suggest she drink from her cup, instead picking up his own and sipping from it. The entire scene was so comical that Riana had trouble biting back her sarcastic laughter.

"What in the world would I have to be paranoid about? It isn't as though you have beaten half to death and kidnapped my sister. Or nearly killed me. Or stolen from me. Or kidnapped me and brought me here against my will," her ears laid back angrily as she spat her words at him, her violet eyes narrowed and venomous. "I mean, if you had been any more a gentleman to me in the past I might be considered paranoid. As it is, I can't even begin to put into words how I feel about you. If you have the words, please let me know."

Malice nodded his head and offered a slight sigh in response to her words. Taking another sip from his teacup, he looked thoughtful for a moment before finally responding to her. "You're right, of course. I've given you no reason to trust me. All I can really say at this point is that I have never been dishonest with you before, and I have no intention of starting now."

"Dishonest? No. I suppose not. Cruel, vindictive, callous, irresponsible, and disreputable, definitely. But dishonest? Not so much, I guess. So what can I do for you? What is it that could possibly warrant you bringing me here and trying to convince me of your good nature?"

"Has anyone ever told you that you have a tendency to run on?" he asked.

Riana's eyes flashed and the table between them exploded into a shower of burning wooden splinters. The sound echoed off the stone walls and caused Malice to half stand up from his chair, spilling his tea in the process. "Don't get lippy with me, Malice. I'm not of a mind to deal with it and there isn't that much furniture in here."

"I suppose you're right. Very well then," he sat back down, dismissively waving away someone who poked their head through the door. The door quietly closed and he returned his attention to his angry guest. "I need to know your intentions concerning the artifacts."

She did her best to keep from flinching, raising a curious eyebrow and looking at him pointedly. "What artifacts?"

He smiled calmly at her. "Now it is you who is playing with me. Come now, Riana, we should respect one another more than that. Even if it is as enemies."

She gave him a long, hard look before continuing, "Fine. I intend to keep them away from everyone who wants them."

"Why."

"Because anything that is so important to so many powerful people needs to be kept out of intentioned hands."

"And you think you are the best suited individual to do that?"

"Well, I've kicked your ass, and you seem to be the best thing going around here." Her eyes flashed again, challenging him to prove her point.

"Let's not forget that it took three of you to defeat me the first time we fought. Not to mention the fact that I had no real desire to harm any of you," Malice responded calmly.

"No real desire?!" Riana's eyes began to glow and a static charge built up in her hair, causing it to float around her head in a menacing halo. "You took my sister captive for months! You threatened me. Stabbed me! I can see how I might have misinterpreted your intentions all this time!"

"Calm yourself!" he shouted, setting his empty tea cup on an end table and standing to face her. "Or my welcoming nature will be put aside to deal with you in kind!"

"Why am I here, Malice? Out with it or I'll make myself an exit."

He collected himself. Turning his back on her, he moved across the room to inspect an intricate tapestry hanging above an ancient credenza that was littered with what looked like equally ancient artifacts, stones, knives, pots, and more. He was quiet for several minutes as he inspected the hanging tapestry, his arms folded across his chest. At last he spoke, keeping his back toward her as he did so, presenting her with a 'can't miss' target. "I assume that you've heard the legend of the warrior that defeated the Lich King using the artifacts?"

"What about it?" she seethed, still surging with power and ready to lash out at him.

"It's curious don't you think? How he was able to defeat the most powerful being Kalijor has ever known, using artifacts of such power that they were secreted away forever, right beneath the eyes of everyone in the world, and yet, no one has ever heard of these items or events before."

"What is your point Malice?" Electricity danced back and forth between her fingertips.

"My point, Riana, is this. I have proof, definitive and incontestable, that the hero survived that battle. Even more to the point, he walked away unscathed from the conflict. Now, my research has revealed that these artifacts can not be taken from a still-living individual, a theory that I am sure you are in a position to validate." He paused for effect, making certain that she knew he was aware of the artifact she wore about her head. "So if he survived the battle, and the objects can not be taken from a living person, then what, do you suppose, happened to him that allowed the artifacts to be scattered?"

The halo of energy surrounding her evaporated in an instant. "What?"

Malice turned to face her, sensing that the chaotic energy had dissipated. "What indeed, Riana. That is the question of the millennium. What force? What magic? What tool? What.... person, could be capable of defeating the most powerful individual in the world? The only person who was capable of defeating the Lich King. What indeed."

"Are you suggesting that there is something, or someone, out there, that is capable of killing a person carrying the five most powerful objects in Kalijor?"

"No, Riana. I am suggesting nothing of the sort. I am telling you that the hero died after the final battle with the Lich King. And I am telling you that the same hero could not have died at the hand of anyone less powerful than the Lich King himself. What you infer from my statements is entirely up to you. However, I would offer you this to think on." He turned back around to inspect the tapestry once more, this time raising his arms toward the fabric, indicating that she do the same.

Riana looked more closely at the hanging fabric. Its quality was apparent even from half way across the room, as was its extreme age. The colors were faded by time, although still discernible, and its edges were unraveling and frayed, but the image in the center of the piece was still easily understood. There stood an impressive figure in the center of the work, his power was evident from the lines of light and energy radiating outward from his body.

He wore a very distinct breastplate with equally impressive pieces on his forearms and head, and a sword of impressive craftsmanship was held aloft in his right hand. He looked almost deific, standing there as if he was allowing the world around him to bask in his radiance.

But as she stepped closer to the hanging she could see the deeper meaning of the piece. The lines of power had dark, black cores to them and the look on the man's face was one of pure hatred and disgust. He wasn't allowing the world to bask in his power. He was burning it down. All around him, what had looked like faded lines and splotches of color from a distance resolved into buildings, towns, entire cities filled with people, all burning away under the wash of power coming from the angry figure. He was killing them all.

"What is this?" she asked, reaching out with her fingertips to gently touch the material, as if to make sure what she was seeing was, in fact, solid and real.

"This is a tapestry that I had smuggled out of the Cohai Observatory some years ago, after I heard the legend of the hero for the first time. Several people died in the stealing of this tapestry."

She cast him a sour look at his choice of words. "As if you care who lives and who dies?"

He sighed heavily. "Riana, I grow weary of this verbal sparring. I have no expectation that you will ever come to understand me on any level other than that upon which we have become acquainted. However, I would ask that you set your witty repartee aside for the time being so that we can discuss the matter at hand more directly."

She glared at him for a long moment before turning back to the tapestry. "Fine. What was the tapestry doing at Cohai?"

He smiled slightly, turning his own attention back to the hanging. "It was collecting dust in the basement."

"And you learned about it how, exactly?"

"A man in my position has ways of keeping in touch with items and events of importance around the world."

"Right. So you heard this thing was there and you what? Attacked Cohai? Funny thing that I don't seem to remember any news about anything having been stolen from Cohai during a raid."

"I stole this long before you were even born, Riana. And do you really think that something being stolen from Cohai would make the local gossip circuit? Such a thing is impossible, as everyone knows. Therefore anyone who knew, was likely silenced immedi-ately."

"Silenced," she echoed.

"Yes," he confirmed.

"As in, 'you talk and we kill you' silenced?" she drew quotes in the air with her fingers as she spoke.

He gave her a hard look of his own making her feel five years old again. It was the same look that a mother would give a daughter who knew the truth of something despite their protestations to the contrary. "I hardly think so."

"So you think that someone, from Cohai, killed witnesses to an art theft?"

"Not someone," he shook his head, then looked back at the tapestry, pointing at the figure in the center. "Look closer."

She moved in close to the tapestry and squinted at the figure in the center. It took several moments before she saw it, barely dis-cernible against the background. In the hero's shadow, creeping up behind him with body poised to strike a murderous blow was the distinct figure of a decidedly less-ugly, blue-eyed troll.

-19-

Riana stepped back into The Crossed Swords in a sort of a daze. The walk from Malice's home had actually been rather short, which probably should have come as no real surprise considering the man's occupation and personality. Although, she had learned a great deal more about him in the last hour or so than she had ever even suspected might exist. Slowly making her way across the room, she slid quietly into a chair next to Jumah while the rest of the group stared at her with open confusion.

Jumah nearly jumped to the ceiling when she sighed heavily and slumped her chin into her hands, supported by the table top. He had been speaking with one of the serving girls and hadn't noticed her entering.

"Riana?! Where have you... what happened? Are you alright?" he stammered.

"Ree!!" squealed Katrina, returning from the back of the room somewhere and, upon seeing her sister slumped over the table, dashed forward and embraced her faster than Jumah could manage from the seat next to her.

"We were very concerned about you, Riana," Desse offered with a soft smile.

"Indeed," Xembak agreed from his stoic stance behind his elven life-mate.

"How many of them did you manage to kill?" Firiel asked, her ears perked up in interest.

"None. I didn't kill anyone. And thank you all for your concern." She sighed, returning Katrina's hug before sliding her chair closer to Jumah and leaning in against him.

The group's faces were haggard, and the table was strewn with magical trinkets that she recognized as divining components, some of them quite expensive. Jumah looked as if he'd run the entire city a dozen times, his hair wind-blown and a slight sheen of sweat on his skin, and Desse, Exodus, and Katrina all looked as if they hadn't slept in a week.

"What happened?" he asked as he wrapped an arm around her shoulders.

"The portal went to Malice's home," she replied.

"What?" Katrina asked. "Why would he want you there?"

"And how is his entire home shielded from our locating spells?" Exodus raised an eyebrow.

"He wanted to talk about the keys and the artifacts," Riana replied, shrugging at Exodus to indicate she had no idea how he had protected his home.

"And what did he have to say?" Desse asked.

"A lot, actually. But mostly it was about how the artifacts were scattered."

"And this was important enough to kidnap you, why exactly?" Firiel raised an eyebrow as she belched and slammed her empty tankard on the table, wiping her mouth with the back of her free hand.

"Could you possibly be any more vulgar?" Katrina asked her with a sideways glance.

"Be calm Katrina," Exodus said, moving up behind her and wrapping his fingers over her shoulders. She immediately leaned back into his grip and half closed her golden eyes, relaxing only slightly.

"So what did he seek?" Xembak asked, watching Riana carefully.

"He wants to make sure the artifacts aren't getting into the wrong hands," She sighed.

"And he thinks his hands are the right ones?" Katrina's voice was sarcastic.

"No, actually." Riana fished a fist-sized object from her belt pouch and set it on the table. "He seems pretty sure of the fact that he isn't the man for the job."

The group eyed the leather-wrapped object for a long moment before Jumah reached out and flipped the loose corners open, revealing the crystal with is glyph floating lazily inside. There was a collective intake of breath before all eyes turned to Riana.

Fully aware of the heavy gazes leveled upon her, Riana sat up straight, poured herself a glass of elven wine and held it to her lips for a moment. After a brief pause, she seemed to change her mind and set the glass down. Reaching across the table, she grabbed one of Firiel's tankards of ale.

Before the redhead could protest, Riana tipped the tankard back and drained it in a single, long pull. She slammed the cup down on the table, doing her best to imitate Firiel's style of doing so, then wiped the foam from her lips with the back of her left hand. How could she relay the events and conversations of the last hour?

She looked up from her empty cup, into the expectant eyes of her friends, all waiting calmly for her to tell them what was going on. She shook her head slightly, reaching out to wrap up the crystal key and tucking it back into her pouch. Casting her gaze around the group once more, she sighed heavily then spoke quietly, as a tears began to pool in the corners of her eyes.

"I'm sorry. I need some time," she muttered, then queued a log-out command and vanished from the room.

By the time Vincent could stammer out some 'I'll check's' and 'I'll call you's', and logged himself out to see what was going on, Riana had already left his apartment, taking all of her things with her.

-20-

Riana had tossed her hastily packed bags into the Kestrel's storage room and climbed into the pilot's seat mere minutes after she'd left Vincent's apartment. She was vaguely aware of some strange and confused looks from some of the people she'd passed along the way, but she didn't really care about what they thought of a young woman carrying a pile of luggage at a break-neck pace through the station.

She was half-way through cycling the ship's engines up when a thought occurred to her. She wanted to be alone, and while the Kestrel would technically isolate her from others, it could be tracked. She knew Vincent would come after her, and she just couldn't expose him to what she was destined to become. The Kestrel would be the first place he would look for her, and if she took it out of its berth, he would almost certainly bring the Neophyte after her. Reaching a decision, she cycled the engines back. Making sure she had her monowire sword secured to her belt, she pulled on one of her chromatic, fitted dusters, and left the ship, securing the door behind her.

The Earth Ring Station was constructed of six mega-cities that were set on opposite ends of three axis. They were joined together by three concentric rings, set at 90 degree angles to one another, that formed the heart of the Ring Station's industrial work zones.

The rings operated as docking stations for the myriad of gigantic ships that plied the trade-routes between planets of the Sol system, bringing in raw and processed goods for final consumption by the majority of the human race. They also served as home to most of the lower middle-class workers and their families who provided the labor back-bone of the rings. These were the people that loaded and unloaded cargo, serviced ships and cared for their crews, as well as supplying food and goods to spacers.

As a final touch, the rings also generated the majority of the Ring Station's power, through solar and thermal processes. This meant that there was the occasional upper middle-class technician living here or there, so that they could be close to their assigned stations if an emergency ever cropped up.

Life in the rings was not great, but it was certainly better than life in some of the harsher environments around the Sol system, such as the methane seas of Titan, or the heavy metal mines of Venus or Mercury. There were two monorails in each ring segment, one for cargo, and one for passengers, that allowed movement between the cities where the bulk of the human race now lived, ever since the nuclear destruction of the Earth's surface hundreds of years ago.

One of the nice things about life in the rings, however, was that it was relatively easy to move around undetected. Since most of the people there were either residents who were just trying to make ends meet, or transients who generally wanted to stay under the radar, one could count on a certain level of discretion. This very prudence had allowed Riana to pass unhindered, or followed, to one of the adjacent mega-cities, Renchi-Kas.

In stark contrast to the rings, the six mega-cities where centers of corporate activity. Each of the massive corporations that made up the Conglomerate, humanity's governing body, claimed one of the six cities for themselves, which meant there was a startling amount of military force present at any given time. The mega-cities sat atop massive space towers that had originally hosted the upper end of orbital elevators. They were filled with people from top to bottom, most of them living in apartments within the structure itself. A huge, bowl-shaped depression, covered by a transparent dome of some indescribably strong materials, played host to the actual cities, making pictures of ancient New York City and Tokyo look like small towns.

There were huge streets, laden with ground and surface-effect transports of every description, sidewalks packed with throngs of people, and the ever-present glow of street lights under the perpetually starry night sky. While the rings produced energy, and moved cargo on and off of ships, the mega-cities produced nothing but bureaucrats and time-sinks. Most of the wealthiest people in the Sol system made their homes in these six cities, which only added to the level of watchfulness of the local citizens and their military protectors.

Renchi-Kas was one of the newer of the six cities, not much more than two hundred years old, which meant that it was even harder for a person to go unnoticed there, since the entire structure had been designed from the ground up with things like security in mind.

It was here that Riana found herself wandering aimlessly, her coat drifting lazily behind her as she walked, without really paying attention to anything around her any more than necessary. Her mind was preoccupied with thoughts of the person who had put their life on the line to save Kalijor, only to be driven mad with the power needed to do just that. Worse, the fact that they had been assassinated by Master Gornin himself, in order to take that power away and hide it from the world.

How could she possibly tell her friends what he had revealed to her? How could they ever help her finish what they had begun? And for that matter, why was she even thinking about going through with it? At this point, she had no real reason to stay on this path. Her mother had sent her after the keys, and Gornin... Well, at least this new information went some distance toward explaining why he was so reluctant to support her. It made her feel a little better about things, knowing that he, apparently, didn't want to follow through with what must, most likely be done.

If she did retrieve all five of the artifacts, ideally for the purpose of keeping them from others, she was committing herself to a life of being hunted down by every person who thought they could defeat her. Not to mention the fact that, according to Malice, anyone who used the artifacts all together, would be consigning themselves to madness.

As she wandered around the city, lost so completely to her thoughts, she failed to notice the figure shadowing her through the streets. The wraith-like form slunk from shadow to shadow, being careful to stay well out of her line of sight, and the presence of hundreds of other pedestrians served to mask it even further.

When her comm link chirped, she nearly leapt for cover. The sound cut through her thoughts like a plasma arc, and it took her three more chirps to even figure out what it was. Her holographic display, one of the advantages of being a cybernetic life form, told her it was Vincent calling and she seriously considered tossing the thing into a nearby waste receptacle. Finally, her feelings got the better of her and she tapped the call button to open the line.

"Ree? Where are you?" His voice was laden with concern.

"Taking a walk," She replied as she took a moment to glance around at the other people on the street. By that point, her shadow had disappeared into an alley and was watching from under the cover of darkness.

"Do you want to talk about it?" He knew she wasn't alright and skipped the question entirely, but his voice remained on edge.

"I would have stayed there if I'd wanted to talk about it," she snapped.

"Fair enough," he answered. "Are you coming back?"

She sighed heavily, eyeing a couple as they walked by, holding hands and smiling as they shared news about their respective days. She longed for that feeling with every fiber of her being, that feeling of being connected with someone. Part of someone. "I want to…"

"Then come back," He made it sound like a statement, but she could hear the pleading tone in his voice.

"It isn't safe," her voice faltered as the emotions built up inside her, but as usual, the tears would not come.

"For who?"

"Either one of us," she stammered, "but mostly you."

"Don't you think I should be the one to decide what's too dangerous for myself?" Now he was in ernest.

"You don't understand."

"I would if you talked to me about it."

"I…" Her eyes flicked across the street toward a dark pool of shadows. She didn't see anything, but she could swear that a moment ago, there had been something there. Something watching her.

"Are you okay Ree?" The concern was edging back into his voice again.

"No," she replied, her eyes lingering on the darkness for a moment before sweeping around the street again. She made her way down the block toward a public park, careful not to look over her shoulder and give her sudden flash of understanding away.

"What did Malice say to you Riana?"

"He shed some light on a few things." She wound her way through a throng of people at the entrance to the park, then moved quickly toward the least inhabited spot she could locate. It turned out to be an area of open, grassy ground, surrounded by a few tall trees. "Namely some of that unwritten history you just found out about."

"You know he's a bastard, Ree. You can't believe anything he says to you."

"That's just it, Vin. He's never lied to me before. Yes, he's been the scum of the earth. He cheats, steals, kidnaps, and probably even murders, but he's never lied to me." She moved to the center of the open space and tried to look like she was really paying attention to her conversation as she tried to see in every direction at once.

"So whatever he told you about the past, you believe?"

"Let's just say that it rings true." She tried not to give off any signs of noticing when the shape leapt from shadow to shadow, keeping to the edges of the clearing.

"And you feel that whatever it is makes you dangerous to the rest of us?"

"I've always been dangerous to the rest of you, Vincent. It's just made worse by what he's told me. I'm damaged goods and you should all keep away from me while you have the chance to get away clean."

"That's just it, Ree. I can't get away. I think I lo…"

116

The conversation was cut off as the shadowed form leapt from a tree, its arms raised over its head, holding aloft a thin blade that slashed through the air with a slight sizzling sound as the figure landed near Riana. The blade, some kind of energy construct that was tightly controlled by what felt like a magnetic field, sliced the air where Riana's head had been a moment ago. Unfortunately, her comm unit was not so lucky. The earpiece emitted a series of sparks and a small cloud of acrid black smoke as it came away from her ear in two pieces.

Riana twisted out of the path of the blade as the wraith landed with a thud that belied its slight frame. Its landing put foot-deep furrows in the ground, while it still appeared graceful and light on its feet. As she turned around to face her mystery assailant, she saw it leap off the ground again, flipping over several times as its sword repositioned itself for another deadly strike at her.

Calculating its trajectory, she stepped forward and met it at its landing spot. Well inside the person's stance, Riana was too close to be hit with its sword, and when her hand closed around an upper arm, there was a slight, feminine, gasp of surprise from the attacker. Fortunately for the woman, she was spared the embarrassment of the gasp as Riana's uppercut to the chin lifted her bodily off the ground and sent her, heels over head, sprawling back toward the ground.

The figure landed lightly, sprawled out on hands and feet, facing her. Gently, the shrouded figure's dark hood fluttered to the ground at Riana's feet, and when she looked up at her assailant, she gasped.

"Surprised?" Firiel asked with a menacing grin. Her flaming red hair uncoiled around her head as she stared Riana down. "Well, this is just the beginning," she added as she charged.

-21-

"What?" Riana's shock allowed Firiel's blade to take a slice out of her side. The flash of pain brought Riana's mind back to the task at hand just before the nanites in her body cut off the signal.

She shifted away from the other woman, ducking through a tight roll and coming up with her monowire sword in hand. The device hummed slightly as the atom-thin wire blade snapped out of the handle, supported by a magnetic field.

"How?" She narrowed her eyes at Firiel, who was crouched down low, staring back at her, sword at the ready.

"You sure ask a lot of questions," Firiel replied, grinning from ear to ear. "So what has your research turned up about me, eh?"

The pair charged one another, their swords clashing together, magnetic fields repelling one another as they pressed them forward. Riana's cybernetic strength seemed evenly matched to whatever science was driving Firiel's muscles, neither one of them able to gain any ground.

"You aren't real," Riana said through her gritted teeth. "There's no record of you anywhere. And you're not a player. How is this possible?"

"Asks the woman with a holographic mother..." Firiel grinned as she lashed out with a vicious kick.

Riana blocked the kick with her shin, cranking her body around as she lifted Firiel's leg up behind her. Pushing forward with her sword and taking a step, she caused Firiel to lose her balance and topple over, but the redhead quickly stuck out an arm and turned the motion into a one-handed cartwheel, pinwheeling over and landing on her feet, facing Riana.

"You know, I would have thought you'd figured it all out by now. I guess you really are as dense as they say." Firiel's energy blade carved a faintly glowing pattern through the air as she twirled it around her, taking a few small steps toward Riana.

"What the hell are you talking about?" Riana turned her body to present the narrowest possible target to her adversary. "Why attack me? I thought we were working together."

"We were working together. Until you got spooked and ran for the hills. Seriously, I have to wonder how you ever managed to kill something like a Death Dragon." Firiel lurched forward and their blades crossed again in a flurry of strikes and parries.

Try as she might, Riana could not seem to gain an edge in the battle. It was as if their skills were perfectly matched to one another. With the exception of Firiel's opening attacks, while Riana was distracted, there had not been a single landed blow.

"I had help from my friends," she retorted, watching Firiel's movements closely, looking for a weakness.

"Of course you did! You obviously don't have the fortitude to handle a fight on your own." Firiel danced around her like a ballerina, striking out with her strange energy sword at random angles and intervals that kept Riana's concentration focused to a razor's edge.

"I get it. You think I'm a coward. What I don't understand is why you care. Never mind how you got out here, and why you're attacking me. Tell me why you give a shit about what I do with my life."

Riana's emotions began boiling up inside her, despite anything Master Jonin or Master Gornin had ever told her. Something about this flame-haired elf just dug under her skin and got her blood pounding through her veins.

"The fact that you have to ask that question at all means you aren't even ready to hear the answer. Not to mention the fact that I am not going to give it to you. You aren't worthy of knowing." Firiel dove in at her again, pressing her sword against Riana's blade and driving forward with all the strength in her legs.

Riana found herself giving up ground under the force of Firiel's drive, and the next thing she knew, her back was slammed into the trunk of a tree. The tree shook from the force of the blow, raining down leaves and pink blossoms around the pair. Firiel continued to press Riana into the trunk with all her strength.

In an act of desperation, Riana lashed out with her right leg, driving her knee into Firiel's groin. The other woman staggered back, inhaling sharply against the pain, and Riana took advantage of the momentary lapse, stepping forward and bringing her sword down in a sharp, overhead stroke aimed at Firiel's sword arm.

The smaller elf quickly rolled to the side, lashing out with her own sword. Both of the women yelped in pain as their blades struck home and a silence fell as they regained their feet. Taking a moment to assess their damages, they were careful not to take their eyes from their adversaries.

Riana traced her fingers across her left cheek, bringing them away to inspect the tips. Even in the perpetual twilight of the megacity, she could easily see the blood on her fingers, which was odd since her nanites should have stopped the bleeding almost immediately. She shifted her gaze from her fingers to Firiel, who was tracing her fingers over the stub of her own left ear. The tip had been cut clean away, leaving her with only half of her long, tapered elven ear.

"So, that's how it's going to be," Firiel snorted as she cast her eyes to where the tip of her ear lay on the ground between them.

"You started this." Riana answered, swiping her fingers down the wound on her face once more, the blood continued to flow unabated.

"And yet, you can finish it any time you want."

"I don't know what you want from me."

"You mean you refuse to see the truth." Firiel narrowed her eyes and shifted back into a fighting stance.

"What truth?!" Riana protested, stepping back into a defensive stance.

"I rest my case. So be it!" Firiel yelled as she charged back into the fray.

Their dance resumed in a clash of magnetic fields, feet, and fists. This time they didn't hold back, didn't hesitate. This time it was going to be to the death of one, or both of them. But still, their skills seemed exactly matched to one another, for every sword stroke, punch, or kick, there was a perfectly placed block, dodge, or roll. Each time one of them leveraged the other into a throw, their victim would reverse the attack, or twist around to land on her feet and then dive right back into the action again.

It was several long minutes before Riana began to realize that Firiel's moves were familiar to her. There was a reason they were so evenly matched, and the longer they fought, the more clear it became, but such a thing couldn't be possible...

To test her theory, she launched herself into a move that she would not normally use under the circumstances, lashing out with a strong right-to-left sword stroke. As predicted, Firiel blocked the attack, but it caused her to turn slightly. Pressing the attack, Riana used the momentum to launch herself into a spin, throwing her legs out and spinning around. When Firiel smoothly ducked under the flying double kick, Riana's suspicions were confirmed, even if they made no sense at all. She caught her feet and spun around in time to block Firiel's next attack.

"That's not possible," she grunted as she intercepted the blow.

"And yet..." Firiel let the statement drop as she sneered back at Riana.

"Why?" Riana questioned as they dove toward one another again.

"Because you know the truth," Firiel answered as their swords hummed against one another, "and it's killing you to not realize it."

"If that's true, then I can stop this any time I want," Riana replied.

"That's right," Firiel grinned as she ducked under a sweeping kick. "Although probably not in the way you are thinking."

"If you're really a product of my own mind, then you can't hurt me if I don't let you." Riana stood up, lowering her sword to her side as Firiel smiled, baring her gleaming white teeth.

The smaller elf drove forward, the point of her blade aimed directly at Riana's abdomen. "This is going to hurt you more than it hurts me," Firiel cackled as the point of the blade pierced Riana's stomach, crossing over the black scar left by Malice's blade.

As the pain started to register in Riana's mind, a third voice cut across her world, causing her to jerk around toward the sound and partially deflect the force of Firiel's blow.

"Riana?!" Vincent's voice touched her ears as she slumped to the ground, bleeding profusely from the open wound in her stomach.

-22-

She came to with a heaving gasp. Sitting up so quickly that she didn't have time to register the pain of the movement until it doubled her over. Falling back to the bed, clutching at the bandages around her waist and gasping for air, it took her several minutes to register the presence of Vincent's voice.

She felt herself being gently rolled over onto her back and straightened out again, her breath coming in ragged gasps as the pain spider-webbed through her body. She winced against the pain and tried to focus her vision on the shape of Vincent as he tucked the covers back over her body and gently brushed her purple hair out of her eyes.

"What… happened…" she panted.

"I was hoping you could help me out with that. I found you in a park in Renchi-Kas. You were on the ground, bleeding from a stomach wound," his voice was filled with that same concern she vaguely remembered from a comm conversation.

"Bleeding? I was bleeding?" She brought a hand to her stomach, feeling the bandages through the covers of the bed. The merest touch of her fingers caused shooting pain to arc up and down her spine. She gasped at the pain, never having felt anything quite like it before. "Why was I bleeding? I'm not supposed to bleed."

"I know," Vincent's tone was serious now. "It took me a while to get it to stop. I finally just plugged up the wound to keep it from bleeding you out."

"Why was I bleeding?" A hint of panic was beginning to edge into her voice.

"I don't know Ree. It looks like a sword wound to me. Was there someone there with you?"

"In the park? I heard you there." Her eyes lost focus as she tried to recall what had happened. She remembered a fight. She remembered something about an impossible fight. Why was it impossible? She pressed her memories, trying to find out what had happened. There was a flash of red across the picture of the twilight park.

"I was there. I tracked your comm link while we spoke. After the line went dead it took me some time to find you. When I arrived you were talking to someone, then collapsed in some kind of seizure or something." He pressed his lips into a hard line. "If I hadn't been there, you might have bled out, Riana. This is a serious wound."

She looked back and forth between Vincent and her covered stomach. "But why does it still hurt? It should be healing."

"Like I said, Ree, I don't know. I was this close to taking you to a med center." He held out his hand with his thumb and forefinger held barely apart for her to see.

"No. No doctors." She waived his hand away.

"I knew you'd say that. It's the only reason I hesitated." Turning to the nightstand, he retrieved a bottle of water and cracked the lid open. Holding the bottle to her lips, he helped her take a small drink, then set the bottle aside. "Whatever happened to you out there, whoever did this to you, they used a weapon I've never seen before. Your wounds are closing, but much slower than normal. Your stomach only stopped bleeding an hour ago."

"An hour? How long have I..." She started to sit up again, but he pressed a gentle hand against her shoulder to indicate she should stay where she was.

"You've been out for around thirty six hours now."

"Thirty six hours?!" She tried to sit up again but the pain, combined with Vincent's pushing, had her flat on her back in seconds.

124

"Yes. And if you keep trying to get up, I'll be forced to call Willhelmina again. The only reason she isn't here right now is that I promised her I would take care of you. Now lie back or you'll aggravate the wound again." His tone was commanding and he eyed her seriously, making her think twice about defying him.

"You called Kat?!" Her eyes turned to near panic.

"You were bleeding profusely, Ree. I had to do something and I knew she is the only person you really trust." His tone was a little sour.

"That's not entirely true..." She winced as she adjusted her position to get a better look at his face. "I trust you too..."

That comment seemed to get him to calm a little, his entire demeanor softening.

Relaxing into the mattress, she gave him a speculative look. "What happened?"

Vincent shrugged. "I don't know. I was talking to you one minute, then there was a shout, and the line went dead. When I finally found you, you were yelling at someone. As I approached, I saw you in a fighting stance, with your sword drawn. You stood up straight, dropped your guard, then staggered back. I shouted your name and you twisted to look at me, then collapsed. I ran to you and found you bleeding all over the place."

"So you didn't see Firiel there in the clearing with me?" She narrowed her eyes at him.

"Firiel? From Kalijor?"

"No, the Firiel from the grocery store down in the mall." She crossed her arms over her chest in a huff, then winced at the pain that even that motion caused.

"No, I didn't see Firiel there with you. Are you telling me she did this to you?"

"Well I sure as heck didn't do it to myself. And even if I did, how do you explain the fact that the wounds are healing so slowly?"

"I wouldn't ever try to explain anything about your body, Ree. The whole thing is pretty far above my understanding." He sat down on the bed next to her and gently pulled the top sheet from her grasp. With soft, probing fingers, he peeled back the bandage covering her stomach and eyed the wound critically. "Come to think of it though, you're pretty lucky that I keep mono-needles around for sewing up my body armor. I doubt I could've done this with a regular suture needle."

She took a moment to drop her own gaze to the freshly-stitched wound on her stomach. The sutures were nice and neat, fairly small, and a better job than she'd seen some field doctors do. The new wound bisected the ugly black scar that Malice had left her with, creating a black and red 'X' mark just above her navel.

"What the heck is wrong with me?" she breathed as Vincent replaced the bandage and pulled her covers back up.

"I don't know. Did Firiel say anything to you?"

"You believe me?" She snapped her gaze up to meet his again.

Their eyes locked across the short distance between them. "Of course I believe you. What kind of friend would I be if I didn't believe you? Especially considering some of the other things I've already seen going on around you."

She smiled at him, more than thankful for her great fortune in finding him amongst all of the other people in the world. Maybe life wasn't so bad after all. "She uh… said she was attacking me because I gave up on finding the keys… Something about, we were on the same side until I quit…" Her fingers moved to massage her temples as she tried to recall the altercation. It had all happened so quickly.

"So maybe we should log back in and get the gang back together?" He raised an eyebrow as if to punctuate the question.

Riana took a deep breath, and sighed heavily, gathering her thoughts before responding. Malice didn't want the keys, he just didn't want them to get into the hands of people who stood to get in the way of his operations, whatever they were. Which, coming from him, was quite a statement. Although she also suspected quite strongly that he mostly didn't want to open himself up to the sort of end that the last person to use the artifacts came to.

Which raised an entirely new point altogether. Was that true? Did Master Gornin actually assassinate the last hero of Kalijor?

She wasn't sure if the old troll was capable of something like that, although she didn't doubt for a second that he was powerful and knowledgeable enough to do so.

Vincent seemed to pick up on her concern almost immediately, even if he had no idea what she was really concerned about. His look spoke volumes about his feelings on the matter, though. Suddenly, she was having a difficult time meeting his gaze.

"Riana, I can't help you if you won't tell me."

"I just told you I was attacked in the park by a person who shouldn't exist in this world. What else do you want me to tell you, Vin?" She still couldn't look him in the eyes.

"Well, I don't want you to tell me anything you don't want to talk about. But if you think you're fooling me, you've got another thing coming."

She let go an exasperated sigh in his general direction, picking at some errant bit-o-fluff on the sheets as she worked at avoiding his gaze.

He waited patiently, his presence a comforting force in the room.

"Malice said some things to me when we were talking…" she offered.

"I find it difficult to believe that anything Malice might say to you would get you spooked," he frowned.

"Normally I would agree with you, but he had physical evidence to back himself up." She frowned too, still not willing to look up to his face.

"Evidence of what?"

Her eyes finally rose to meet his, studying him closely as she considered her words. "He has a tapestry in his house. It's obviously extremely old. He says he stole it from Cohai."

"Okay," he prompted her to continue.

She offered up another heavy sigh before allowing herself to carry on. "It depicts a person wearing what looks like the Obscuri artifacts. He's obviously gone mad with power, and is burning the countryside, tearing down cities, and killing people."

Vincent took a long moment to consider her words before responding, his voice slow and measured, "And you think he is trying to tell you that this will happen to you if you get all of the artifacts?"

"He didn't really go so far as to hint, it was more of an outright statement."

"I see," he nodded, folding his arms cross his chest and offering her a hard look, "And you believed all of this?"

"The tapestry was real enough," she sighed.

"Okay. So who is to say what circumstances might have led to such an event? The man could have taken a bump to the head while fighting the Lich King."

Now it was her turn to offer him a hard look, wrapping her own arms around her chest in parody and wincing as a jolt of pain shot through her. "That's dumb, Vin."

"Not any more so than you believing word one that falls out of Malice's mouth. The man is a proven self-serving, manipulative bastard, Ree. You can't believe a thing that he says."

"He's never lied to me, though."

"What?" Vincent's look was beyond incredulous.

"Seriously. He's been and done a lot of things to me, to Kat…" She took a deep breath before continuing, looking Vincent directly in the eyes now, "But he's never lied to me about anything as near as I can tell."

Vincent sighed, rearranging himself on the edge of the bed so he was looking at her straight on. "Alright, so let's say he's telling the truth. That still doesn't mean it will happen to you."

"I know, but that isn't the worst bit," she breathed.

He raised an eyebrow at her. "The possibility of going mad and slaughtering people isn't the worst part?"

She shook her head, dropping her eyes to the shape of her body beneath the sheets.

"Talk to me, Riana." He placed a comforting hand on her thigh and gave it a gentle squeeze.

"There was another person in the tapestry."

"Okay?"

"How do you suppose the artifacts got hidden away?" she changed tack, looking up at him once more.

"I don't follow…"

"Well, we know from first-hand experience that the circlet can't be removed, right?"

"I suppose so, yes."

"Well if any of the other artifacts are even similar, then how, after the battle was over and the hero victorious, would the artifacts be removed and hidden away?"

"I thought the Hero and the Lich King killed one another?"

"Okay, then how did the hero go mad and start killing innocents if he died fighting the Lich King?"

Vincent thought for a moment, then nodded. "Fair enough, so he survived, then went mad. How was he stopped if he was on par with the Lich King for power?"

"Exactly." Riana tried to sit up, but Vincent was quick to press her back down into the pillows with a clicking of his tongue and a shake of his head. She grunted and gave him an exasperated look, but capitulated, sinking back down into the bedding.

"So, who was the other figure in the tapestry?"

She looked back up at him, her eyes hard and confused. Finally she managed to force the words out. "It looked for all the world like a blue-eyed troll..."

"A blue-eyed..." His eyes went wide. "Master Gornin?!"

She nodded.

"You think Gornin would be capable of such a thing?"

She shrugged. "I don't know. If anyone in Kalijor is powerful enough to do it, it would be him."

He nodded. "I'll grant you that. The old troll is certainly the strongest person I've ever met, next to you of course."

"What?" Her look was somewhere between amazement and incredulity.

He smiled warmly at her. "Riana, I've never met anyone as strong as you before. Look at all of the stuff you've been through in your life and all of the things piling up on you to be done. Most people would crack under that kind of pressure, those expectations."

She snorted at him. She would have laughed outright, but she feared that might rupture something vital at that point. "Obviously that was someone else at the concert with me. Because you sure didn't witness my breakdown…"

He smiled at her, squeezing her thigh again. "No one can be expected to take such things in stride without the occasional complaint, Riana, but you continue to do what you have to, despite any momentary complaints you might have. You draw the most amazing companions to you and you lead them with emotion and skill."

"Lead? I'm no leader, Vin. I'm just trying to get all of this crap off my plate so I can get on with my own life. I don't want any part of all this legacy stuff!"

"And that is what makes you mighty, Riana. You don't want it. You want nothing to do with any of it, in fact. But you still do it, because you know no one else is going to if you don't. In my eyes, that trumps any hand Master Gornin, or anyone else for that matter, might be holding."

She looked at him, eyes glassy with phantom tears. She wished for all the world that she could shed them, but they still wouldn't come to her. Instead she sniffled and blushed at her friend's words. "I don't know what to do, Vincent. I'm confused, and scared."

"I can only imagine, Riana. But you need to know that I am here for you. I'm not going anywhere without you, and I'm not letting you go anywhere without me. It's been my experience that people doing what they have to can always use plenty of help."

The lack of tears was almost as crushing as his words were embracing. "Thank you." Her face must have looked comical, with her desperate need to shed tears of fear, and happiness, combined with her look of love for the man sitting with her.

"So what do you say the two of us log in and go ask Gornin? No more of this second hand innuendo business?"

She nodded at him as he leaned down and embraced her gently.

-23-

They appeared in the Cohai courtyard, amidst the immaculately manicured gardens, meditating students, and sparring matches. Riana was either oblivious to, or just too lost in her thoughts to care about the strange looks that were cast their direction as they did so.

Jumah however, was not. "Ree?"

"Yeah?" She replied as she turned toward the keep and began stalking toward the main door.

"Didn't we log out in Rathalon?"

"So?"

"So, what are we doing in Cohai?"

"We came to talk to Gornin, didn't we?"

"Well... yeah..."

"Then let's go talk to him," she offered as she pressed her shoulder into the huge keep door and heaved the heavy, wooden panel open.

Jumah just stared in awe, unable to break free from his train of thought long enough to help her. On the other side of the door, stood the large, misshapen form of Master Gornin, blue eyes shining brightly in the darkened interior of the keep's great hall.

"Hello Riana. Jumah." Gornin inclined his head to each of them as he spoke.

"Master Gornin," the pair chorused, bowing to him.

He eyed them both for a long moment, as if trying to divine some deep, inner secret that they may be hiding before he spoke again. "How may I be of service to you?" There seemed to be a weight of some kind in his voice, making it lower than usual.

"We've come to ask you some questions about the past," Riana said, giving him a hard look.

"I will share what I can." He beckoned them to follow him as he turned and led the way into the keep. A few twists and turns saw them entering another of Cohai's tiny stone rooms where Gornin closed the door behind them, then turned to face the pair. "Proceed."

"I had a chat with Malice the other day," Riana began, her ears turning red and laying parallel to the floor.

"He is not the sort of person I would imagine you sharing long conversations with," Gornin's tone was still low and more cautious than usual.

"Nor would I. In fact, he had to have me abducted to make it happen, but regardless, he brought up some interesting points that I feel should probably have come up sooner rather than later."

"Be careful Ree," Jumah whispered, his hand finding its way to her shoulder.

She tossed Jumah a sideways glance before returning her attention to the troll and pressing her lips into a hard line. "He has a tapestry in his home that he says he smuggled out of Cohai. It depicts the unnamed hero of Kalijor burning down villages."

She paused, but Gornin said nothing, as if he was waiting for the other shoe to drop. So she obliged him, "And in the background, the hero is being stalked by a blue-eyed troll."

The room was silent then, all three of them looking toward one another, reading reactions and waiting for someone else to speak.

It was Gornin who finally broke the silence, his voice still heavy with some unknown weight, "He no doubt told you that the only way to take the artifacts from someone is for that person to die." It wasn't a question.

"Yes," Riana nodded.

"I told you, Riana, that I do not condone your pursuit of the artifacts."

"Because you knew you'd have to kill me later?" She folded her arms across her chest and glared at him, meeting his clear blue eyes with her own violet orbs.

"No fate is writ in stone."

"But you did it, didn't you?"

"Yes."

The room fell silent again as his admission settled in.

"How?" Her shoulders slumped and her ears fell flat. Jumah moved up next to her and wrapped his arms around her, pulling her in tight to his body.

"The artifacts are powerful, Riana. More powerful than any other items of power that Kalijor has ever known. That kind of power is not meant for the mortal mind. It changes a person. Plumbs their depths, reveals truths about them that they never knew themselves. He was powerful, but not invulnerable."

"So the power drove him mad?"

"Essentially. He thought he was doing good. He thought he was making the world safe. He swore that he was upholding the law." Gornin paused to take a deep, sorrowful breath as he recalled the experience, relived the events in his mind. "He was a good man. It was the most difficult thing I have ever done."

"But you did it anyway." She squeezed her arms around herself, feeling suddenly cold and naked in front of the person she had looked to as a father figure for years now.

"I did what was necessary to protect all of Kalijor. Just as you now do what is necessary to protect all of Kalijor, and your own world as well."

"And you'll end me as well. If you have to…"

"If I must."

She looked up at him again, her eyes shiny with tears as she locked them with his. The intensity of their exchange heated the cold, stone room. "Can you do it?"

He paused to consider. Clearly she was not asking if he could live with himself after the act, that much was already apparent. "I have not taught you everything I know, Riana."

"But you've said yourself that I am..." She stopped, thinking better of her words and changing her mind. "That I could be, one of the most powerful magic users Kalijor has ever known. That, with the artifacts, and the fighting skills you've taught me..." She kept his gaze. "Can you? If..."

"I will do, in the end, what I always have done, Riana. Just as you do now."

"And what is that?" she sniffled.

"What I must."

-24-

"Did you two find anything useful?" Riana's tone was somber as she looked toward Katrina and Exodus across the dining room table.

They'd moved their gathering to the Thorindal family home in Rathalon, since there was no longer any need to stake out Malice's haunts. It had been three days, in Kalijor , since they'd spoken with Master Gornin, and Riana's mood had remained serious despite the passage of time.

"We found a few spells that will make the trip into the Dead Sea possible," Exodus answered, his hands resting on the open pages of a rather large, and ancient tome. "Protection from toxins, breathe without air, those sorts of things."

Riana nodded at him, "And the guardian?"

"That's been something of a tougher subject," Katrina pipped in. "There aren't any really reliable accounts of any monsters in there. Lots of conjecture, though. Our best guess is that it's some sort of Leviathan."

Jumah raised an eyebrow at Katrina. "I thought the Leviathan was a kind of monster."

"Well, it is," Katrina replied.

"Well obviously, but I meant, a specific monster. Anyone I've ever heard talking about a Leviathan has made it sound like some kind of giant squid or something."

"It may very well be," Exodus said.

"But no one knows for sure. The simple fact is that nobody who's fought one has ever made it back to civilization to talk about it," Katrina finished.

"Well that's encouraging." Jumah leaned back in his chair, balancing it on two legs. "But you found out something more, I take it?"

"Why would you think that?" Katrina replied.

"Because I know you. And I know your sister. That level of compulsion does not go to the Great Library and come back without something useful and exciting." Jumah was grinning from ear to ear as he spoke. His feet were now in the air as well, the ancient wooden chair groaning slightly in protest to his treatment of the heirloom.

Katrina's face reddened, her ears drooping in embarrassment. Riana actually chuckled, offering her sister an encouraging smile.

"Fine. We found something more..." She pulled one of the tomes they had brought back with them from the stack and leafed through it until she found her bookmark, then let the book fall open on the table and turned it so the others could see it.

The page in question had quite a few passages, written in a flowing, complicated script that hadn't been a living language in over a thousand years. The majority of the space, however, was dominated by the image of some kind of huge, tentacled beast. It had a mouth full of wicked teeth that looked as if it could swallow a small boat in one try, and probably over a hundred tentacles of various sizes and lengths protruded from its body without rhyme or reason.

The creature seemed to be involved in the act of destroying some kind of settlement, with splintered huts and crushed bodies beneath it. "I present to you, Leviathan." Katrina's voice was somewhere between pride at her accomplishment and horror at what she had found.

"That looks fun," Jumah whistled.

"Such a creature has not been seen for aeons," Desse breathed after stepping forward to inspect the image in the book. Xembak followed her from where the pair had been standing at the other end of the table and quirked a scaly eyebrow at the representation, but said nothing.

Firiel didn't even bother looking at the picture. Instead, she kept her icy glare drilled into Riana's forehead, where it had been since the group reconvened hours ago. She hadn't said a single word to anyone, just sat there, her one whole ear twitching idly, and the half-ear on the other side still raw along its cut edge, watching Riana.

They had both remained stoically silent about the events in the park. Riana partly for fear of her friends thinking she was insane, and partly because she wanted to find out more before she started in on the elf again. Firiel seemed to feel the silence was in some ways just as torturous as an out-and-out battle would be. And she was, in many ways, very right about that, judging by the palpable tension between them.

"Does it say anything about how we might kill it?" Riana asked, looking up at her sister and Exodus.

Katrina shook her head. "Nothing yet. We only just found this text before you called us back here to meet. A quick look seems to indicate that it is vulnerable to fire, but that won't be much use to us at the bottom of The Dead Sea."

"Must we immediately move to death and destruction?" Desse's voice was a bit haggard. "Perhaps the creature can be reasoned with. Or avoided entirely."

Riana looked up at the elf and raised an eyebrow of her own. "Maybe. But we should be prepared with a contingency in case that doesn't work for us. Agreed?"

Desse looked at her for a moment, her whole body seemingly ready to protest the fact that the creature might have to be destroyed. When Xembak set his hand on her shoulder, her whole demeanor changed slightly. She pressed her lips together into a hard line and nodded at Riana. "Very well."

"Good. Then maybe you and Kat should spend some time going over these texts and see what you can come up with for both possibilities." Desse and Katrina both nodded and Katrina began collecting books into a pile, preparing to head back to the Academy library.

"I assume we will need some reagents to work the underwater spells?" Riana added.

"Yes, we have compiled a list," Exodus replied with a nod, "Some of it will be difficult to locate, but I know a few out of the way places we can check."

"Okay. Would you and Jumah mind taking care of the list for us?"

Jumah and Exodus exchanged looks and then nodded in unison.

"Sure," Jumah responded.

"Of course," Exodus said at the same time.

Riana pulled her coin purse from one of her belt pouches and handed it to Jumah. "Here, take this."

Jumah accepted the coin purse with a hard look, tucking it into his own belt pouch. "Are you okay, Ree?"

She nodded at him, offering a wan smile, "I'll be alright, as long as I have you all here with me."

The group sat in silence for a moment, then a flurry of activity began. Katrina and Exodus exchanged hugs, then she, Desse, and Xembak headed out with their stacks of books. Jumah embraced Riana, kissed her briefly, then turned and nodded to Exodus, and they left as well, leaving Riana and Firiel alone in the dining room, staring at one another in silence.

-25-

"So. What's it going to be between us?" Riana crossed her arms over her chest and eyed Firiel accusingly.

"I'm sure I have no idea what you're talking about," Firiel's voice dripped ice, and her acidic green eyes never left Riana's violet orbs.

"It was you, wasn't it? In the park."

Firiel just smiled at her, leaning back in her chair confidently.

"Why?" Riana queried.

"Because you have to be made to understand the seriousness of what is happening here." Firiel crossed her arms, mirroring Riana

"Maybe if someone would tell me what was going on, I would have an easier time getting on board with the program…"

"You'll figure it out."

"So you won't tell me either?" Riana sighed in exasperation.

"That's not my job, Riana."

"What exactly is your job, then?"

Firiel shrugged, a mischievous grin spreading across her face.

"Is this going to be one of those cryptic 'I'm not allowed to tell you anything of any relevance' conversations?" Riana traced her fingers through the air as she spoke.

"No. I just don't feel like telling you anything useful at the moment."

Riana stared at her dumbly.

Firiel stared back for a minute, then her face broke into an even wider grin as a realization struck her. "You mean all the people in your life... the ones you trust and who's advice you value, have been telling you all this time that there are rules to their game?"

"Wa..." Riana stammered.

"Ho, this is rich!" Firiel hooted, slapping her thigh. "They've got you all turned around, don't they?"

Riana felt the fire rising within her. She began to seethe as Firiel's words dug deeply into her very soul. The possibility that Gornin, the Obscuri, even her mother, Ezrina, had been withholding information from her all this time, was something she simply didn't want to consider.

"Fine then," she cut off Firiel's laughter. "Can you at least tell me who you are?" Riana sat down in a nearby chair with a dramatic sigh, folding her hands over one another on the surface of the ornate, wooden table.

"I am Firiel," the elf grinned.

"But I know you," Riana narrowed her eyes, trying to figure out where she'd seen this elf before. Her green eyes and shocking, flame-red hair. Everything about the woman screamed of their having met before. But she hadn't seen an elf quite like her since... "Oh my gods!"

Riana's eyes went wide as the realization hit her. At the same instant, Firiel laughed openly. A full, hearty, belly laugh. "The light dawns!"

"Are you... her?" Riana's hand twitched toward the handle of Elkorine, but she stopped herself. She still didn't know anything, really, and Firiel still seemed willing to talk.

"No," Firiel finally responded after taking a moment to recover from her laughter.

"Then who..."

"Ambrai was my mother," her voice turned serious and took on a hard edge. She sat down in a chair across from Riana, her gaze boring into her.

"I did what I had to do, Firiel. She'd been possessed and the darkness in her was going to do something terrible." Riana's eyes began to tear up a bit as she spoke. The battle on the shores of The Dead Sea, more than a couple of years ago now, in real time, came crashing back around her like a wave. That had been the day she'd left Kalijor and found out the truth about the world. It had seemed a cruel joke then. Even now she was constantly reeling from blow after blow, all centering from that one, fateful day.

"I know why you did what you did, Riana. You don't need to apologize to me. My mother died the day she helped remove that curse from Kilishandra and Ezrina. Dad said she was never right again, after that day."

"She didn't die. She was still in there. Still fighting for air." Riana's eyes were unfocused, hazy with tears and painful remembrances. Before the battle that ended both of their lives, Ambrai had been calm, lucid, and had begged Riana to end her life. "She was able to suppress the beast within her for short periods. She was still in there. Fighting for her very soul."

Firiel's eyes narrowed at Riana's words. Her breath caught as she considered what had been said, and what she should say in return.

Riana filled the space first. "She begged me to do what I did. To take her life before the darkness could fulfill its plan. In the end, it was her that saved us all, Firiel. She was so strong. That thing had us all beat. At the last second, she seized control of the monster in her mind and made it pause long enough for me to…." her voice trailed off as her eyes refocused on Firiel's sharp features. The other woman was staring at her hands on the table, eyes tearing up.

"Thank you," she finally managed, wiping her tears away with the back of her hand. "I know you did what you had to. I am very happy to hear that she died well."

"She died a hero, Firiel. I've never met a stronger person in my life. And I hope that you have her strength."

Firiel looked up at Riana, locking eyes again, both clouded with emotion, that undercurrent of animosity still present, but somehow it seemed to smooth over their differences, creating a sort of bond between them. "What do you mean?"

Riana's look turned hard as she spoke again. "I've found out that the artifacts can have adverse effects on the person who uses them all in concert. I need you to promise me that, if the time comes, you'll do for me, what I did for your mother…"

-26-

Vincent's ceiling came into sharp relief as Kalijor faded from her view. Riana looked down the length of her body to see the dressing over her recent sword wound and sighed as she raised her arms, plucking the ODN patch cord from her right wrist with a subtle 'popping' noise. She eyed her wrist as the skin sealed over the hole where the cable had been inserted, then slowly leaned forward, testing the stomach wound carefully.

Much to her surprise, there was none of the previous pain or discomfort as she sat up in one fluid motion. Tentatively, she touched the dressing, and when she felt no stab of pain, pressed a little harder. Still nothing.

Finally, she stood up, and peeled the bandage from her stomach, looking down to see that the new wound was completely gone. The jagged black line that Malice had left her with was still present, but the one caused by Firiel in the park was, now, nothing more than an uncomfortable memory.

"Weird," she commented as she reached for her duffle bag to rummage for some clothing.

"What's weird?" Vincent's voice asked as he stepped into the bedroom with his typical grin on his face.

"You mean aside from you?" She raised an eyebrow at him.

"Obviously," he chirped. "And if there's anything weirder than me around here, I want it captured and beaten," he added with a serious nod. Then he looked at her and cocked his head to the side, his long blonde mane shifting like a cascade of water. "Then again… You're pretty weird yourself…"

Riana snatched a pillow from the bed and lobbed it at him, striking him squarely in the chest. "Nice. Not exactly the best way to endear yourself to someone, blondie," she chided.

"Well you keep logging out in the middle of plans…"

"This time it isn't escapism. I got a message. Something that needs to be dealt with." She tossed her duffle on the bed and started to dig around inside. Finally, she extracted one of her black body suits and tossed it on the bed, then she dove back into the bag after the rolled up suit of reactive body armor, tossing it next to the other garment.

"Wow. Looks pretty serious," Vincent commented as he moved up behind her and wrapped his arms around her waist, pulling her into a tight embrace.

Riana leaned into him, laying her head back against his shoulder and turning her face toward his, "I have to go, Vin."

"So who's stopping you?" he purred as he placed a light kiss on her lips.

"At this point, I think it's me," she replied, kissing him back, "But I have to stop it. This is important."

Vincent kissed her once more, then released her. "Anything I can help with?"

"I don't know." She started peeling off her bedclothes and pulling on the bodysuit. "You remember Daray?"

Daray was Solidarity Online's most recent personnel acquisition. She was an industrial espionage specialist who had been extensively rebuilt at a genetic level as part of her new hire package. She was made faster, stronger, smarter, and female… Before she'd discovered the heinous secret that Aegis Online was writing a virus for the purpose of killing all of the users logged into Kalijor, she'd been a young man. In order to keep him safe and better arm him to go back to AO and get the virus code, they'd reprogrammed Darren's DNA to be Daray's. Both Riana and Willhelmina had been enlisted to help her adjust to her new body and abilities, and even Vincent had pitched in some, going so far as to kiss her in a public setting, knowing who she had been and planning on her less than favorable response.

Vincent rubbed his jaw as the memory of Daray knocking him across a crowded dance floor played itself out in his mind's eye. He swore his jaw still hurt, and that had been months ago. "Uh. Yeah."

"Well, she just sent me a message saying she saw Shantal over in Neo-Tokyo."

"You're really going to go pick a fight with this guy?" Vincent shook his head in disbelief. Very few people in the solar system went looking for a mercenary of Gregory Shantal's reputation for violence and ruthlessness. Even if they did feel he had wronged them horribly.

She finished sliding into the bodysuit and waited a few seconds for the neck to shrink back down and find its spot, then reached for the armor and began working her way into it. The stuff was a nightmare to get in and out of, but it was much more flexible than hard armor, and easier to carry around in her bag as well.

"I have to."

"No you don't. You're just upset that he tricked you."

"He tried to hurt Kat. Played a part in her abduction…"

"And you got her back," his tone was flat. He was intentionally keeping the edge out of it, but the message was obvious to anyone who cared to listen.

"He isn't working alone, Vin. Someone paid him to do what he did."

"You may have heard, but some folks you know are involved in this whole 'saving the world, thing' in Kalijor. That seems like the sort of activity you might want to be involved in…"

"This is part of that," she replied, pulling the fastener on the front of her armor closed and reaching for her bag again.

"How?" he asked as he snagged the lip of the bag and dragged it out of her reach.

"I don't know," she eyed him, "But then, very little of what's been going on in my life the past few years has made much sense to me, so I don't see why this would be much different."

145

"Fair enough," he acquiesced. "So…"

"So… what?" She snatched the duffle back from him and pulled a complicated-looking tangle of straps and buckles from it. She started straightening the mess as she waited for his explanation.

Vincent seemed to play with the notion of giving into her need for him to get testy, but then smiled and pulled open one of his dresser doors, sliding out his bolt caster. The weapon was the sort of thing that would intimidate anyone staring down the barrel of it. The barrel measured about three inches across and looked like a stubby little grenade launcher from the old 20th century action films, only it sported quite a few high-tech upgrades.

Riana had no idea where he'd gotten the thing. She had looked into the weapon and discovered that they had stopped manufacturing them nearly a hundred years ago. Partly due to the expense of the ammunition, but mostly because they tended to cause a significant amount of collateral damage whenever they were used. The fact that there were anti-matter rounds for the weapon, of which, Vincent claimed to have a few, just cemented her belief that the weapons were abandoned for fairly good reason.

He hit the lever that allowed the barrel of the weapon to break open and tilt forward, then pulled a fist-sized cartridge from the same drawer and slid it home in the tube with a hollow 'thunk' noise. He looked up at her and smiled again as he jerked his hand upward and the barrel snapped closed with a definitive click.

"What are you doing, Vincent?" she asked as she watched him strap on his belt and slide the weapon home in the holster across the small of his back.

"I'm coming with you," he smiled, reaching down to strap the regular holster on his right thigh above his knee.

"No. You aren't." She stepped into her combat webbing and began pulling and tugging it all into the appropriate places, tightening straps and snapping buckles shut as she went.

"Sure I am." He retrieved a simple, black pistol from the drawer, inspected the breech critically, then slid the magazine home inside the handle and cocked the weapon.

"This isn't your fight, Vin." She closed the last couple of buckles in the center of her chest then started pulling hardware from the bottom of her duffle and clipping it to the harness's various attachment points, pouches, and dangling straps.

"I'm sure that can be said." He jammed his pistol home in the thigh holster, then moved to his small closet and pulled his flight jacket off a hanger. He took a moment to examine it for any damage, wear, or other issues with the concealed armor plates strategically placed inside its lining, then pulled the jacket on and turned to face her. "Of course it could also be said that I love you, and that I care about what happens to you, and that makes this, by said association, my fight." He pulled his comm link from his jacket pocket and secured it to his ear as he waited for her to process his words.

Riana stopped what she was doing and stared at him, mouth open. It took a whole minute for her to realize it was open and decide to do something with it, "Uh…"

"Speechless? At a complete loss for words?" He grinned as he moved toward her with an exaggerated swagger. "Exactly how I like my woman to be!"

Riana stopped staring and wrapped her arms around him in a tight embrace. "I love you, too," she gushed, unable to think of anything else to say that might live up to the moment.

-27-

In her lessons about human history, Riana had been instructed by Willhelmina to watch a thousand year old feature-length video about a group of rebels and their efforts to overthrow a despotic, totalitarian dictator. It was a science-fiction epic (for the time) that was filled with space ships, gun battles, swords and sorcery. The characters were formulaic, but well played archetypes and much of what the movie predicted in the way of technology had since become reality. From directed energy weapons, to plasma swords that would slice through nearly anything, even people who could move things, and influence other's with their minds.

In the movie, the old mentor figure referred to a bar in a dingy little space-port town as 'a wretched hive of scum and villainy'. This line kept repeating itself over and over again in her head as they walked down the street in Neo-Tokyo.

The street was filthy, and the rest of the city seemed to get worse from there. It was dark and oppressive, populated with people who looked as if they'd just as soon shank a traveler and steal their clothing as look them in the eyes when they passed in the street.

Riana strongly suspected that them being well armed was the sole reason they had not been attacked already. Although she was certain that plenty of people were still contemplating the possibility of a mugging, which only made her smile inwardly. They had no idea what they would be getting themselves into if they actually acted on those thoughts.

"So, tell me again why this place is such a cesspool..." Her voice was quiet and directed at Vincent through the side of her mouth. Sounding like a tourist would only encourage an attack.

"Officially, there aren't any favored cities by the big five," Vincent began.

"Those being the companies that make up the Conglomerate..."

"Right," he confirmed, "But as it happens, each of those corporations has a major facility or headquarters in one of the six megacities of the Ring Station."

"Leaving one city without a corporate power-seat," she nodded.

"Right. So Neo-Tokyo has sort of become the de facto head of all things illicit and carnal. The Conglomerate military maintains a minimal presence inside the city, preferring to keep their soldiers at the exits to keep the scum from getting out, rather than spend the resources trying to clean things up. Plus, the black market needs a place to operate from, so they kind of have to leave the city alone."

Riana turned her violet eyes to Vincent. They were large as saucers and her ears twitched as if irritated by some unseen insect. "Wait."

"I know," he smiled.

"You're telling me that the Conglomerate lets the black market thrive here?"

"They have to, Ree." He shrugged his shoulders as if that was it.

"Not that I really care either way, mind you, but why would they do that?"

"Turn left here." He pointed to a small intersection they were approaching, then continued. "It's like this... The Conglomerate needs certain resources in order to run smoothly. But their citizenry has become used to a certain lifestyle, and a certain kind of labor. Most of which does not involve much in the way of real hard labor, especially in hazardous environments."

"So they should be using robots and remotely-controlled automatons to do those tasks, right?"

"You might think so, but no. Robots are not generally sophisticated enough to make good on-the-spot decisions and judgement calls, so while they are great for hard, physical labor, their lack of intuition and inability to improvise limits their usability. So instead, the Conglomerate creates an unofficial arrangement with the people that choose to live outside their system..."

"The dissidents?" Riana cut him off.

"What?"

"Dissidents. I've heard that term used to describe people who choose to live off the grid." Her ears drooped as she spoke, unsure if she'd used the correct term.

"We don't tend to think of ourselves as dissidents."

"You're..."

"I was born in the Dregs." his smile was less jovial than usual.

"I'm sorry, I had no idea..."

"It's okay, Ree. Sometimes I forget how short a time we've really known one another. All that time in Kalijor sort of compresses timelines... Anyway, the Conglomerate sub-contracts a lot of its more dangerous extraction, refining, and assembly work to free agents, then allows Runners, like myself, to bring the goods in from outside the system."

"So, Neo-Tokyo is used as a sort of black market clearinghouse for smuggled goods that the Conglomerate consumes?"

"Exactly. And the criminal element is more or less allowed to thrive here in order to facilitate the exchange of essential materials in from the free agents, and other goods back out to those same folks."

"So not only does the black market exist at the behest of the Conglomerate, but they are also given free reign of this entire city."

"Yup."

Riana nodded her head in understanding, ears perking back up again. "There was a time when I thought the governments of Kalijor were overly complicated and politic in their operation."

"Then you found out how things really are, eh?" Vincent grinned at her.

"Something like that," she nodded, "but getting to know real human beings, and all of their infinite complexities, has shed a certain amount of light on things."

"I suppose it would at that," he nodded, *"The Ether-Bean* is just up ahead there on the left."

"So, do you still have family in The Dregs?"

Vincent quirked a grin at her. "Yeah, my mother and sister. Mom has actually been running a small shipyard since dad passed a few years ago, and my sister owns a restaurant, damn good cook."

"So when will you take me to meet them?"

He raised an eyebrow toward her, "You'd go to The Dregs with me, Miss Thorindal?"

She wrapped an arm around his waist and pulled herself into him, stopping their progress long enough to give him a quick kiss. "I would go to the ends of the universe with you, Mister Torres."

Vincent returned the kiss, chuckling as they covered the last half block leading up to the building. "I'd love to introduce you. I don't get over there much, we…"

"You don't get along because you didn't stay to take over the operation of your father's business…"

"What?"

"Was that wrong? That seems to be a recurring theme in media…"

Vincent looked confused for a moment, then started laughing almost hysterically. He actually stopped walking again to bend over and brace his hands against his knees.

"I've said something wrong again, haven't I?" Riana's ears drooped as she stood there, helplessly, and watched him laugh.

Finally, Vincent managed to get himself under control enough that he could speak again. "No, you're right…" He paused to wipe tears from his eyes. "That does seem to be a pretty common theme in the movies, doesn't it? Anyway, no. Mom does a hell of a job with the shipyard, and she has no issues with what I do, except that maybe it's a little more dangerous than she'd like. What I was going to say is that she really, really, wants grandchildren..."

Riana's eyes went wide again as the meaning of his words sank in. A moment later she was blushing furiously and jogging toward The Ether-Bean with a sniggering Vincent hustling after her.

-28-

The Ether-Bean was a sort of combination cafe, dance club, and digerati's haven. It occupied the bottom two floors of a ten-story building made of glass and gleaming metal. The sidewalk and street outside were filled with teens and young adults dressed for dancing and partying, sharing conversations about their various adventures.

The first floor was filled to overflowing with oversexed youths, drinking coffee (an expensive indulgence, with so little arable land and facilities trying to feed so many people across the solar system) and a myriad of other drinks, eating various treats and meals, and dancing and cavorting to loud, driving beats that permeated the hot, sweaty room.

The masses were being served by a veritable army of barely-clad men and women bearing trays and smiles that seemed to grow as their bodies were squeezed and caressed by the clientele in the course of doing their work. They appeared to be from a multitude of origins, black, white, tall, short, many with genetic alterations, small horns, tails, pointy ears, wild hair colors, and more, but the one thing they all had in common was an extreme beauty, and a lack of modesty.

Pressing their way through the crowd, Riana and Vincent finally mounted the wide, curving staircase that led up to the second floor mezzanine. The stairs curved around a large, round stage in the center of the main floor that currently had a holographic projection of a band playing the music that so permeated the huge, writhing space. As they climbed the stairs, passing the half-way point seemed to be like moving through an invisible curtain of some kind as the pounding rhythm was suddenly drowned out, dulled to nothing more than a background vibration.

The area was a wide, dimly lit balcony, overlooking the sea of grinding bodies below, and played host to several dozen sunken alcoves, each one with an overly-comfortable chair in the center and surrounded with dozens of holographic screens. The occupants of the sunken computer terminals were going about various tasks that Riana almost instantly recognized as illicit.

"What do you suppose this is all about?" Vincent asked, indicating the computer pits with a nod.

"I don't know exactly, but they seem to be getting into some pretty secure systems. This is exactly the sort of place Gregory Shantal would hang out."

"Based on what I know of him, I'd have to agree with you." Vincent scanned the space with a wary eye. "But you should know that he's probably not the most dangerous person in here."

"What does that mean?" Riana cast him a questioning look.

"It means that this is Almon Genloe's place."

"And who is Almon Genloe? Some kind of amazing warrior?"

"Not exactly, no. He's sort of a kingpin. He funnels and channels the majority of the black market goods and services that come in and out of Neo-Tokyo. I don't know how impressive his fighting skills are, but I can tell you that he almost certainly has a lot of body guards that are almost definitely excellent warriors."

"And he's kind of a bastard, too," a female voice interjected from behind the pair.

They turned around to see a thin woman, just over five feet tall, with a curtain of short, strawberry blonde hair framing her dark, cobalt eyes as she looked up at them. She was dressed in a skin tight, rubbery cat suit that reflected the dim lights of the holographic displays in its dark, midnight blue color. The low heels of her boots added no more than an inch to her diminutive height, but that didn't stop her carrying herself with the confidence of a seasoned warrior.

"Daray!" Riana beamed, wrapping her arms around the smaller woman and grinning.

"How're you holding out?" Vincent asked the young woman with a raised eyebrow.

"As well as can be expected, under the circumstances." She shrugged as she disengaged herself from Riana's embrace. "How about you two?"

"We're doing well. Lots going on. World in imminent danger, you know, the usual stuff," Riana quipped.

"I gathered as much. It took APRIL the better part of a day to locate you." Daray smirked, referring to the advanced artificial intelligence that cohabited her reengineered brain. She motioned to a small table nearby where the three of them seated themselves.

"I'm surprised she was able to get to me in Kalijor," Riana admitted.

"Yeah. She said the firewalls were pretty tough, but there was something really odd going on in sub-space. Something about massive amounts of data flowing in and out of the Kalijor servers."

"Well, there are millions of people playing. That's a lot of data," Vincent commented, his eyes fixed on a door at the far side of the mezzanine. The door was flanked by large, burly men with cybernetic arms and legs.

"No, she says it's much more than that," Daray responded, then looked to the side as if listening to another conversation. After a moment she looked back at them and added, "I don't quite understand everything she's saying, but it seems to be several hundred thousand times as much data as should be expected. It's like the entire sub-space realm that Kalijor uses for input/output is filled up almost to overflowing."

"That's in line with what we found a little while ago," Riana confirmed. "We think there may be something going on in Kalijor that was caused by the same accident that created my consciousness."

"We do?" Vincent gave her a quick look.

"Jax, Kat, and I found some indications of this a few months ago. Jax is watching the traffic but it's still too early to tell for sure what's going on." Riana put her hand on Vincent's arm and smiled. "I'm sorry I haven't told you before, things have been so busy that I'd forgotten."

"Let's call it even," he grinned at her before returning his gaze to the door and its sentries.

"So what do you think is going on in there?" Daray asked, indicating the door.

"I think Genloe's got someone in there doing business," Vincent replied.

"I think it's alive," Riana responded at the same time.

"What?" Daray and Vincent asked in unison, turning to fully face Riana, confused.

Riana blinked at them, the tips of her ears twitching slightly. "I think that whatever caused me to become sentient, is affecting the rest of Kalijor as well. I think I was only the first."

"But your sentience almost crashed the servers, didn't it?" Vincent replied.

"APRIL says there isn't enough processing power aboard he *Ty-conderoga* to handle that kind of AI complexity," Daray added.

"It did," Riana nodded toward Vincent, then turned her attention toward Daray. "She's right, and Jax is looking into it, but he's just one guy, working in his spare time. Although, he seems to think it is related to the sub-space domain somehow."

Turning back toward Vincent, Riana squeezed his arm. "Why do you think Almon has someone in there?"

"Those two big cyborgs usually only look that edgy when there is something significant going on behind the door they're guarding," Vincent answered, with a nod toward the door's guards.

"So Almon's making a big deal," Daray nodded. "I saw Shantal go in there over two hours ago. APRIL says she's sure he's still in there, although she's having trouble getting through The Ether-Bean's firewalls discretely."

"You're telling me that Gregory Shantal is in that room?" Riana started to stand up, but was restrained by Vincent clapping his free hand over the one she had placed on his arm.

"Hold up there, Ree. If you go charging in there, all hell will break loose and those guards are cyborgs. Even with your skills, if you start a fight with them, there's no way you'll be able to deal with Shantal as well."

"I can take care of them," Daray chirped.

"There you go," Riana beamed at Vincent. "She'll get the guards, we bust in, you keep this Genloe person under control while I take care of Shantal."

"Good plan," Vincent nodded, but still didn't release her hand as she tried to stand up again. "Except for the part about us having no idea why he's even in there and why you feel this need to attack him."

Riana dropped back into her seat with a huff, turning an annoyed expression toward Vincent. Her ears cocked back at a severe angle as she glared at him.

"He's a bastard, Vin. He helped kidnap Kat, betrayed us both, stole SO property, and he's somehow in league with Malice."

"And he's a really crappy dresser," Daray added brightly.

"Uh-huh." Vincent gave Daray a hard look, which merely bought him a little smirk in return, but the withering look from Riana was enough to chill his blood. "Look, Ree, I know you want to get this guy, but you need to slow down a bit. If he's in there with Almon, then there is something being planned. Almon is a major player and Shantal is as big as anyone can get in the world of hired muscle."

"All the more reason we should get in there and break up whatever's going on," Riana frowned.

"Plus, I owe those guards a good trouncing," Daray grinned.

"Is APRIL having any luck getting through the firewalls?" Riana eyed the comparatively tiny Daray.

Daray looked up and to the side for a moment, listening to APRIL's voice in her mind, before shaking her head as her attention returned to the group. "No. She says she needs at least an hour to do it without setting off every alarm in the place."

"Fine. Then we'll do it the old-fashioned way." Riana stood up, turning to face the door, serious intent written across her features.

Daray hopped to her feet, her hands reaching for the narrow sheath slung across her back to retrieve the pair of simple, metal sticks held there. The look on her face was a cross between cold business and schoolyard glee.

Vincent came out of his chair so quickly that it clattered to the floor behind him. His arms shot out to grip each of the women's nearest arms, although he knew there was no chance at all of him actually restraining either of them.

"Ladies, I really think we..." his thought was interrupted by the sudden opening of the door. In the void, stood the wiry, denim overall-covered frame of Gregory Shantal. Even from their table, Riana could tell he had changed. His wispy silver-grey hair had been replaced with a strange, light blue-grey coif that was much thicker than his normal hair. His body seemed even thinner than she remembered, and his features were much softer, more effeminate. He stepped through the doorway, speaking over his shoulder for a moment as his heavy boots clomped along the smooth surface of the floor, and when the door slid closed behind him, his head swiveled forward, hard grey eyes instantly locking on Riana. He grinned from ear to ear and immediately made his way across the space to the group.

"Good evening, child. I haven't seen you in months!" his voice was merry, and carried a tone that made the listener want to bathe in acid.

"What are you doing here, Shantal?" Riana hissed at him through clenched teeth. Vincent's hand on her upper arm seemed to be holding her back, despite the fact that she was easily ten times stronger than him.

"Why, business of course. What else would I be doing here, child?" His grin revealed a set of teeth that were all immaculately white and spaced just a little too far apart to make an appealing smile.

"I see you've replaced your hand," she spat, the menacing grin spreading across her lips telling him that she was more than willing to repeat the amputation.

Gregory raised his arm to reveal a small, slender hand with delicate fingers that looked more feminine than even his slight frame

158

should have. "Quite right, child! And I must thank you. Without your complete failure, I wouldn't have had the opportunity."

Riana started toward him again, but Vincent pulled her back, moving up beside her to get a better grip on her arm. Daray had slid the metal bastón from their sheath and held them both in one hand. Her cobalt eyes shifted between the skinny man, and the anxious-looking guards flanking the door. They were watching the exchange with interest, their hands working in and out of fists in preparation for action.

"Are you okay, Ree?" Daray locked her eyes on Riana's.

"Sure," Riana replied, her eyes narrowing to slits and trying their hardest to burn a hole through Gregory's head.

"I'm going to go powder my nose then," Daray slid past the man, moving toward the pair of cyborgs with a casual gait.

"Don't, Ree," Vincent cautioned.

"I have to, Vin. I'll understand if you want to go," her eyes never moved from Shantal's as she spoke.

Vincent sighed heavily, released her arm, and took a step to the side. He looked around the mezzanine again, then back to the man standing unassumingly before them. Riana's ears sagged slightly, but her eyes remained drilled into Shantal's as he grinned at her.

"Alright, but I want it known that I think this is a terrible idea," Vincent breathed.

Riana's ears perked back up, and in the space of a heartbeat, had lunged forward, her fist cocked back, aiming a thunderous punch at Shantal's nose.

In that heartbeat, the room exploded into a flurry of violent activity. Shantal ducked to the side to avoid the punch, narrowly avoiding it as well as a shot fired from Vincent's handgun.

The cyborg guards sprang into action, pushing off the wall and breaking into a run. Daray followed suit, dashing toward the cyborgs with surprising speed. With twenty feet still between them, she tipped herself forward into a somersault, then pushed off the floor with her hands, launching herself at them feet first. They tried to break to either side of her, but she spread her feet out at the last second, catching each of them squarely in the side of the face and sending them sprawling to either side.

"You should have listened to your boyfriend, child. This is not going to end well for you," Gregory preached. From his position to her side, he spun around, leveling a quick backfist at the side of her head.

"I beat you the last time we fought, old man." She blocked his attack with her upper arm, wrapping the rest of her arm around his. She shifted under his captured limb, bracing her hips against his, and heaved him off the ground and over her shoulder.

Instead of crashing to the floor, however, he twisted himself around in mid-air, getting his feet beneath him again, and landed in a solid stance, with his arms gripping hers and a smile on his face. "Yes, but last time, I let you win."

A brief flash of panic lit Riana's eyes as he reversed the throw, sending her crashing through the table they had been sitting at. Another shot from Vincent's handgun rang out. This time the bullet actually tore through the fabric of Gregory's dirty white t-shirt.

Gregory spun around, launching a reverse side kick toward Vincent's chest that was narrowly avoided by stepping to the side. With a quick movement, Vincent pressed the barrel of his gun to Gregory's calf and fired off two quick shots that sent sparks and bits of metal flying from beneath the wound in his artificial skin.

"Nice shot, honey," Riana said as she kipped up and launched a kick of her own, hooking her foot in toward his face as he retracted his wounded leg.

"Thanks, Ree. It was tough to miss on that one," Vincent smirked, barely ducking under Gregory's body as it lurched to the side from the force of Riana's kick.

"And later on you can explain how you're keeping up with the fight," Riana added as she stalked forward.

"Sure thing," Vincent nodded, following suit.

Across the room, Daray had her hands full keeping the guards busy. They were fast, strong, and competent fighters. Between the two of them, it seemed all she could do to keep them occupied. She ducked and wove, hand-springing over kicks and rolling under punches as she threw her arms and legs out in intricate circles and winding patterns that made it look more like some sort of acrobatic dance than an actual fight. If anything, she was slowly wearing them out, as she seemed to have a boundless source of energy tucked away in her tiny frame. Her genetically-engineered body matching their mechanical bodies two-to-one.

"You don't get it, do you child?" Gregory's annoying voice chided. "It doesn't matter how many henchmen you bring along. You can't beat me." He kicked out with his wounded leg, catching Vincent in the shoulder and sending him sprawling, with a loud thud on the floor.

"Hey!" he protested as he slowly collected himself and stood back up. "I'm no henchman! I'm more of a thug..." He fired several rapid shots at Gregory, "or maybe a lackey..."

Gregory easily bent backward out of the path of Vincent's bullets, but that put him in line for another kick from Riana, her foot nearly in his face already, but somehow he managed to twist around, grab her ankle, and drag her to the ground, landing on top of her with a heavy thump.

"Get off me, you old pervert!" she growled, cocking her hand back and cutting loose with several rapid punches to the side of his head.

"Of course, child," Gregory grinned, twisting around atop her, still clutching her ankle. He seemed to flow like water, rippling and churning rather than actually moving. The next second, he was facing opposite her, one leg wrapped around her captured limb, bracing her knee in the locked position, and his other heel digging into her stomach and ribs painfully, hydraulic fluid and sparks raining down on her. "You really should go back to school, it doesn't seem as if you've studied very hard since the last time we met."

"Let her go!" Two sharp cracking sounds indicated more shots from Vincent, and the bullets tore holes in Gregory's forehead, revealing a gleaming metal skull beneath the artificial skin.

"Your weapon is useless at that range, especially against my armor. Now be a good thug and let the child and I speak." Grinning, he turned dismissively away from Vincent, refocusing on Riana and giving her captured ankle and foot a little twist to reinforce his position of power over her. "Now then, I'm afraid I wasn't expecting to see you here this evening. It's a bit too soon for you to be creeping back into my affairs, child. I'm going to have to make sure you stay out of the picture for a while. But don't worry, it won't hurt for too long before your wonderful little nanites cut off the pain receptors in your leg."

At that, he began to arch his back and further twist her ankle, creating an impossible physical arrangement for her leg. It was only a matter of moments before even her metal bones snapped under the intense pressure. Riana gritted her teeth against the pain for a moment before, just as he'd said it would, the pain stopped, leaving only the surreal understanding that her leg was about to be splintered into shards, and that she could neither feel it, due to her cybernetic construction, nor do anything about it, due to the way this man had her pinned.

"I said… Let. Her. Go," Vincent's voice came back again, this time it was punctuated by the loud clicking of metal on metal. Both Riana and Gregory looked up at the same time to see the huge muzzle of the shotgun-like bolt caster, leveled at Gregory.

"You wouldn't risk it!" Gregory chortled, amusement clear on his face.

"Sorry, I'm just a thug. The boss lady tells me to kill the bad guy, I kill the bad guy. Not my fault if she doesn't cover all her bases."

At the sound of the emphasized word, Riana instantly wrapped her arms in front of her face and twisted as much to the side as she could. A heartbeat later, there was a hollow 'thump' sound as the linear accelerator propelled the huge cartridge out of the weapon, followed by the sound of the projectile slamming into Gregory's body.

Riana felt a lurch as Gregory convulsed, then she felt his body go limp, releasing her leg and allowing her to roll over backwards. Coming to a crouching position, she looked at Gregory Shantal's body on the ground in front of her, twitching and spasaming. A gaping hole in his chest revealed a machine shop of bent and mangled parts, many of which were now hanging out of the hole for all to see.

"What was that?" she gaped.

"A one pound metal slug going twelve-hundred feet per second," Vincent smiled as he opened the breech on the bolt caster to eject the spent cartridge and insert another.

"You don't get it… do you… child?" Gregory's voice was broken, but just as annoying as always. He lifted his head up to look at Riana with his cold eyes. "This only speeds things along." His new hand raised off the ground to point at her and she could see a deep gash around his bare neck and shoulder. The wound was wide, probably close to an inch, and seemed to be filled with some kind of fluid, shiny and wet.

"What did you do to yourself?" there was actually a tone of concern in her voice as she shivered from the site of the wound.

"You. You did this child. And soon enough, you will reap the rewards for your actions."

"Um. I hate to break this up, touching as it is and all, but I think we'd better get a move on people." Daray sauntered up to them, discarding a cybernetic arm casually. "APRIL says there is like, a whole army headed this direction. Seems someone started some trouble or something and they're all hot and heavy for a fight."

As she finished speaking, a large group of armed and armored soldiers piled through the front door of The Ether-Bean and began to make their way through the crowd toward the stairs.

"This is not a good thing," Vincent said, sliding the bolt caster home in its back holster.

"Yeah. Those guys look a little upset about something," Daray smirked.

"I'll lead down the stairs. Daray, you're with me. Vin, you work your way around the action, cover us as you are able, but the air looks to get pretty thick, so watch for stray fire."

"Right," Vincent nodded, pulling his pistol and replacing the magazine.

"Lead on, o-cybernetic one," Daray grinned, bowing slightly toward the stairs.

"You'll never make it, child. Give up now and hope they go easy on you!" Gregory sneered.

"Shut it!" Daray replied, kicking him in the side of the head and unhinging his jaw. "The sound of your voice makes me want to step out an airlock!"

Riana chuckled as she pulled the bull-pup from beneath her jacket and cocked the weapon. "Okay. Let's be off."

-29-

"Well, it was nice to see Daray again. I'm glad she's adjusting to things," Riana commented as she wiped blood from her neck.

"Yeah." Vincent replaced the empty magazine in his pistol and jammed it roughly into his thigh holster. "Can we talk about what just happened back there?"

"What do you mean? We just found out that Gregory Shantal was working some deal with a known criminal figure and stopped them from doing whatever it was they were planning." She pressed her lips together in a hard line as she rubbed at a rough spot on her shoulder.

"We didn't stop anything, Riana. All we did was go in there, in a very public place, and start a fight with a man who deals with criminals and the government in equal measure."

"Well he won't be bothering anyone for a while."

"Riana, he wasn't bothering anyone today!"

She turned her violet eyes on him, her ears were drooped down low and the tip of one twitched randomly. "He bothers everyone. He's a menace."

"So you say. But he didn't -do- anything Riana. Having a meeting with someone is not against the law!"

"Maybe not, but he had it coming." She turned back to her own affairs, clearing the breech on her bull-pup and wiping some of the blood from it's sleek black frame.

"Riana, what the heck is going on? You aren't like this."

"I'm not like what, Vin? Huh? What am I not like? You don't know me well enough to tell. No one does!" now she was pointing at him, and yelling, her ears pointing straight back.

"I know your heart, Riana. And there isn't any place for revenge in it. Something else is going on here..."

"Yeah, well maybe you don't know me as well as you think," she punctuated her words by slapping a fresh magazine into her weapon and drawing back the charging handle. Then she turned to look out the window of the monorail. Mere feet away, on the other side of a thick, transparent wall, spun the blue-green orb that was Earth. White, wispy clouds drifted lazily across its surface.

"Sometimes I think I know you better than you do, Ree. Are you going to tell me what's going on?" He shifted out of his seat, sitting down next to her and putting an arm around her shoulders.

"I don't know what's going on, Vin. I'm lost. I don't know what to do, or where to go, or even who I am. All I know is that people keep expecting impossible things of me, and want me to do them without any explanations..."

"And that's why you went to The Ether-Bean looking for a fight? So you could exercise some control in your life?"

"No," she sniffed, still unable to produce the tears she so desperately needed to cry. "He hurt Kat. Helped lock her up for months..."

"And you think he needs to suffer for it? You cut off his hand, Riana. And he's left you alone since. Going after him like this is only going to incite him to retaliate."

"Yes! He does need to suffer for it. Besides, he tore off my hand first." She looked down at her hand, flexing the fingers beneath the black glove a few times, remembering the excruciating pain he had caused when he'd crushed it, even if it had only lasted a moment before her body had shut off the pain receptors.

"So it's going to be 'an eye for an eye'? Riana, that sort of thinking doesn't lead where anyone should ever want to go."

"She's all the family I've got, Vin. I can't let anything happen to her before..."

"Before what?" Vincent looked at her, questioning.

She turned away from him again, looking back out onto the jewel beneath them. It looked so peaceful and serene. One would never know that it had been rendered uninhabitable by nuclear weapons hundreds of years ago. "It really is beautiful, isn't it?"

"What?"

"The Earth. Whenever I'm here, I just spend all my time staring at it."

"You can see the earth from where you eat your meals on the *Tyconderoga*, Riana. Are we changing the subject for a reason?"

"Not like this. Not without the rings and platforms covering up parts. There's no view quite like this one."

"No. I suppose not." He squeezed her to him. They were obviously done talking about it for a while, but he was by no means letting it drop. Still, there was no sense in aggravating the situation, or the super-strong, over-emotional cyborg either, for that matter.

"You know, what you said earlier..." she spoke to his reflection in the window, still not taking her eyes off the planet beneath them.

"Earlier when?"

"Back at your place. Before we left for Neo-Tokyo."

"Yes. I remember."

"Did you mean it?" She finally turned to him, a hopeful, child-like look on her face.

"I wouldn't have said it if I didn't mean it."

"Would you..." She dipped her chin down, looking at her hands as they minced together for a moment. "Would you say it again?"

"I'll say it any time you like." He hooked his bent finger under her chin and lifted her eyes to his. With a loving smile he spoke, "I love you, Riana Thorindal."

Riana's heart melted. Her glassy eyes still refused to shed tears, but she knew they would have been there if they could. Leaning into him, she kissed him on the lips for a moment, then broke away and whispered in his ear, "I love you too, Vincent Torres." Then she leaned back in and embraced him in a hug that lasted until the monorail stopped in På-rymi an hour later.

-30-

"Are we ready?" Riana asked the collected group. Their response was largely a series of nods. Katrina and Exodus, however, did not have good news.

"We were unable to find one rather critical bit needed to cast the spell," Kat frowned.

"But we've got a line on where we can get it," Exodus added.

"Okay. What is 'it' exactly?" Jumah raised an eyebrow at the human.

"The root of a Sapsorrow's tooth," Katrina piped in.

"Are you out of your minds?" Jumah returned, his blue eyes as big as saucers.

"It is unlikely that such a thing can be found at market, for any price," Xembak interjected in a very serious tone.

"It is also unlikely that such a beast will willingly allow the extraction of any of its teeth," Desse added from her chair in front of Xembak, who stood behind her in his usual defensive posture.

"Agreed, and to make matters worse, the root needs to be fresh. No more than twenty-four hours old. Which means we need to find it fairly close to the Dead Sea," Exodus confirmed.

"Which means we will be asking a very large, very old Sapsorrow to give up a tooth, since only the oldest of them live that far into the Plain of Sorrow." Jumah folded his arms across his chest.

"A Sapsorrow?" Riana finally asked.

"Yeah, Ree, you know, a Plains Ray?" Katrina admonished her.

"Why would I know that? What the heck is a Plains Ray?"

"What? Did you skip your cryptozoology classes at the Academy?"

"Yes, Kat! I skipped them! I was learning to use more than just my brain while you were buried in books remember? Could someone tell me what we're dealing with please?"

"It's hard to explain," Katrina frowned. "It's kind of like a large fish, or worm, with a flat head that…"

"Look, Violet, it's a flatworm that buries itself in the muck of the Plain of Sorrow, and lures creatures in with unresistable bait, then grinds them to bits in its toothy maw," Firiel grinned evilly at Riana as she spoke.

"Did you just call me Violet?" Riana's eyes flashed at Firiel, who stood there and smirked at her with a challenge in her eyes.

"Can we try to stay on topic here please?" Jumah touched Riana's arm, which caused her to wheel around and glare at him for a moment before the venom drained from her eyes and her look softened.

"Fine, so it's a big worm. How do we find one? Do they have any weaknesses we can exploit?" She tossed Firiel a look before turning back to the rest of the group.

"Well, that's part of the problem," Exodus confirmed.

"They can stay buried for years, decades even," Katrina added.

"And even if you wander right out on top of one, they don't always attack. If they are in deep torpor, or have recently eaten, they may let you wander right into their trap and back out again without ever revealing themselves," Jumah added.

"The beasts are difficult to locate, unpredictable, and fierce adversaries in combat," Xembak growled.

"Yet, we need to locate one, and defeat it, in order to descend beneath the surface of the Dead Sea safely," Desse smiled.

"Do you ever get upset or excited?" Riana raised an eyebrow at the elf.

"All things are part of the pattern, Riana. You, me, the Sapsorrow, even the Dead Sea. If our cause is just and our motivations on the side of right, then we will prevail," her voice remained serene and her smile never faltered.

"Right. Just cause. So, does the pattern include a thread on locating these monsters?" Riana's ears flattened out as she replied to Desse.

"As a matter of fact, I think I may be able to help with that," Desse said.

"Great. So what else do we need?" Riana turned her gaze to the rest of the group.

"Well, here's the really bad part about this whole affair," Katrina spoke up again. "Because the tooth must be so fresh, we'll have almost no time to recover after the battle with the Sapsorrow."

"Desse can heal us up though, right?" Riana turned her gaze back to the elf.

"Of course I can. However, my energies are limited. If we sustain too much damage battling the Sapsorrow, then I will be of little use during and after any battle with the guardian," even delivering this news, her face remained calm.

"So is there an alternative for healing that we can get ahold of?" Jumah piped in.

"We picked up a few potions and elixirs at the bazaar, and we can grab a few more in Bête Noir before we head south," Exodus replied.

"Great. So is there anything else we need before we go?" Jumah beamed at the group.

"I'd like to bring Xanthe along. He's been feeling a little neglected of late."

"Why are we bringing your pet?" Firiel scowled.

"He's not my pet, he's my friend. We're bringing him because he wants to help and I think he can. So, if it's not too much for Exodus to handle teleporting?" she looked at Exodus pointedly and received a smile and a nod. "Then he'd like to come with us and do what he can."

"And in the meantime he can eat our food and drink our water. Have you ever even been in the Plain of Sorrow before, Violet?"

"Stop calling me that!" Riana yelled. She couldn't figure out why, after the conversation they'd had, Firiel was still treating her like this. "Xanthe can live off almost nothing. He won't tax our resources."

"Can we move past whatever this is, please?" Jumah's calm voice slid between the daggers the women were shooting at one another with their eyes. "We need to get this operation under way. Let's take thirty minutes to make final preparations, then meet outside the west gate to collect Xanthe and go. Agreed?"

"Fine," Riana and Firiel chorused, still glaring at one another.

"Very well," Desse replied, standing up and taking Xembak's hand. They left the house, followed closely by Firiel, who took another moment to glare at Riana before the door closed, separating them.

"We'll meet you two at the gate." Katrina smiled, then snatched Exodus's hand and dragged him out of the house as well.

"I thought that wen't rather well," Jumah smiled.

"Really? It felt kind of like impending disaster to me." Riana slumped into a chair.

"So, what's going on between the two of you?" Jumah leaned against the table, positioning himself so she could easily make eye contact.

"She doesn't like me."

"Yes, I gathered as much. Is there something I should know about?"

"It's nothing to do with you," she grumped, folding her arms across her chest and crossing her legs.

"Riana, I love you. You have a very peculiar idea about how things work."

"Oh?" She raised an eyebrow at him.

"Yes. You see, when you have a problem, that problem affects me. Likewise, when you have a problem with another member of this group, it affects the rest of the group."

"Don't worry about us. We'll both be on task when the time comes." She turned her head to hide the true meaning of her words, looking out the window at the city wall.

"Who is she? You found out, didn't you?"

Riana remained silent, eyes focused on the blue skies over the top of the wall.

Jumah knelt down next to her, placing a hand on her tattooed thigh and squeezing slightly. "You don't have to tell me. But whatever it is going on between the two of you, it's dangerous. For you, and for the rest of us as well."

"She's Ambrai's daughter," Riana blurted out. Turning to face Jumah, tears welling in the corners of her eyes. "She was almost my sister."

"Ambrai?" He asked, then a light dawned. "You mean the woman you had to kill at the Dead Sea."

"The one who resurrected my mother and turned her into a ghoul, then tried to give birth to evil incarnate? Yeah, her."

"You did what was right, Riana. She asked you to do it. Begged you even."

"That doesn't change the fact that I killed her. I killed Firiel's mother and that's why she hates me."

"I doubt she hates you," Jumah reassured her.

"She stabbed me," she exclaimed.

"When did she stab you?"

"In the park!"

"Oh yeah." He ran his fingers through his hair and took a deep breath. "Was that before or after you found out who she is?"

"Before." She leveled her best 'what are you getting at' look on him.

"And after you found out who she really is, the wound healed right?" He returned her look with his own, 'wait for it' look.

"So you're saying that she doesn't hate me, but she does feel the need to insult and call me names?"

"Love that sibling rivalry," he grinned.

"We're not sisters!"

"Uh huh, I know. But still... mothers possessed by evil forces, learned to fight those forces because of it. Strong, independent, head-strong, quick wit..." His grin widened a bit. "You are as close to being sisters as any two unrelated people I've ever met."

"What about Kat?"

"As far as I'm concerned, you two actually are sisters." He patted her thigh as he stood up again, then held out a hand to help her up.

She stood, pressing up against him and wrapping her arms around his waist. "What did I do to deserve you?"

"Well, we all make mistakes in life. Yours seem to have saddled you with me," he joked.

"I'll be sure to figure out whatever law that was, and keep breaking it then. I don't think I could bear loosing you."

"I'm not going anywhere," his words were punctuated by their lips meeting.

-31-

The Plain of Sorrow was just as gloomy as Riana remembered it being. The dry air and constant warmth played a stark contrast to the sodden, orange, clay-like ground that ran off as far as the eye could see in every direction around Bête Noir.

Contrary to what most people thought, Bête Noir was not the name of the city, but was, in fact, the name of the smoking, black mountain that thrust obscenely out of the ground, creating the northwest wall of the city. In reality, the city didn't have a name, everyone just called it Bête Noir. The founders, fearing that they would be eradicated by the armies of the light side of Kalijor if their settlement appeared permanent enough to have a name, chose to never christen it. Since that unknown day, everyone had just taken to calling the city by the name of the volcano shielding it from the eyes of the light side.

In stark contrast to the ugly plain surrounding it, the city was alive and teeming with activity at all hours of the day and night. The group had appeared, thanks to Exodus's mastery of spatial manipulation, just outside the city wall and gotten right into the city through one of the less-used western gates.

The guards had offered Xanthe a wary glance or two, but otherwise let the group through unhindered. Now, they wandered the streets of the strange city, its kaleidoscope of different architectural styles almost overpowering the senses.

As they made their way through the winding, cobbled streets, Riana came to a stop, staring across the street at a large building, a strange look spreading across her face.

The building was three stories high and easily four-hundred feet on a side. It was constructed of an incongruous mixture of stones that looked almost haphazardly piled up into something resembling walls. Its roof was a ramshackle mixture of tiles and thatching that looked as though a stout wind would send it wholly into the open maw of the volcano. The doors and windows were all framed in various materials ranging from burnt lumber to pristine hard-woods and even solid slabs of wrought stone. The front doors were double wide and large enough to admit two ogres standing shoulder to shoulder, allowing a steady stream of people to flow in and out of the building.

The oddest thing was that most of the building appeared to have been twisted, or deformed in strange ways, with whole sections of walls jutting out over the road below for no apparent reason, and huge wooden beams bent at impossible angles. It was like a caricature of a building really, misshapen and oddly proportioned.

"What's up, Ree?" Katrina's voice penetrated her scrutiny of the structure.

Riana broke her gaze and turned to face her sister, who was standing there with a weird, half-smirk on her face. "Nothing. Just an old memory, from a previous life."

Katrina turned to look at the building, narrowing her eyes at it for a moment before they opened wide, brightening in recognition. "Oh! The Shadow of the Mountain! That's where we stayed before," her voice trailed off, not sure about her sister's feelings on the subject.

"Before our lives got really interesting!" Riana smiled, wrapping an arm around Katrina's shoulders and squeezing her sister to her. "You have to admit though, the place has a look none of these other buildings can pull off. I'd say a little reality-warping has done it a huge favor."

Katrina giggled, remembering the incident that altered the look of the building all those years ago, before grabbing Riana's hand and skipping off around the corner, dragging her sister behind her. Before she knew what was going on, Riana found herself in front of another familiar building.

A massive wooden structure with a hanging sign above its huge front door read:

Animal boarding and sales
Common, exotic, magical,
tack, feed, supplies

Katrina pulled Riana inside, putting her face to face with a short, skinny man, with a set of curved horns wrapping around his head and a knowing.

"Well hello again," he greeted them.

"You remember us?" Katrina asked with a raised eyebrow.

"Of course I do. The pair'o you came in here a couple years ago. Not t'gether though. You," he pointed at Katrina, "came in ask'n about her." He pointed to Riana. "As I recall."

"That's right," Katrina nodded.

"So, that's how you tracked me down…"

"Well, I'm certainly no bloodhound."

"And how's Mr. Xanthe doing?" The man moved between the sisters and reached out to Xanthe, who Riana had not even realized was there with them.

Xanthe cooed happily, lowering his head so that the man could scratch him behind the eye ridges. "Y'don't say," he whispered to the Equun-Draco conspiratorially, casting a suspicious eye back toward the elves.

"Did he say something?" Katrina asked.

"Nothin' much. Just that you two are get'n in it pretty deep of late. He says t'be sure you aren't leav'nim out, since he can be quite helpful." He patted Xanthe a few times on the neck then advanced back toward the women. "Still, he seems in good spirits. I told you the two o'you would work out alright." He winked at Riana as he moved past them and started spreading some fresh hay in an empty stall. "So, what can I do for the two'o you?"

"Nothing really," Katrina responded. "I just wanted to stop by while we were here and say thank you for pointing me in the right direction back then."

"What was I goin t'do lass? Let yer friend bleed t'death out in the 'sorrow?"

"Still, it wasn't something you had to do. I just wanted to let you know that we were both okay, and that we really appreciated your help," Katrina pressed on.

"Don' make a big thing out'ta it. I was just trying t'be neigh-borly."

"And thank you for Xanthe. He's become my dearest friend," Riana smiled as Xanthe lowered his scaly head onto her shoulder, and she wrapped a protective arm around it, hugging him to her.

"Jus' you three watch each other's backs. Lots'o folks out there wouldn't mind seein' the likes'o you done in."

"How do you know that people are working against us?" Riana eyed him.

"Never mind that," he turned to face them again, leaning on the handle of his pitchfork. "Just watch your backs, and tell that chee-tah friend'o yours to watch'is step down at the bottom o'the world." As he spoke, he pointed toward the huge door and their heads turned to follow his direction.

The doorway was open, empty, and there seemed to be nothing there of interest. When they turned back toward the man again, his pitch fork lay against the upper rail of the stall and there was no sign of him at all.

"How're we doing ladies?" They both started at the sound of Jumah's voice, spinning around to see him standing mere inches from them, grinning his usual, mirthful grin.

"Where did you come from?" Katrina slapped him on the shoulder. "You shouldn't sneak up on people like that."

"All in good fun ladies," he bowed.

"Especially when they can vaporize you with a word," Riana added.

"There is that," Katrina agreed with her as Jumah tried to figure out whether or not they were joking.

Finally, he decided on a subject change. "We have procured the necessary potions and tonics, bolstered our rations, and are ready to depart for parts unvisited. We await only your joining us at the south gate." He bowed low in a parody of some graceful dance move, indicating the door of the stables with his outstretched arm.

"Alright already, no need to get overly dramatic about it," Katrina rolled her eyes as she turned and headed for the door, patting Xanthe as she moved past him.

"I liked it," Riana retorted as Jumah stood up again and their hands found one-another, fingers twining. She grinned at Xanthe, who chortled in response and fell in beside the pair as they moved toward the exit together.

"It was just for you anyway. I like your sister and all, but that whole 'killing me with her mind' thing is a little bit on the iffy side."

Riana punched him in the shoulder as they made their way to the south gate.

-32-

If the Plain of Sorrow, with its ruddy orange color and annoyingly adhesive properties could be considered a festering sore on the face of Kalijor, then The Dead Sea was a puss-filled, open wound. The water, if it could still be called that, was a sickly green color and bubbled every so often, as if it were a giant witch's cauldron. A thick fog hung over the surface of the sea, making the green water look even more like pea soup, and reducing visibility to a few dozen yards before all that was visible was the acrid fog itself.

The beach, while composed of the same orange soil as the rest of the Plain of Sorrow, was even wetter, allowing their boots to sink a few inches and creating slurping sounds every time they lifted their feet to take a step.

"Is it my imagination, or is this place even worse than it was the last time I was here?" Riana shook a glob of the nasty mud from her boot and offered a sour look to her companions.

"The last time you were here, your head was imploding. I don't think you're qualified to make that call." Katrina sniggered.

"Oh sure, rub it in." Riana leaned on Jumah for support, frowning as she put her foot back down and it sank into the quagmire again. "So... Is it?"

"Is it what?" Jumah asked her, unsure if the question had been directed at him.

"Is it worse than before?" Riana eyed Katrina.

"Yeah, I think it might be." Katrina pulled Chavan, the magical staff she received as a gift at the same time Riana had acquired Elkorine, from the mud and looked at its length. The dwarven runes were caked full of mud up to about two feet.

"Are you kids done? Maybe we should get back to this whole, 'saving the world' thing?" Firiel pushed between the sisters, slogging her way through the soupy ground further up shore, where the ground was a little more solid.

"Yeah. Right," they both answered in unison, casting the tiny elf a whole set of critical eyes.

"What's with her?" Katrina asked under her breath.

"She hates me," Riana answered with a shrug.

"Nonsense," Desse interjected as she moved past them, her boots not even touching the ground. "She simply feels that you could focus more on the issue at hand. It is her way."

"I'd just like it if her way didn't involve constantly tearing me down." Riana sloshed after the rest of the group as they made their way up the rise of the beach.

"Maybe she's just jealous…" Jumah offered, holding out his hand for Riana to take as they moved toward Firiel.

"Or she could just be constipated," Katrina added brightly.

Xanthe snorted at them both, striding past them with ease, his large feet allowing him to stay on top of the muddy ground instead of sinking into it.

"So does Xanthe hate you too?" Katrina chuckled at her sister.

"No, he just thinks we spend too much time chatting when there's so much work to get done," Riana replied with a nod to the large animal as he moved up beside Firiel and began surveying the area. "Although I think he may still be a bit upset about being left behind the last time we went out on an adventure," she added in a hushed tone that she was all too aware would not make any difference, given the mental link she shared with him.

"Really?" Katrina raised an eyebrow, her ears perking up in interest.

"Yeah. He's a smart one and he knows it. He's upset that we left him behind, especially considering how vulnerable I was, being blind and all." They hadn't had much of a choice though. They'd been imprisoned in Avian for a crime they hadn't committed, then released by the king, disguised as a commoner, through a series of secret passages that would not have permitted Xanthe to get through, even if they could have freed him form the stables. By now they had joined up with the rest of the group, who were all standing atop a small rise in the beach, looking off in all directions for signs of their quarry.

"So what are we looking for again," asked Jumah.

"It's a sort of a huge sea ray creature, with teeth, and a bad attitude," Katrina responded with a nod, placing her flattened palm to her brow as if trying to shield her eyes form the sun. Of course, there was no actual sun on Kalijor, especially not in the dismal, overcast, and perpetually foggy landscape of the beaches they now wandered.

"And when it isn't floating around terrorizing people, it looks like what?" Riana asked.

"They tend to bury themselves in the sand, with nothing but their feelers protruding above the ground level," Exodus filled them in.

"Feelers which look like what? Giant whiskers? Long, insectile protrusions?" Jumah continued.

"Shrubs," Riana replied.

"Eh, yes actually, small shrubs. How did you know that Riana?" Exodus responded with a tone of awe to his voice.

"Know what?" Riana blinked at the group.

"That Sapsorrow feelers look like shrubs sticking out of the ground," Exodus replied.

"I didn't know that. Why would you think I knew that?" A guilty look fell over her face as she turned from person to person in the group, ears laying down flat from her head.

"You just answered Jumah's question though," Exodus was clearly confused.

"I did?" she turned to look at Jumah for an explanation.

Jumah shrugged, then smiled slightly, and finally repeated himself, "I had asked what their feelers look like, and you responded 'shrubs' which, apparently is the answer."

"Oh," she shrugged, then turned to Exodus and added, "no, I didn't know that."

"Then why did you say shrubs, dear," Desse chimed in, her face still placid and unimposing.

"Because I see shrubs over there," Riana pointed in a direction parallel to the shore of the sea where, off in the distance, far enough away through the pea-soup fog and dim lighting, she could make out the vague silhouettes of a small patch of shrubs, laying low to the ground.

"What shrubs?" Katrina asked with more than a little skepticism.

"Those shrubs, right there," Riana pointed at the grove.

"Anybody else seeing this?" Firiel's voice made no attempts to conceal how irritated she was.

"I don't see anything but fog," Katrina shrugged.

"Nor I," Exodus said, then added, 'but my eyes are merely human. Riana's are both elven, and magically enhanced."

"That is true," Desse added. "While my elven eyes do not see the shrubs in question, I know that Riana has a certain acuity that most others are not blessed with."

"Maybe…" Xembak's voice silenced the group in an instant. "We should stop accusing the girl of being vapid and go have a look." He shifted his polearm to his left hand as he patted Riana on her shoulder with his right, then set off down the rise in the direction she'd indicated. Desse fell in at his side, and Xanthe was not more than a couple paces behind them.

"I like the way he thinks," Jumah smiled at Riana, taking her hand in his and heading after them.

Katrina chuckled as she and Exodus fell into step, leaving Firiel alone on the low hill. She watched them all move off into the fog for a moment, then snorted derisively, shifting the weight of the myriad swords and daggers hanging from her belts, before setting out after the group.

-33-

They almost gave up before finding Riana's copse of shrubs. After heading toward them for the better part of an hour, the entire group was ready to admit she was out of her mind and move on to greener pastures. Her continued insistence that the mysterious shrubs were still ahead of them and, indeed, getting closer with each passing moment did nothing at all to reassure anyone. Katrina pointed out they needed to look somewhere for the creature and that this direction was as good as any other, all things considered, so they kept moving toward the unseen destination.

Riana's mood quickly descended into a funk that even Jumah couldn't bring up, even though he had remained in support of her from the beginning. Finally, she'd climbed up on Xanthe's back and leaned forward into his serpentine neck, only looking up to check on the enigmatic shrubs whenever someone else actually stooped to asking if they were still 'on course'.

When Desse finally announced that she too could see the shrubs, Riana's mood was officially unpleasant, and nothing anyone else tried to do about it seemed to be having any beneficial effect.

"Ree, they said they were sorry," Jumah tried again, his voice in earnest.

"That's nice. The problem is that no one believed me before, and they were all ready to call me insane, or even stupid, until Desse saw them too."

"You have to admit, it was a little far-fetched Ree, I mean, seeing something like those," Katrina pointed to the dark shapes that she could now just begin to make out in the distance, "seen from what? A mile and half away? Through this nasty fog? Even you have to admit that's a little difficult to believe."

"Fine, whatever," Riana snorted as she spurred Xanthe to the head of the group and out in front of the rest as they approached the tiny grove.

"What's her deal?" Katrina murmured under her breath.

"Perhaps she is upset because no one expressed even the slightest hint of support for her. Instead, we all chose to believe our own senses, and 'logical processes'," Exodus finally chimed in.

"Maybe. But it wasn't just me, and she's being pretty hard on me about it."

"You are her sister. This automatically makes you a target for the brunt of her emotional outbursts."

"Well Jumah was right there, and he's as close to her these days as I am," she groused.

"Yeah, but I never said I didn't believe her. She surprises me every day, usually for the better. I've learned to defer to most of her 'crazy ideas'," Jumah waved his hand toward the fog as he spoke to them. "Except of course, for social situations in the real world. She seems to be a bit behind on a lot of that still..."

"And her ears work pretty well to boot," Riana hollered back at them, drawing a chuckle from Firiel and a chortle from Xembak.

"I wasn't finished Ree. I was also going to add that you continue to make significant strides. I will always have faith in your abilities and be here to help support you when you need..."

"Everybody back off!" Riana's shout cut Jumah's words off as a wet slurping sound filled the air.

Xanthe reared back on his hind legs and roared at the rising swell of the ground ahead of the group. The tiny grove of miniature shrubs seemed to be sucked under the muddy surface of the ground as the bulge grew up behind where it had stood, the sound filling their ears.

Hollow breathing sounded around them, accompanied by the putrid smell of rotten flesh, washing over them in a wave of hot air

184

as the creature rose up from the sand. It loomed over them as its rippling, fleshy wings picked it up from the ground. Dark, cold eyes reflected the entire group in their inky blackness and its massive, tooth-filled maw opened wide, as if trying to demonstrate how easily it could swallow the entire group whole.

It's body hung in the air, the constant motion of its wings creating a searing, humid downdraft beneath it, and its wide, flat tail, equipped with a wicked-looking stinger at the end, swayed gently from side to side, almost as if the beast were trying to hypnotize them all.

"What the hell is that?!" Riana shouted over the din of the creature's raspy breath.

"That," Exodus replied dead-pan, "is a Sapsorrow."

-34-

The Sapsorrow lunged at them, scattering the group like leaves in the wind as they dove for cover from the creature's massive, tooth-ringed maw. Riana thought of a shark's mouth, as wide as its body, and lined with rows and rows of teeth, but this was different. This was an animal large enough to swallow a team of horses whole, and its gaping jaws seemed to form an almost perfect circle, ringed with row after row of sharp, hooked teeth, all pointing straight back into the thing's body so that prey stood little chance of extricating itself from the black tunnel of death.

Standing up from the ground where she landed, face first, after leaping off of Xanthe's back to avoid the creature's attack, Riana ran her hand down her face, sloughing off a pound of the orange, caked dirt. She snorted in her sister's direction, "Bloody thing's faster than it looks."

"Mind your back, Ree!" Katrina yelled, a tongue of flame lancing away from her extended hand like a flamethrower and arcing over Riana's shoulder.

Spinning around to follow the line of the flame, she saw it scorching down the creature's underbelly as it wheeled away from the pair to escape the heat. Aside from drying a long swath of its underbelly, the flame seemed to have little effect.

"No kidding. Thanks Kat," she responded, yanking Elkorine from the sheath on her hip. Her eyes flashed as she summoned a sphere of crackling, black energy in her left hand.

A bolt of lightning lurched out of the sky, burning away a large portion of the fog surrounding the battle and slamming into the monster. Tiny sub-bolts crackled across the creature's damp hide, racing back and forth for several seconds. The Sapsorrow's wings stiffened under the assault, its body falling several feet toward the ground before it recovered, nosing into a shallow dive to regain some lift as the wings took up their writhing motion once more. Steering itself toward Exodus, whose staff was still coursing with electricity from the lightning bolt, the man gestured with his free hand and blinked out of existence an instant before being gobbled up.

"That was unexpected," his voice was calm, issuing from between Riana and Katrina as he appeared there without any warning at all.

"This thing's full of surprises," Riana agreed, hurling the ball of energy at the monster and charging toward Xanthe, feet sinking deeply into the mud with each step.

"She enjoys this sort of thing, doesn't she?" Exodus looked to Katrina, who had just hurled a small cloud of razor sharp icicles at the monster. The barrage of icy spikes tore into the burnt circle of flesh that Riana's Sphere of Annihilation had created, allowing the thick, black, life's blood of the Sapsorrow to finally be seen seeping from the tiny wounds.

"Yeah, she's always enjoyed a good fight. I think that's why I took to studying instead of bashing things."

"Not the bashing type?" Exodus joked as he wove another spell by creating intricate, mystical patterns in the air with his hands.

"Not so much. I enjoy a good knock-down drag-out from time to time," Katrina cast another spell of her own, creating a shimmering wall of burning heat around Firiel as she leapt off of Xembak's shoulders, swords drawn and held over her head, sailing through the air toward the monster. "I just wanted to actually ~win~ a fight from time to time. And it turned out to be the mental ones I was always best at," she added.

Firiel's attack succeeded, if a bit awkwardly. The monster dipped a bit to avoid Exodus's newest blast of lightening, which caused Firiel to miss the beast's flank, as it was suddenly lower than she had planned. Instead, she found herself tumbling across its back, scorching a trail of burnt slime in her wake thanks to Katrina's spell. She slashed out with one of her swords, burying its tip in the creature's thickly muscled back in order to arrest her slide and keep from falling off the other side.

"Excellent work, Firiel!" Desse called out, her hands weaving a spell of their own, which caused the ground beneath the creature to start shaking and rippling with some unseen force, "Everyone! We must force the creature to the ground so that we may better end its suffering."

"More easily said than done, love," Xembak replied, his halberd working through the air at a blinding pace as he defended himself and Desse from the creature's wildly thrashing, stingered tail.

"I think Firiel has the right idea!" Riana added as she reached Xanthe, who lowered his tail into the mud and allowed her to run up its length. "All we need is a little bit of elevation!" She charged across Xanthe's back, and along his neck until, just as she reached his head, he lifted it abruptly, catapulting her into the air.

As she pinwheeled toward the Sapsorrow, Riana shifted her vision into the magical spectrum that allowed her to see the truth of things in Kalijor. The creature's body melted away into an outline of blue points of light framing a bright orange spot just behind where she imagined its head might be, if it weren't seamlessly merged into the rest of its body.

"Firiel! Hit it there!" she hollered, conjuring up another sphere of energy and hurling it at the orange mass before tumbling onto the monster's back and sliding nearly off the other side before finding purchase in the same way Firiel had, Elkorine carving a deep gash across its back.

The sphere of annihilation impacted the spot and Firiel immediately went to work on it with both of her weapons, slicing and hacking at the monster's impossibly thick hide. "Thing's tough as dwarven armor," she grunted as she worked her blades through the monster's skin over and over again. "Could use some help up here scaly!"

"As could I, Firiel. However, its tail seems to have a mind of its own," Xembak grunted, knocking away another thrust of the stinger. The hollow, sword-like protrusion was dripping thick, mucousy gobs of, undoubtedly unpleasant, fluid.

A roar issued from Xanthe's huge, open mouth as he suddenly charged across the space beneath the creature and clamped onto the end of its tail, just behind the stinger. Xembak hoisted himself up onto the constrained tail and shimmied his way up to its back, using his claws for purchase through the slime, although he was forced to abandon his halberd to make the ascent. He scooped Riana up with his left hand, hoisting her to her feet as he drew the claymore from its scabbard and charged toward Firiel without ever breaking stride.

Riana extricated Elkorine form the creature's hide as she fell into step beside Xembak, her eyes flashing and symbols across her body glowing into high-relief as she charged the magical sword with spell energy.

With Xanthe holding onto its tail and three of their comrades on its back, Desse, Katrina, and Exodus changed tack, combining their spell strength to try and keep the creature as immobile as possible. Katrina raised a series of icy pillars in the shifting sands of the beach, which had promptly sprouted thousands of rapidly-growing vines. The vines climbed up the pillars and began working their way across the Sapsorrow's underbelly, but they couldn't find purchase anywhere on the smooth, slimy underbelly.

"My vines are unable to find purchase in its hide and it is simply too wide for them to get a grip in any other way," Desse declared, lines of concentration writ across her face.

"Yeah, I'm not having much luck spanning it either," Katrina confirmed as she drew another mystical symbol in the air with her outstretched hands.

"Maybe if we scored its skin somehow the vines and ice could get a better grip," Exodus suggested after firing off a bolt of stunning force that hit the creature squarely in the underside of its head. The blast seemed to cause no discomfort as it continued to thrash and wail beneath the attack.

"Alright then. A little surface scoring, coming right up," Jumah responded, stepping up between the three magic users and drawing his two short swords from the scabbards across his back.

"Where've you been?" Katrina cocked an eyebrow at him. She was absolutely glowing with magical energy as the three of them pulled the mystical forces from the world around them and wove it into their various spell effects.

"I'm sorry, I had to check up on something real fast," his tone was truly apologetic, and a quick glance from Katrina revealed what she thought were a series of claw marks across his back as he dashed off down the low rise. In an instant, he was moving so fast that she could barely make out where he was, let alone discern any kind of details about potential damage to his person.

Jumah pressed his aching body into overdrive, speeding down the hill and leaping the short distance to the first pillar of vine wrapped ice. His feet pressed into the surface, legs coiling beneath him for an instant before they extended, propelling him through the air toward the next closest pillar. He made several such leaps, all in the span of a second, raking the tips of his swords across the creature's underbelly in long, shallow arcs as he went. Within moments, he had left a shallow hashmark pattern in its slimy flesh.

"Try it now!" He shouted back at the casters, then dove off the pillar of ice he'd landed on, raising his swords over his head and bringing them down in a mighty arc. Selendria's, twin blades bit into the hard surface of the Sapsorrow's stinger, slicing the rock hard needle cleanly from the creature's tail as he landed solidly on his feet. He gave silent thanks to his clan for the use of their familial weapon as he squeezed the handles of the magical blades.

Xanthe twisted his head around to look at Jumah, who simply inclined his head at the creature, smiled, and then scampered up the still-captured tail as if climbing a short set of stairs.

"They're taking much better now," Desse spoke through clenched jaw, every iota of her being focused on the growing of the vines which were now spreading across the creature's underbelly like a thick carpet of green.

"I'll say," Katrina confirmed as another gesture produced a similar growth spurt in the bands and blocks of ice that were working to entomb the monster.

Firiel eyed Jumah as he came to a sudden stop with the other three atop the Sapsorrow's body. "Where've you been?"

"Helping the caster-core get this beast's squirming under control," Jumah replied. "So what's the plan here?"

"There's some kind of critical part just under this spot here," Riana chimed in, taking another swipe with Elkorine. Lightening arced from the blade and coursed back and forth across a large wound the trio had carved in the creature's back, "A nerve cluster or something."

Jumah eyed Riana, then took a spot next to her and joined them in carving through the creature's thick hide. The addition of another magical blade seemed to help tremendously. Within moments, the huge animal was wailing and shaking violently, attempting to get away from their attack, but restrained by the thickening mass of the vines and strong ice growing up around the tips of its rippling wings.

As they finally struck bone, Firiel, Xembak, and Jumah stood back while Riana conjured another sphere of annihilation and hurled it into the wound, hoping to end the creature's suffering as quickly as possible. Energy exploded as it struck home and the Sapsorrow gave one last, tremendous shudder before collapsing atop the frozen pillars and vines beneath it. There was a great creaking noise as Katrina's pillars tried to take the creature's full weight, followed by the sounds of cracking and splintering as the body fell to the ground amidst a shower of exploding ice and shredded plant life.

The quartet on its back scattered, heading in opposite directions to try and escape the violence of the death knell. Jumah was clear within seconds and caught Riana in his arms as she dove from the monster's back. Firiel and Xembak found their fall arrested by a blanket of yielding vines that set them softly on the ground amidst the cacophony of the monster's death.

-35-

When the eight of them regrouped atop the tiny rise where Katrina, Desse, and Exodus had been casting spells, everyone looked as if they'd just run a marathon, except for Firiel, who promptly sat down on the muddy ground and resumed picking at her nails with a knife.

"We need one of its teeth. A large one," Katrina said as she pulled a thick mat from her large pack and set it on the ground. She quickly pulled several other items from her pack as well, including a small iron kettle, several glass vials filled with various odds and ends, a squat candle that Riana vaguely recognized from the enchanting labs at the Magic Academy, and numerous other small parts.

She lit the candle and set it under the cauldron as Jumah and Riana moved toward the Sapsorrow's dead form. "So," Riana began, but let the word hang in the air between them.

"So," Jumah responded, letting the word be its own punctuation mark.

"Tough fight," she added.

"I guess. We seem to have fared alright," he shrugged.

"Most of us anyway." She eyed him, looking up and down his body at the various scratch marks. They criss-crossed his body and almost glowed red they were so fresh.

Jumah looked down at his wounds and then cast an understanding look at Riana as they stopped in front of the creature's mouth. "I'll get Desse to take a look after we get the tooth."

"Okay," she replied, again letting the word hang in the air.

"I don't really want to talk about it right now, Ree," he growled, placing his shoulder under the creature's body and heaving with his legs to raise it off the ground a foot or so.

"Talk about what? I didn't ask you anything." She crouched down and peered into the creature's mouth, shaking her head at the sight. "The things I get myself into…"

"Yeah, well you aren't asking me anything louder than any question you've ever actually asked before. I'll tell you all about it when the time is right."

"Hopefully I'll still be around," she muttered as she slipped into the tooth-filled maw. Her eyes flashed as she conjured a ball of fire in her left hand so she could see where she was going, searching for the largest tooth she could find.

"What's that supposed to mean," he grunted back at her, the weight of the creature taking its toll on his strength reserves.

"Sorry, that wasn't meant to be a barb. I just meant this thing might still eat me," her voice echoed back out of the creature's mouth.

"Oh," he replied, bracing his hands on his thighs to better support the creature's weight. "I don't suppose you could speed things up? This thing is kind of heavy."

"Yeah, I think I found a good one here." She looked down on a curved, sickle-like tooth that reached up to her knees. "Now I just need to get it out of here. One sec."

She grabbed the tooth in her left hand after perching her fireball in mid-air and releasing it to hang there on its own, then drew Elkorine and used its tip to cut the flesh around the base of the tooth free. Even with Elkorine's magical blade, it was tough going. The creature's flesh was stronger than any armor she'd ever encountered. Several minutes later, she emerged from the monster's maw, two teeth dangling from her hand, and smiling at Jumah.

Jumah smiled back, stepping out from under the monster and letting it fall to the ground with a loud thump. "Two?"

"Just in case." As they moved back toward the group, the faint thump of her fireball exploding could be heard from deep inside the monster's mouth. Riana simply shrugged.

"Wow! Now those are some teeth!" Katrina gaped at the implements as Riana handed them over. She and Exodus quickly set one aside and began scratching and picking at the other, their portable alchemy set already bubbling and churning away.

"They were the biggest ones I could find in there. Please don't ever, ever, ask me to do that again." Riana ran a hand down an arm, sloughing off a giant gob of slime onto the ground. The rest of the group just stood and stared at her in amazement.

"That's really gross," Firiel chuckled.

"You don't say," Riana gave her a nasty look as she continued to squeegee the goop from her body.

"Maybe you should consider wearing some actual clothing, when you go adventuring out in the unknown wilderness," Firiel glared back at her.

"I like my outfit. It's very comfortable, and it doesn't hang on to monster stink," Riana actually stuck her tongue out at Firiel before moving off to sit on the other side of the little hill and wait for the announcement that they were on the move again.

"I'm sorry Jumah, I can not seem to heal these wounds," she heard Desse saying and looked over her shoulder at them. "Where did you get them, they don't look like anything the Sapsorrow might have caused."

"Thanks for trying Desse, I'm sure they'll heal up alright in time," he replied, locking eyes with Riana for a moment before returning his attention back to Desse. "I'm not sure where they came from. Everything happened so quickly…"

"I see. Well, take this salve and apply it to the wounds. I'll see about making you a poultice to put on them while we rest this evening," she smiled.

"Thanks again Desse." He accepted the small pot of salve and moved over next to Riana, sitting down beside her. "Hey there." He smiled at her, leaning over a little so their shoulders could touch.

Riana looked over at him, tears pooling in her eyes. "What happened Jumah?"

"You won't let it go will you?"

"Not likely. I know you don't injure like this, unless it was something magical…"

"That's true."

"So…" She waited impatiently.

"So?"

"Dammit Jumah, what are you doing here?"

"I'm here to help, Ree."

"And yet, your off on some secret errand the very moment we need your help. And you come back all torn up, but refuse to talk about it. What am I supposed to think?"

"Just please, Ree, take it on faith. I can't talk about it just yet, but I really want to tell you. Once this is all over, and we get a few minutes to ourselves, I'll explain it to you."

"I don't like being treated like some youngling, Jumah."

"I would never think of treating you like 'some youngling'. This was something that I had to do. It was intensely personal and I am not able to speak about it just yet. But when I can, believe me, you will be the first person I speak to. I'm here now and I'm not going anywhere else without you until we see this through. I'm sorry."

"Alright," she sniffed, leaning back into his shoulder for a moment before wrapping an arm around his back and squeezing him. "I hope the other guy is worse off at least."

"He is," Jumah's voice was kind of sad as he wrapped his arm around her waist and they pulled one another closer, staring out over the fetid, green water of the Dead Sea in the waning light of the evening.

-36-

"Okay, this has to be the strangest thing I've ever experienced," Riana's voice gurgled as it passed through the putrid water between her and the rest of the group.

"I told you it would be weird," Katrina's voice bubbled back.

"I know, but I wasn't really expecting this." Riana held up her hand, looking at it through the water. Even the powerful enchantment that Exodus and Katrina had concocted for them did not seem capable of completely penetrating the soupy medium that enveloped them.

"What were you expecting," Exodus asked. He might have raised an inquisitive eyebrow, but the action would have been lost on anyone more than a foot away.

"I don't know... A bubble? Or something?" She shrugged.

The five of them were slogging through the muck and sludge that covered the bottom of the Dead Sea. They'd worked numerous enchantments into their magic, including one that had them levitating several feet above the true floor of the sea, which was the only reason they were able to see one another at all. Otherwise, they would have been several feet below the surface of the sifting, putrid silt that blanketed the floor of the sea, rather than knee deep in it.

Another enchantment allowed them to breath without filling their lungs with the nasty water and move without restriction due to the volume or pressure of the water. It even allowed them to speak, and hear, almost normally. Their eyesight worked, although it did not cut through the thick, pea-soup liquid very well, allowing them to see perhaps a dozen feet total, but only a fraction of that with any real clarity.

Riana's ability to shift her vision into the surreal, computerized space allowed her to keep them all appraised of what was going on around them. Not that there was much going on within the poisonous water. After five hours of wandering across the bottom of the sea, they still had yet to encounter any living, or un-living, thing.

"We looked into that, but it wasn't going to work," Katrina answered Riana's question. "Any bubble we created would keep us from interacting with our environment, so in the end we decided to just protect ourselves from the harsh environment and make sure we could move and communicate," Exodus's clinical explanation did nothing to fully describe the situation.

Riana's inspection of her own hand yielded nothing new in the way of sensory information. She could still feel the slimy goop that was the water up against her skin, sliding over it like some kind of mucous. She still couldn't see well, beyond a foot or two, with her regular vision. She couldn't smell anything at all, and anything she heard was tinged with the bubbling, reverberation caused by the sounds traveling through the aqueous medium.

"Yeah, that makes sense. I guess. It just feels so… wrong…" She shook her hand as if trying to slough off the sludge, then looked at the blurry form of Jumah, walking along next to her. "Or is it just me?"

"No. This is definitely a new experience," Jumah confirmed. "Although I didn't really have any preconceptions about what to expect."

"This is not a natural medium for air-breathing humanoid life forms to exist in," Desse responded with a little less of her normal tranquility.

"Let's get one thing straight right now," Firiel interjected, "this is not a normal medium for ~anyone~ to exist in." Even her normally abrasive nature seemed to be faltering under the adversity of their situation.

"I find this environment to be somewhat comforting," Xembak added, eliciting a grunt of agreement from Xanthe, who was having a bit less trouble moving through the sludge than the rest of the group.

"Yeah, well you two are just plain weird," Riana retorted.

"Your own failure to see the benefits of this environment," Xembak responded, dead-pan.

Riana stared at him a moment, trying to figure out if he was being serious or making a joke. In the end, she decided to just let it go and changed the subject, "I'm seeing the beginnings of a structure up ahead. It looks like a similar sort of structure to the ziggurat we found the first artifact in."

"Where," Firiel bubbled.

"Just over there," Riana pointed off at an oblique angle to the direction they'd been moving.

"How far?"

Riana cast the redhead a sour look before responding, "It's nearly impossible to tell with my vision like this. It could be twenty feet, or a mile and a half."

"Do you have any idea how un-helpful that is?"

"About as un-helpful as you pestering me about it I suppose," Riana glared through the murk at Firiel. "Have you ever seen an entire world in computer wire-frame models, with little wisps of colors leading back and forth across the network to where things originate from? Because if you have, I'd sure love to compare notes on how to manage depth perception issues."

"Riana, please calm down." Jumah's hand gripped her shoulder lightly, but she shrugged it off and set to slogging ahead through the silt in the direction she'd pointed.

"No, I don't think so Jumah. I think I'm well beyond calming down. She's been riding me since we met, and for no good reason." Or at least no reason she was going to tell the rest of them.

"It isn't my fault you can't take it, you spoiled little rich girl."

"What the heck is going on here?" Katrina shouted at them. "Are you two insane?"

"Kat, how can you be a part of my life, and still ask me that question? Of course I'm insane! That doesn't change the fact that I don't need to be hassled by her for things that are beyond my ability to control." Riana had stopped and turned to face the rest of the group and was pointing an accusing finger at Firiel, who was simply shaking her head at the aggravated elf.

"Don't bring me into this. You're the one who can't take a little friendly ribbing."

"There is nothing friendly about you! You've been mean and antagonistic since I first saw you!" Her eyes flashed, and a corona of energy began forming around her, the water bubbling and boiling in growing eddies, swirling about her body.

"Uh guys…" Exodus tried to break through, but was quickly cut off by Firiel.

"I may be mean to you, but at least I'm not pretending to be something I'm not."

"I'm not pretending to be anything! I thought we had an agreement to just get over this and carry on with things, but you just won't stop will you?" The water around Riana was actually boiling now, and even Jumah had to take a step back from her to avoid being scalded by the magical maelstrom.

"Ladies, please calm down," Desse began.

"We do have an arrangement, and I'll keep my end of the bargain, don't you worry. That doesn't mean I have to like you, or even pretend to get along with you. You're a spoiled brat, who doesn't deserve a single thing she's ever had and I will not pander to you!"

"Guys," Exodus's voice was washed out again.

"Well if you don't think I'm capable of taking care of myself out here, why the hell did you sign on to help us?"

"I'm here because my companions are here, and because you asked me to take care of you," Firiel's tone was still level and her voice had yet to raise beyond a conversational level despite the fact that Riana was just about screaming at her.

"Impudent, ignorant women!" Exodus finally shouted at them, silencing the group in an instant. All eyes turned to him, and both Riana and Firiel looked as if they might band together long enough to reduce him to ashes, but he was busy pointing in the direction

Riana had started moving. "I think we have a problem here. The silt is moving."

"What?" they all replied in unison, turning in the direction he was pointing just in time for some kind of massive form to erupt from the silt beneath Riana, showering the group in muck and filth. A cloud of fine, putrid dirt billowed up around them, obscuring their vision utterly and knocking them all off their feet.

All except Xanthe, who wailed out a great, pained ululation, as if his very heart was breaking in two. The group rallied quickly, regaining their feet and moving toward the sound of Xanthe's keening.

"Who's here? Sound off!" Jumah called out.

"I'm here," Katrina called out.

"As am I," Exodus confirmed.

"Xembak and I are here," Desse spoke through the dark cloud.

"Present," Firiel enthused.

Her voice was followed by a lack of voices that, even with the sound of Xanthe's howling as a backdrop, sounded like utter silence.

"Ree?" Katrina called out.

"Riana?" Jumah echoed, cupping his hand to his mouth to amplify his voice.

"It is returning," Xembak added as the cloud darkened even more. They could all sense, more than actually see, the massive form of the beast looming over them. It paused for a moment, Xanthe's keening coming to an abrupt halt as the strange pause hung in the air between them.

At last, the creature, whatever it was, let out a wail that shook the silt around them and caused the water to vibrate and ripple with the monster's energy. Then, it plunged down toward them, jaws open wide, and tentacles writhing in every direction at once.

-37-

The shadowy form loomed over them for an instant, then dove at them, scattering the group as they all leapt out of the path of its attack. They still couldn't see the thing through the cloud of silt and muck the thing had raised, but Jumah felt its presence as a writhing tentacle wrapped itself around one of his ankles and dragged him down. He kicked and pulled at the boneless limb, even as the creature continued to slide through the silt as if it was running on the beach.

"What the hell is that thing?" Firiel swore, a pair of magical blades appearing in her hands as she peered through the cloud.

"Leviathan!" Katrina and Exodus shouted back in unison. They both began chanting, glowing magic coalescing around them as they gathered it for their spells. The light of their magic actually illuminated them through the muck, giving the others a rallying point.

"How do we fight that thing? I can't even see it. It doesn't have any appreciable body heat, and the water's filled with crap!" Firiel's voice actually carried a tone of frustration for once, that maddening calm having finally been shaken.

"Perhaps we should blanket the area with sending circles, so we will be alerted as to where it will breach the surface of the silt layer," Desse suggested.

"Not bad Desse, but lets start with this," Katrina called back after she finished chanting the words to her spell. Over the course of about five seconds, the world came into sharp focus for them, their eyes somehow adjusting themselves to see through the cloud of filth that hung about them.

"Why didn't we use that spell earlier?" Firiel asked as she spun around, surveying the area around them with her newly clarified sight.

"Because the spell only lasts about half an hour, and it used up five-hundred gold pieces worth of components," Exodus responded.

"And we had to cast it twice just there. We only have enough reagents to cast it once more," Katrina added, looking around at the group, "Riana and Jumah are both gone."

"Good riddance," Firiel growled, pointing the tip of one of her more wicked-looking blades at a disturbance in the silt that was making its way rapidly toward them. "Here beasty comes again!"

The bulge rolled up to them like a wave, keeping low to the ground before it stopped a dozen yards ahead of them, leaving them all stumped for a moment before Firiel shouted at them, "Under your feet, move it!"

They all scattered again, mere seconds before the thing erupted from the silt, mouth open wide to swallow its prey whole.

Firiel wrinkled her nose at the monster, its long, worm-like body towered a hundred feet overhead. It's segmented body was ringed with knots of long, skinny tentacles, including a crown of them around its huge, circular mouth. That mouth was currently pointed in their direction, baring what looked like a twenty-foot wide tunnel, lined every inch with teeth.

"Is that…" Katrina began, pointing up at the monster's mouth.

"Jumah," Xembak confirmed, narrowing his eyes at the tiny form of the werecheetah, still held fast in one of the creature's crown of tentacles. He was being held by his ankle and tossed about like a rag-doll.

"He looks like he's having a good time," Firiel joked. "Any ideas on what to do with this fellow?"

"Yeah, we never really did figure that bit out..." Katrina frowned.

"Nice you two!" Firiel shook her head and charged at the monster's body, slashing at it with her twin swords several times before the Leviathan shifted its body mass to one side and began leaning further over, preparing to to attack them.

"So, what do you think life-mate? This creature is a singular thread in the tapestry. I've never seen its like before," Desse turned her questioning brown eyes on Xembak for a moment.

Xembak offered Desse an appraising look, then shifted his stance, returning his gaze to the monster. "I suspect that hacking at it with blade and club will fail to damage the creature to any significant degree."

"This is why we needed more information," Katrina grumbled, then threw herself into the casting of another spell.

"Yes, but there wasn't much to be found. I don't think more time would have been of too much more benefit." Exodus fell in casting beside her.

"Yes, a plan would be of much benefit in our efforts. In the mean time, I shall go and assist Firiel in the apparently futile efforts in which she is engaged," Xembak added, hefting his halberd and charging out to assist Firiel against the thing and waving Xanthe in beside him.

-38-

The light washed over her like bottled fire, suddenly let loose everywhere at once. The air was calm, cool, and definitely processed. This was not Kalijor.

Riana opened her eyes. What she saw was most certainly not anything she would have expected. Leaping to her feet and spinning around to face the little old man, sitting quietly on his knees at his coffee table, she blurted out, "Master Jonin! Oh my god, I'm so sorry!"

The man looked up at her, his mirthful eyes shining in amusement. He had carried much the same look almost every time she had seen him over the last couple of years. Time in which he had trained her in the arts of hand to hand combat, as well as spiritual coping skills to help her in her life's transition from Kalijor, to the real world. He was the resident combat trainer on the Tyconderoga, and one of the few remaining class one hand-to-hand combatants still alive after the decimation of the Earth and its many ancient cultures. "Sorry for what child?"

"I don't know. I must have... drifted off... or something..." Now the confusion began to set in with significantly more weight. Hadn't she she just been on the bottom of a putrid sea, arguing with Firiel and... something about a monster beneath her feet?

"You did not," he paused for a moment to consider the phrase, rolling it around in his mouth before speaking it, "drift off. I was having tea, you arrived."

His tone was anything but surprised, which she imagined would be the normal reaction from anyone who had another person suddenly appearing in their space. Which was another point to consider...

"How did I..."

"I suspect you met an untimely end at the behest of some gruesome creature or other. Or perhaps fell to your doom? Either way, it matters not. Tea?" Master Jonin motioned with an open hand to indicate the spot on the floor opposite where he sat.

Riana stared at him for a moment, then lifted her eyes to cast her gaze around his home. Everything was there, exactly as she remembered it from the few times she'd visited. Although, the last time she'd been there, she'd been more or less blind, so some of the details may have changed since then. There was no way for her to be totally sure. "I can't have tea Master Jonin, I'm sorry. I need to..."

"Assist your friends. Yes, I know. Please, sit with me," He motioned to the tea set again, his face still utterly unperturbed by events.

She dumbly stumbled the few feet to the table and dropped to her knees opposite him, her violet eyes seeming to have trouble focusing on things.

"As the honored guest, would you like to pour?" He motioned to the tea setting, a small smile spreading across his face.

Riana looked down at the ancient teapot and bowls arrayed about the surface of the table, the water was steaming hot, and smelled of his own sweet blend of home grown, and dried tea leaves, not the synthetic amalgam that was served in the station's commissary. The number and placement of the implements seemed to indicate that he had not only been expecting company, but had a good idea of when they would be arriving as well.

Riana shook her head, trying to ward off the fog in her mind, and reached for the pot's bamboo-wrapped handle. "Master Jonin, forgive me, but it seems as if you were expecting me."

"Observant as ever my child." He nodded at her, watching with keen interest as she poured first his own tea, then hers, before setting set the pot down and turning it to insure it was positioned just so. "Despite your best efforts to appear otherwise, you have always been quite bright." Riana flushed, ears drooping and eyes falling to the table for a moment, until Master Jonin picked up his tea bowl and offered it to her across the table.

Riana straightened up a bit, accepting the bowl with both hands, then turning it so the back of the bowl was facing her. She held the bowl up and bowed her head slightly, then sipped at its contents, wiping the edge with the chakin and offering the bowl back to her host with both hands, head inclined toward the table in respect.

Master Jonin received the bowl, turned it again, then drank, prompting her to take up her own bowl and join him. "In answer to your question Riana, I have been expecting you. I do not know the circumstances, or method of your arrival however."

Riana returned her bowl to the table and looked thoughtful for a moment, hands perched on thighs in contemplation, "I was at the bottom of the Dead Sea, with Kat and our friends. I was arguing with Firiel. Exodus interrupted us and the ground moved and everything went dark for a moment," she looked back up at him and finished, "and then I was here."

"You have long let your temper be your master Riana, this is a condition that you must endeavor to rectify or it will, one day, be your undoing."

She burned scarlet from embarrassment. He was right and she knew it. She'd always known it. What she hadn't always known, or even knew now, was why she continued to let it happen. "Master Jonin, I think I was eaten by some kind of creature."

"I suspected as much."

"But how did that get me here? I was in Kalijor. At worst, I should have woken up where my body is right? I wasn't even on the station," Riana pondered out loud.

"This is true. You were not on the station. Now you are." He sipped at his tea again, giving no indication that his words should be anything other than glaringly obvious.

"I see that, but how? Is this some sort of hallucination?"

"Do you think you are hallucinating?" he raised an eyebrow at her.

She looked around again. Everything seemed right, felt right. The tea was hot. The air was that same, constant temperature she'd become accustomed to, the one that every facility from Mercury to Pluto kept their systems set to. Briefly, she reached down and pinched her forearm, the burst of pain was quickly shut off by her cybernetic systems, but it had been there, just as expected, however briefly.

"No, I don't think so," she conceded.

"Nor do I."

"So, how did I…" she stopped mid-query, he'd already told her he didn't know. She should know better than to ask the same question more than once.

"However you did it, it wasn't the first time, was it?"

Her breath caught short in her artificial lungs. How the hell did he know that? She wasn't even sure of it herself. She'd thought it had been a hallucination then too. Outside the door of their first assignment as couriers for Solidarity Online, on the moon, she'd suddenly been in the Burning Expanse, looking down on a decimated camp, and the body of her mother, Ezrina. It had seemed so real then, despite its utter impossibility. Now, however, the light seemed to be slanting on the situation from an entirely different direction. She slowly shook her head, "No, I don't think so."

"No," he confirmed.

"What does all of this mean Master Jonin? Why is it that people are able to cross over from Kalijor to here, and back again?"

"You are referring to the others? The fiery elf, your mother?"

Riana nodded, poking her tea bowl with her index finger.

"I am not a technical person Riana. I do not pretend to understand how Xavier's computers work. But I do know, that life will always find a way to beat the odds." He continued to sip at his own tea, taking the occasional pull from the bowl between statements.

"Life. So it is alive. Kalijor, I mean."

"You would do well to trust your intuition Riana. Do not seek the affirmation of others at the cost of taking timely action. You knew this long ago."

"But you can't explain how people can move back and forth between worlds, and I certainly don't understand it." Riana scowled at her cup, frustrated.

"You may not understand it. But this lack of understanding does not seem to be interfering with your own movements."

"Understanding would allow me to go back to help my friends."

"Then you must reach understanding."

"How?"

"I can not explain what I, myself, do not understand."

"But you knew I would be here!" She made an effort to calm herself, and noticed his smile change, ever so subtly, to a knowing smirk.

"It has taken me over one-hundred years to understand my own gifts Riana, it is unreasonable of you to expect me to also understand yours. You are your own person, with your own gifts. You must understand them on your own, and in your own time."

"That doesn't help my friends," she grumped.

"Not at present. However, all things occur in their own time. Your friends will make due."

"Why here?" Her ears perked up suddenly, eyes brightening and refocusing on him.

"Why indeed?"

"Because I look up to you," she admitted. It wasn't anything he didn't already know, the old goat. "And because, despite all your double-talk and aggravation, you always help me see things in just the right way."

"And what are you seeing now?"

She paused, eyeing the room. In truth, she had no idea what she was doing. Looking for a needle in a haystack the size of a planet, a whole solar system in fact, maybe larger. How had she come here? What did she know about the circumstances?

She'd been angry, vocal, unwilling to compromise. There was an interruption. Exodus had yelled at them, called them both names, then the ground had heaved. There was darkness, tumbling in free fall, then she was here. What had she done? And how?

"I don't know what I did," she admitted.

"Nor do I. However, I am not the one who must discern what happened. That is a journey for you to make Riana. I will help in any way that I can, but in the end, the path is yours, and yours alone."

"So what is my first step?" She didn't know the first thing about something like this. She didn't even know the barest tip of what would be involved in moving a physical body from one location to another without it crossing the distance between. In Kalijor, such a thing could be blamed on magic, but Willhelmina had told her, in no uncertain terms, that magic was a thing of fantasy. Only in the game, in Kalijor, could a person harness the ambient energies of magic and bend them, and reality, to their will. So this had to be something different. Didn't it?

"What troubles you child?" Master Jonin's voice cut through her reverie.

"I was just thinking about what could make such a thing possible. Am I really here? Or am I some kind of projection, and my body is still there, with Vincent, plugged into the computer?"

Quicker than the old man had any right to move, Master Jonin snaked a hand out across the table and gave her a harsh pinch and a twist. Again, it hurt, for just that brief instant before her enhanced body killed the feeling.

"Ouch!" she complained, yanking her arm back from him. "What the hell was that?"

"If you were not here, I could not have hurt you."

"You've a fine way of making a point," she grimaced at him.

"But the point is made. You are here."

"So it would seem. But I still don't know how."

"What were you thinking before I pinched you?"

"It's stupid...," she hedged.

"Explain please."

"I was thinking that the only way to bridge two locations, without crossing the distance between them, is by using magic. But magic is only a fictional force that exists in Kalijor."

"Is it?" his question was almost a slap in the face to her. Was he mad? Or was Willhelmina?

"I'm sorry Master Jonin. Willhelmina told me that magic wasn't real in this world. That it was only something that existed in fantasy, in Kalijor…"

"And yet, here you are. Having tea with me. When mere moments ago, you were, I believe you said, at the bottom of the Dead Sea, fighting some kind of monster."

She raised her own eyebrows at him this time, and perked her ears up for good measure too. "Are you telling me that there ~is~ magic here?"

Master Jonin shook his head slightly, causing her ears to droop a bit, but then he said, "No Riana, I am saying that, no matter what force is at work when you do these things, what does it matter what you call it? If you want to call it science, call it science. If you want to call it magic, then call it magic. All that matters is, that you learn to harness it."

Those words threw some sort of switch in her head, like an electrical breaker. She hadn't thought about it like that before. In point of fact, she'd been trying not to think about it at all. She didn't want Gayle and her cadre of doctors and scientists coming after her with probes and scanners for telling someone she'd been having visions, or hallucinations, of other places. If this were true, if there was some force here that she could manipulate, to a similar effect as magic in Kalijor, then it would help reinforce so many fraying edges of her life that it would almost be a new experience all together.

"Magic," she mused.

"The name is immaterial. If I told you that you exhibit an unheard-of ability to intuitively manipulate the subspace realm that Kalijor resides within, and with that control comes the ability for you to create localized, environmental effects, largely through sheer force of will, would it make any difference? Would it make any sense? All that matters, is you, and what you choose to do with this ability. Just as in Kalijor, your ability to use magic is not dependent upon the magic itself, but rather the will that is bending the magic into place."

"Control subspace? Me? What sort of control? How is that possible?"

"Riana, you must sooner or later realize, truly believe, that you are a child of two worlds. As such, you are permanently linked to both of those worlds. They both influence you, every moment of every day. You are tidally locked between them, and it is time for them to start feeling the effects you are capable of exerting upon them. Stop acting as the passive force upon the tides and take an active role."

"What kinds of effects?"

"I do not know what is possible. But I do know that you are the bridge between this world and that one. Through you, one can flow into the other."

"So, I'm some kind of conduit? Are you telling me, it's my fault that Firiel and my mom can slip back and forth?"

"Some things you must still learn for yourself, Riana. You learn nothing by my telling you."

"Actually, I'm learning quite a bit, thank you. But why we'd want that to keep happening instead of reverting to the normal method of you speaking in tongues, and me trying to decipher your riddles is beyond me," she was getting angry again.

"There goes your temper again young one. I assure you this does you no favors."

"Please stop calling me 'young one' and 'child' Master Jonin. I can not tell you how irritating that is," her face was as sour as her tone.

"You should not let these little things trouble you so, Riana. They are merely words. Words can only wound if you allow them to. I mean you no harm, in fact, I have done everything in my power to see that you have the tools you need."

She deflated significantly, bowing her head as she spoke, "my apologies Master Jonin."

"Your apology is not necessary, Riana. All I ask is that you open yourself up to the world around you. Become aware of the smaller things in life. The nuances, the ebbs and flows, eddies and currents. The universe is a living, breathing thing Riana, and you, each of us, are connected to it. Most people close themselves off to this connection. It is either too subtle or scares them because of the enormity of its consequences. Do not let this be you. That is all I ask."

Riana blushed and turned her head to the side, trying to avoid his eyes. Her ears drooped. "I'm afraid," her voice was quiet, almost a whisper.

"I know. Any sane person would be. Use the fear. Temper your will with it. Fear can be the most powerful weapon in your arsenal, and not the fear that you may induce in others. When you embrace your fears, and use them to your benefit, you can accomplish great things."

"I just wish I knew what things I was meant to accomplish…"

"Do you?" He poured himself another bowl of tea and topped hers off, in an attempt to reheat what was there.

"Why wouldn't I? All these people, in this world, and that one, all of them pushing and pulling me in different directions. Asking of me but never explaining why, or what for. I feel as if I'm destined for something, but I have no idea what, and nobody else is explaining it to me," her exasperation seeped into her words.

"That is because no one else ~can~ explain it to you Riana. Sooner or later, you will come to the conclusion that there is no destiny. We each forge our own way and no one can tell us where we are 'supposed' to end up," Jonin's voice remained calm.

"But what about these artifacts? And the prophecies? Master Jonin, I've been told that Master Gornin might try to kill me if I follow through with this."

"To die while pursuing right is an honorable passing. Do you feel that the path you are walking is the right one?" He sipped at his tea.

Riana finally turned back toward him, picked up her tea bowl and sipped at it thoughtfully for a moment before she responded, "I think so. It's difficult to know for sure. Xavier tells me one thing, and Malice tells me something else. Gornin said he doesn't agree with me, but he still supports me. My mothers, both of them, seem to think I am doing right. All I really know is that the keys are being found, and everyone agrees that nobody should have the artifacts that they unlock."

"And so you have determined to collect them?"

"I don't want them. I never did. All I've ever wanted is to explore, to live, and be free. I guess it seems as if someone who doesn't want the artifacts, might be a better person to carry them than any person who would seek them out for their own purposes. Don't you think?" She looked across the table at him, setting her cup down and folding her hands in her lap.

"You do not need my acceptance Riana, nor my permission. I only asked, because I wanted to know if you believe in what you are doing."

She paused, that was certainly an unexpected reply. "I don't understand Master Jonin. What does it matter what I believe?"

"It matters Riana, because a person who walks the wrong path will find nothing but pain and suffering that will eventually end their existence, having accomplished nothing. While a person who walks the correct path, whether perceived, or actual, can weather the same tribulations, and die in the end feeling as if they have done right and made a difference."

"That makes sense," she agreed, "but what about good and evil? Right and wrong? What if the path I walk, even if I believe utterly that it is correct, is wrong? Evil."

"Good and evil have long been the subject of much debate, you are correct. However, it is important to understand that few people would actually consider themselves evil, even when doing the most despicable things. It is the strength of their convictions that drive them, and history becomes the judge of their rightness or wrongness. We can never truly tell, when we are in the here and now."

"Just believe," she responded.

"Just, believe." He echoed with a faint smile.

She nodded solemnly as the room darkened around her and she was suddenly overcome by the sensation of falling. The walls seemed to close in on her and the space around her grew damp and oppressive. The fetid smell of the Dead Sea, mixed with the abhorrent scent of some kind of bile and she could faintly hear the sound of weapons slashing at armored flesh and the bellowing sound of Firiel's anger.

-39-

"We aren't having any effect on it at all!" Firiel screamed as she dove out of the way of the Leviathan's descending body. The beast was now moving back and forth, dropping heavy loops of its wormlike body on the group and attempting to grab them with its various rings of tentacles.

"Its hide is too thick, even for magical weapons," Xembak agreed.

The group scattered again, leaping into the silt and rolling away as the tentacles tried to wind around limbs, weapons, belts, gear, anything they could find.

"Our spells aren't doing much better!" Exodus hollered back, reaching out a hand to help Katrina back to her feet.

Desse drifted back to the ground slowly, her own levitation spell allowing her to leap into the air and drift about much more easily than the others. "I can not get any plant life to take root and grow in this putrid water."

"At least its tentacles aren't quite as tough as its body," Firiel commented, hacking off the tip of a writhing, snakelike appendage as it tried to wrap itself around her ankle. The severed tip sank into the silt and disappeared, still undulating as it dropped from sight.

"What the hell is Jumah waiting for up there? His swords can cut the tentacles as well as our weapons," the flame-haired elf added, glancing up at the tiny form of Jumah, still held limply in the creature's mouth tentacles.

For his part, Jumah was simply biding time. He knew Riana had gone down the monster's throat when it had initially surfaced beneath them, and since then he had made every effort to 'accidentally' get snagged in its mouth tentacles. He was currently doing everything he could to avoid being swallowed himself, since the purpose of these tentacles was to move food items into the monster's mouth. It wasn't as easy as it might look from elsewhere either. He was constantly batting away other tentacles, repositioning himself and throwing his weight around. Not to mention the need to regularly grab another tentacle in order to gain leverage against the one that was holding him fast.

Luckily the Leviathan had not yet wised up and just released him, although he couldn't imagine that moment was too far off at this point. No matter what happened though, he had to maintain this position, because when it happened, it would happen very quickly, and there would be precious little time to change positions, or alter trajectories.

And then it did happen. A low, rumbling, guttural noise began rolling up from beneath him. The monster straightened out a bit, all of its tentacles pausing mid-movement as it seemed to be trying to sort out some strange new feeling. All at once, it lurched further out of the silt, its body now over two-hundred feet long, and belched out a sickening cloud of smoke, followed by hundreds of gallons of bile, slime, half-decomposed animal carcasses and worse.

Wasting no time, Jumah broke free of the monster's tentacle, swung himself up on top of it, planting one foot on its fat lip, just outside the topmost row of teeth, and sprang into the space above its open maw, directly into the cloud of sickening debris.

-40-

While she had no idea where exactly she was inside the monster's body, there was little doubt that she was indeed, inside its huge body. The surface beneath her feet was soft, wet, and just as putrid as the silt-covered Dead Sea bottom had been. Only this surface was also covered with what smelled like a terribly nasty corrosive.

"Some kind of digestive acid," she mused. "I wonder why it isn't digesting me…"

The light cast by the fireball in her hand was flickering, and didn't spread very far, but even with its marginal assistance, she could tell she was standing knee deep in the nastiness, but she was very obviously not being burned away by it. She knew this, because of the complete lack of pain and suffering that she was quite sure would accompany the process of being digested alive.

"This won't do at all," she mused as she examined her surroundings, dragging her free hand along the squishy wall of the creature's digestive tract. There was no chance of her climbing out, not on her own. She was going to have to come up with a different plan, and afterwords, she would devote some musing to the experience she'd just had in Master Jonin's quarters.

Looking around again and seeing nothing that screamed out at her as an alternative, she shrugged and flung the fireball into the wall of the creature's stomach. The fireball exploded into a wall of flames that rolled up the fleshy surface and overhead, burning brightly for a few seconds and then fading away into an utter darkness.

The good thing that happened, was that the monster shuddered. The walls of its bowels actually constricted around her. Not so much that she was in any danger of being crushed, but it was a close call while the space was on fire. Now that she thought about it, this tube seemed a bit small for as large as the creature had seemed when it first surfaced beneath her feet. It briefly flitted through her mind that it might have multiple, smaller stomachs, like a bovine. She shook the thought off and returned her energies to the task at hand. She needed to get free, and she knew that her magic was effective on this thing's inner walls, but not so much that it would provide an immediate exit. She needed more. Something bigger.

Then it occurred to her, in a flash of insight, tinted with what Master Jonin had said to her. Why did it matter what you called it? As long as it produced the necessary results. That having been said, it was time to apply a little science.

She slid Elkorine from its scabbard, spun the blade around into an Earth-grip and dropped to her knees, jamming the blade into the flesh at her feet. This produced a satisfying squeal form the monster's innards. Closing her eyes, she concentrated on the spell she wanted, the mystical tattoo glowing into vibrant color in the darkness of the creature's stomach.

Lightning coursed from her body, down through the blade of the magical sword and into the monster. She kept the flow of magic slow and constant, producing a steady current and channeling it through the weapon. It took only a moment before she smelled the hydrogen gas wafting up from the acid around her, so she took a deep breath and held it, all the while pumping magical lightning through Elkorine's blade.

She pushed and pushed, concentrating on the spell, channeling the energy, holding her breath. She pushed until her lungs burned and her blood felt like it was boiling, then she pushed some more. When she felt certain that her lungs would surely burst any moment, she changed tack. A shift in concentration brought a magical shell of solid rock out of the ether, surrounding her body like a

217

seamless castle wall. She closed her grip on Elkorine and conjured another fireball.

She felt the explosion all around her. The concussive waves compressed her stone hide in on her tortured lungs. She felt the sudden lurch of acceleration as the heat of the blast began melting away her stony protection, but she dared not open her eyes, or take a breath, not yet.

The cacophony of the explosion mixed with the sounds of the monster's protests at its presence and the feeling of acceleration continued for what seemed like hours, especially in her oxygen-deprived state. Still, she waited in tortured, pained depravation, until she felt that instant of free-fall.

Blessed free-fall. That was the apex of her trajectory, the highest she would get, it was now or never, and her head was spinning, with little white pulses of light peppering her awareness. It took a heart-beat for her to remember how, as if she'd simply erased the knowl-edge of how to breath in order to hold her breath for so long. Then, finally, her mouth opened and she sucked in mightily, the cool, sweet-smelling, magically processed air provided by Katrina and Exodus's water spell filling her lungs. She opened her eyes to see the monster's jaws rapidly approaching again, only this time it was her moving toward it as she fell back toward gravity.

This was the part she hadn't quite worked out yet. Landing. She had brief flashes of herself slamming into the hard surface of the sea's bed, hundreds of feet below the loose silt they'd been walking on. A tiny, red smear that no one but the toxic carrion eaters would ever find. She certainly didn't want that. At the same time, she had no idea what to do. None of her spells could save her, they were all combat related.

As she began to panic, watching the toothy, vomit-caked maw of the monster approaching her, she felt strong arms wrap around her body and a familiar, comfortable warmth pulling her into its embrace. She looked up from her impending doom and saw Ju-mah's bright blue eyes smiling down at her.

"How did you...," she stammered.

"Just a moment dear," he grunted, then his body heaved and lurched, followed by another split second of weightlessness and another lurch. Then they stopped. Jumah held her in his arms and smiled down at her as the Leviathan collapsed in a heap behind him and sank into the silt. "Now, what were you saying?"

"How did you get up there to catch me? I know you're fast but..."

"Shush you. I hope you don't seriously believe, even for an instant, that I would ever leave you alone in the face of danger."

She just stared at him for a long moment until she realized that the rest of the group had gathered around them and were all staring at her in awe. "Thank you," she finally managed, unable to think of anything else that seemed even remotely appropriate.

"Think nothing of it, m'lady." He held her to him for another moment, then helped her get her feet back onto the virtual ground they'd created in the silt.

She took a moment to slide Elkorine back into its sheath, then sloughed some of the monster's stomach contents off of her body before turning to face the group and smiling awkwardly. "Hello."

"What was that?!" Katrina gushed, diving forward and wrapping herself around her sister. "That was the most amazing thing I've ever seen before in my entire life! That was cooler than the time you convinced that griffon to give you its feathers!"

"Truly an amazing performance. We feared your thread had been cut short, Riana," Desse smiled.

"And quite brave as well," Xembak bowed to her. She blushed, turning her face away slightly.

"Guys, I'd love to take credit for it, but the truth is, I got caught unawares because of my emotions and the monster swallowed me. Everything after that was pure luck." She took a deep breath and turned to face Firiel, who was standing behind Desse and Xembak giving her a hard stare.

Riana pressed her way between the fair-haired elf and the reptilian, and presented herself before Firiel, arms held at her sides, hands open, and lowered her eyes respectfully. "Firiel. I'm sorry. I lost my temper and let it get the better of me. I want you to know that, I respect your abilities, and..." She looked away for a moment, then forced herself to meet the other woman's eyes again, blinking back tears, "I'm a bit jealous, that you got to know Ambrai, before the darkness took her. Kilishandra loved her, with all her heart, and the fact that you got to know her, while she was still the person my mother loved... Well, I just wanted you to know, I think that's why I've been so combative, and I'm sorry."

Firiel, and the rest of the group, all stared in silence for a long moment before Firiel finally smirked. She reached up and placed an open hand on Riana's shoulder, squeezing it reassuringly. "I get it Riana, I really do. And that was a pretty cool trick back there with slimy. But you know this soul-searching revelation doesn't change anything between us, right?"

Riana nodded, reaching up and placing her hand on Firiel's shoulder, "I know. I wouldn't expect otherwise."

Firiel smiled then, cuffing Riana's shoulder a couple times as the smile turned to a grin. "Alright then. I think we can be friends."

"I'd like that," Riana nodded as they broke apart again and she turned to look at the rest of her companions. "Okay, let's get back to it. This place is disgusting."

"It looks as if there is a structure over this way," Xembak broke the silence that followed. He pointed toward a small, cut stone outcropping that jutted out of the sea bed not too far away.

The mood was much different now that they could actually see something solid through the murk. Not that the thought of their destination was any more appealing... Being able to see it offered at least a small degree of comfort as they approached their next challenge.

"This is truly an ancient design," Desse commented, running her hands along the frieze surrounding the partially exposed stone door.

"These structures were constructed before Kalijor's current, known history picks up in any detail," Katrina confirmed.

"Known history? What does that mean?" Firiel eyed the robed elf.

"It means we've been lied to, most of us, for our entire lives. There's something bigger going on here, and the keys, and artifacts are a huge part of it. It's happened before, and it was covered up." Riana spoke as she rooted through her pouch for the crystal key, pulling it out and unwrapping it.

"Nothing can stay buried forever," Exodus sighed.

"And innocents inevitably become caught in the middle when the past begins to resurface," Desse remarked as Riana held the key in her palm and pressed it up against the stone slab, pushing it out of the way with no apparent effort.

"I don't know about the rest of you, but I'm no innocent," Riana commented, waving the group through the entryway as she held the door open for them. "All I know is that I'd rather spend the rest of my life running from the big dogs, than let any of them have these artifacts."

"That's odd," Firiel chirped.

"What's that?" Katrina responded, looking toward Firiel with a curious expression.

"I agree with her," Firiel pointed at Riana as she slipped past her into the darkened corridor with a chuckle. "I never thought that would happen..."

One by one, they all filed in past Riana, even Xanthe, ducking his head and pulling his legs in a bit, until Riana stepped through and the stone door closed behind her, leaving them in total darkness for a moment before a faint glow began to suffuse the space.

A few moments later, almost as if the darkness was adjusting to their presence, the glow began to brighten until they could make out the exquisite craftsmanship of the stone structure around them. They stood in an octagonal hallway, its walls lined with ancient symbols that resembled Riana's magical tattoos.

"What," Katrina wrinkled her nose and waved her hand in front of her face as a putrid odor washed over them, "is that smell?"

"Uh... I think that might be me..." Riana winced. The entire group turned to look at her. She was standing in a small puddle of bile and slime from the Leviathan's stomach. She stepped gingerly out of the puddle, examining herself as she moved. The rest of the group took a collective step back from her as she moved.

"It's okay, I think it all slid off whatever spell you guys used to protect us from the water when it was cancelled. She touched her arm tentatively, then sniffed at her fingers and forearm, finally nodding to the group.

"Speaking of which," Jumah stepped up to her and embraced her for a moment before turning to face the group, "where did that spell go? Can we cast it again when we need to get out of here?"

"I'm afraid that was a one-time thing," Exodus grimaced, "As to what happened to it, I'd have to put forward that this place has some sort of enchantment on it that cancels out other spells and enchantments as they enter. It's a fairly complex and ancient form of defensive magic, but not unheard of."

"That's not all it cancelled…" Katrina tried to cast a spell, but nothing happened. No mystical symbols shimmered into life around her, and no magical charge suffused the air. She even rapped her metal staff on the ground to try and create its orb of light, but that didn't seem to work either.

"Great. No magic or magic objects," Firiel chimed, sliding a sword home in its scabbard and then drawing a wicked looking hand axe over her shoulder. She tested the weapon's balance, then nodded approvingly.

Xanthe grunted, shifting his weight uneasily and projecting a feeling of deep concern and discomfort into Riana's mind. Clearly the enchantment was effecting him as well, and he wasn't enjoying it, although the fact that the corridor was significantly wider than the door had been, seemed to ease him somewhat.

"Okay, so no magic. No worries right? All we had to do last time was answer a riddle, so we should be alright," Riana cast a hopeful eye around the group as she spoke, but was met with a half dozen doubtful looks in response.

"Something tells me our luck just isn't going to be that good," Katrina commented.

"Alright you two, pipe down and let's get a move on." Firiel shook her head and turned to move off into the ziggurat.

Jumah draped an arm across Riana's shoulders, pulling her up against him as they fell in behind Firiel and Xanthe. The two other couples brought up the rear.

-41-

The dragon was larger than she remembered.

Riana shifted uneasily on her feet as the great, red beast stared them all down. Its hot breath washing over them in great, heaving gusts, mussing their hair in its wash.

Even Firiel seemed, at least to some degree, impressed by the creature. She had lowered her weapon in supplication, even though the creature had yet to address them.

"Riana Thorindal. Katrina Thorindal. Jumah Wataru. Exodus. I see you have found your way here at last." Its voice was low and rumbled through them like an earthquake, vibrating their bodies as if they were tuning forks. "And you have brought more friends with you." The giant red dragon swiveled its head slightly, focusing its glowing eyes on Firiel, Desse, and Xembak thoughtfully.

"Guardian. We have the key, and have come to retrieve the artifact," Riana stepped forward as she addressed the dragon. "Ask your riddle."

"You have much to learn youngling. When we spoke before, I told you that artifacts were best left alone. Yet you persist in their unlocking. There will be no riddle this time!"

Without warning, the dragon reared up on its hind legs and spread its wings, filling the massive chamber they'd found themselves in. It let out a roar that shook the walls and then descended on the group, teeth bared, and steam rising from its scaly lips.

Riana stood, stunned by the dragon's attack. At the last second, Jumah tackled her to the side, knocking her bodily to the ground with a loud huff while Xembak pushed Desse to the side, then leapt into the air, landing on the dragon's wrist. He dug his own claws into the tiny gaps between the dragon's scales, halberd held at the ready in his free hand.

In an instant, weapons were drawn and the group was reforming to face the dragon, who wasted no time in continuing his assault, his clawed arm moving through the air toward them.

Firiel jumped, pinwheeling through the air with her weapon dragging behind her, raking the razor sharp axe blade across the scaly hand before landing again on the other side. Katrina dived for the ground, narrowly avoiding the sharp claws, while both Riana and Jumah slashed at the creature's palm with their swords. Riana rolled to the side as she sliced, and Jumah braced himself for the impact, holding the points of his swords against the dragon and leaning into its attack.

The dragon shrank back from the onslaught, but not before forcing Jumah to the ground and flinging Xembak upwards, breaking his grip on its scales. The resulting movement tossed him through the air where he gracefully flipped over, spread his feet and tail out, and landed firmly on the dragon's back. He brought his halberd down in a powerful stroke, driving the blade home between the dragon's shoulders.

An eerie keening sound filled the room, its warble and pitch easily washing out the roar of the wounded dragon. Xanthe stopped the noise after the room seemed to pause, then charged the dragon, teeth bared and a roar of his own filling the room. The sword-like blade on the tip of his tail slashed back and forth as he charged, looking as if he meant to clamp onto the dragon's throat, but at the last second, and as the dragon moved to avoid the obvious attack, he ducked his head and made to dash under its belly, his tail slashing forward and thrusting into the dragon's exposed sternum.

The red beast staggered back a few steps, opening up its front for Firiel and Riana to dive in and slash at its forearm.

"This is not going to end well if we can not access our magical powers," Desse hollered as she flanked the beast, scimitar in hand.

She cut a wide arc with the curved blade and left a long, white scratch along the dragon's flank.

"Yeah, and I'm not feeling terribly helpful over here," Katrina added, brandishing her narrow dagger in one hand and Chavan in the other. She had yet to approach the creature more than a few paces, not being used to physical combat and every movement it made caused her to jump back again. Being squished flat was a valid concern.

"Stay back Kat!" Riana shouted over her shoulder, taking another swipe at the dragon's forearm.

"And you pay attention to your surroundings!" Firiel shouted at Riana while blocking another swipe from the dragon's claw, redirecting it over the taller elf's head. "I can't watch your back all the time you know."

"Nor can I watch yours!" Riana shouted as she ran past Firiel and pierced Elkorine's tip through the advancing tail of the dragon.

"Do you realize how much more effective you could each be if you devoted all of your energy to the fight?" Xembak snarled at the elves from where he stood, halberd still buried in the dragons back, as a handle to hold onto while he slashed at its neck repeatedly with his claymore.

"At least as effective as they are now," Jumah quipped. "Although I think their constant back-talk may actually help their focus a bit." He was busily dodging stomping fore-leg while slashing at the limb.

Xanthe growled again and slashed at the softer underbelly with his claws and tail, but a deep, rumbling bellow from the dragon, followed by it rearing up on its hind legs and throwing its wings out wide, simultaneously dislodged the entire group, tossing them like bowling pins in every direction as it stepped back, drew in a deep breath and belched a gout of flame directly at Katrina.

"Kat!" Riana shouted, throwing herself in front of the jet of flame, arms and legs spread wide to absorb or deflect as much of the blast as possible, and steeling herself for the inevitable, searing pain.

The room fell silent. The pain didn't come.

Riana opened her eyes to see the entire room had stopped. Everyone stood still, silently staring at her, Katrina a few feet ahead of her with eyes as wide as saucers.

Slowly, Riana dropped her arms to her sides, and turned around to see tiny tendrils of fire frozen in place, in the shape of her body as it had begun to envelop her. The frozen column of fire was easily twice her height and equally as wide. There would have been no chance of her blocking the whole thing.

"What is this?" she asked the room.

"You mean that wasn't you?" Firiel moved up next to her and stuck the tip of her axe into the column of flame. It passed harmlessly through the fire.

"Not me," Riana confirmed.

"Not directly you," a familiar voice added from behind the cone of frozen fire.

Riana took a few steps to peer around the face of the fire. The dragon had backed up another few paces and was now sitting on its haunches, looking down at them. If it had been possible for the creature to do so, Riana felt sure it would be wearing a knowing smirk.

"I did this?"

"In a manner of speaking," the dragon confirmed.

"Oh good, more riddles," she groused. The rest of the group began to gather their wits and moved to join Riana as she addressed the dragon.

"No. No more riddles. Your actions have proven your selflessness. The day is won. The artifact is yours to take." The cone of flame reformed itself into a swirling column of flame that spun around wildly for a moment, then receded into the floor, revealing a stone pedestal with wide, polished metal choker on it.

"Well. Alrighty then…" Jumah chuckled, eyeing the dragon, "That's a heck of a way to say hello you know."

"My apologies Jumah Wataru. The specific conditions of the enchantment must be upheld."

"And the anti-magic effect in this place?" Katrina asked with a sniff. She still clung to her dagger, as if her life depended on its presence in her hand. She was clearly still shaken by the entire proceeding.

"The enchantment is now broken. You may use your spells normally," the dragon replied.

"Thanks for that..." Katrina groped around on her belt for the dagger's sheath, finally snagging it, then looking down at it to make sure everything was properly aligned before sliding the weapon home with a huff.

"Alright. Grab your toy so the world can be safe and we can get out of here," Firiel grumped, glaring at Riana. Xanthe growled a warning at the elf, who simply rolled her eyes, then moved over to the giant red dragon and began poking at it with her finger.

"Alright. Here we go then." Riana moved to the stone dais and inspected the item. "Wasn't the original user of these items a man?"

"He was," the guardian answered.

"Then why is all of this stuff... sort of feminine?" She turned to look at the dragon.

"What are you talking about?" Firiel complained, "That piece of armor'd fit anyone, man or woman."

"I suppose it would, but what man would wear a metal choker?" Riana blinked back at Firiel.

"A what? Have you gone crazy?"

"The artifacts take whatever form the user's mind finds most useful," the guardian interrupted.

"So, I see a metal choker..." Riana began.

"And I see a nice leather jerkin," Desse finished.

"To my eyes, it is a fine, steel breastplate," Xembak added.

"Regardless, its function remains the same, and once it is worn, everyone will see it the same way its wearer does," the guardian explained.

"Well, isn't that convenient..." Riana turned back to the choker, and slowly reached out her hands.

She was about to grab it when they were all interrupted by a new, but all too familiar voice, "I find it exceptionally convenient, as I have no desire to be seen in anything quite so... subservient..."

The whole group turned to look toward the sound of the voice. Standing in the doorway was Malice and his entire band of brigands, weapons drawn, warpaint applied, and ready for a fight.

-42-

"Malice!" Riana spat, her fingers curled around the metal band, but still not touching it.

"Astute as ever," Malice sneered at her.

"You told me you weren't after the artifacts! You said you just wanted them kept out of the hands of your enemies."

"Yes well, it wasn't all lies. I still don't want them in the hands of my enemies. I really am fortunate that you're such a gullible twit though. Otherwise I might have had to deal with the dangers you faced on your way here."

"So you just let us risk our lives and waited for what? For the anti-magic enchantment to drop?" Katrina growled.

"You see? All that schooling really is beginning to pay off!" Malice grinned at her as Katrina fumed silently, her eyes narrowed and sending a stream of daggers his way.

"Just grab it and put it on Ree. Then he won't be able to take it from you," she finally managed to say through clenched teeth.

Riana nodded, then gasped. As she tried to wrap her fingers around the object to pick it up, she found that she couldn't touch the thing. "What the hell?"

"The artifact can not be claimed as long as its ownership is contested," the great red dragon rumbled.

"So none of us can grab it until everyone in the room wants the same person to take it?" Riana looked up at the dragon.

"That is correct."

"I thought only the 'chosen one' could possess the artifacts…"

"Silly youngling. You should have stayed in school. Then, maybe, you'd have a clue."

The dragon shifted its gaze between Malice and Riana, finally resting them on her and saying, "Only the 'chosen one' may unseal the items. Once they are unsealed, anyone may claim them. Provided they are uncontested."

"And you're determined to be difficult about this, aren't you?" She eyed Malice, who simply smiled in return.

"Fine. Then I challenge you to single combat!" Riana pointed at him. "There's no reason for any of the rest of these nice people to put their lives on the line. This is between you and I."

"Ree!" both Jumah and Katrina protested at the same time, but she waved them off without breaking her eye contact with Malice, who seemed to be considering her offer.

Finally, he motioned to his collection of minions, and they all seemed to deflate a little bit as they backed away.

"Be ready. You know he won't keep his word," Riana whispered to her companions as she moved around the the dais and into the open space of the room to face Malice.

"So when I beat you again, you will relinquish your claim on the object?" He smiled at her as he ran his fingers through his wild, dark hair.

"If you beat me. Then yes, I will relinquish my claim," she confirmed.

The two of them stood about five feet apart, staring one another down for several minutes. The words of Masters Gornin and Jonin echoed through her head.

'Victory is in the mind.' Master Jonin had told her the first time they had sparred, and he had tossed her cybernetic body around like a rag doll.

'If you can envision a clear path to victory, then the battle is all but won.' Master Gornin had suggested as he'd watched one of his students, a tiny little gnome woman with wild, orange hair, wade uncontested through a group of ten different attackers twice her size.

'A battle is like a game of chess, you must read your opponent's intentions in their moves, then plan your own moves to intercept them where they will be, not where they are.' Master Jonin's words to her before he had released her to active duty after her hands had mended themselves, just before she'd rescued Katrina from the oubliette she'd been imprisoned in for months by the man standing across from her.

These visions played themselves out in her mind's eye as she paced her breathing, and flexed her fingers around Elkorine's handle, violet eyes narrowed at Malice, who was casually swinging his huge, black sword around, waiting for her.

All her life she'd studied the art of combat, both armed, and unarmed. Then she'd worked to combine her magic with her techniques to create an entirely new form of combat. The fact that he'd beat her before stemmed from the same roots as when Gregory Shantal had beat her the first time. She'd grown angry, lost control of her emotions. In essence, she'd defeated herself. She wasn't about to let that happen again.

She stood there and waited for him to make his move. She suspected he would attack her all out, try and finish her as quickly as possible with his most powerful attacks. He may have tried his hand at subtlety, by lying to her and trick her into unlocking the artifact for him, but she knew that at heart, he was not much more than a simple brute.

When the attack finally came, she was certain it would be abrupt, and intended to intimidate as much as possible. She was not disappointed. He lunged at her, hands held up by his shoulder as if there were a weapon in them, and bellowing like an enraged orc. Mere feet from her, she saw the sword he wore across his back vanish for an instant, then reappear in his hands, held ready to strike.

Riana took a step back into a defensive stance, raising her left hand and casting a shield spell. One of her tattoos glowed to life and a shimmering barrier appeared just in time to stop the blow of his sword. Sparks showered from the point of impact, which Riana used to cover the round kick she threw with her back leg, catching Malice in his upper thigh and causing him to stagger to the side.

"Nice one Ree!" Katrina shouted, pumping her fist in the air.

Riana kept her eyes on Malice, and her senses focused, quickly sliding Elkorine out of its scabbard and into her right hand.

"You still bear the mark I gave you the last time we crossed blades," he taunted as he regained his balance and spun his blade menacingly.

Riana narrowed her eyes at him but said nothing, shifting her stance to better accommodate his new position, the point of her sword raised to around belt level.

"Nothing to say eh? I suppose it's only natural to remain silent in the presence of one's betters!" He took what looked like a drunken step to the side, spinning his weight at the last second to bring his black blade around, aimed at her mid-section.

Riana managed to get the blade of her sword into the path of his hidden attack, but his strength was much more than she had anticipated. The blow jarred her arm, shaking Elkorine loose form her grip. The magical blade clattered to the floor at her feet and before she could think about how to recover it, he was pressing his attack. A few more short swings had her ten feet from her weapon in a matter of seconds, and a wide grin plastered across his face.

"And now you've dropped your little toy too!" he howled at her, his grin widening to the point of being comical.

Riana just smirked at him as he advanced on her with a massive swing of his sword cutting through the air. He was obviously intending to finish the fight with the swing, which made her next action all the more satisfying. She quickly stepped inside his stance as he advanced on her, grabbing his forearm with both of her hands and pressing her hip into his as she twisted his arm and shifted stances, moving her hip out as she pulled on his arm. His feet came off the ground as his head was directed to take their place.

Shifting her weight ever so slightly, she staved off the breaking of his elbow, opting instead to further twist his forearm and force him to drop his own weapon just before he slammed into the ground with a cacophony of metal on stone.

"You little bitch!" he snarled as he rolled onto his knees and reached for his sword.

Riana's eyes flashed as she conjured up a focused, gale force wind that pushed the blackened metal weapon across the floor to

Jumah who stopped it with his foot, resting the toe of his boot on the blade and smiling at Riana.

"Come on Malice. I won't use my magic. We can settle this like civilized warriors can't we?"

Getting his feet back under him, he slowly raised himself back to a standing position, rubbing his jaw as he stared her down. "It seems I have little choice in the matter."

They squared off again, Malice's eyes narrowed at her, firing daggers of hatred across the gap. Setting himself in a strong, offensive stance, he waited less than a heartbeat before he came at her again, swinging his arms in a round-house punch that Riana stepped to the side to avoid, grabbing his forearm and giving it a twist as she wrenched it around behind his back. She just as quickly released his captured limb, with a solid push that had him staggering away from her as she settled into a defensive stance to prepare for him again.

Recovering his balance, Malice spun back around to face her, swinging his left leg toward her in a sloppy round kick that Riana tapped aside, only to get caught in the side of the face by the other leg an instant later as he reversed his own technique.

The blow sent Riana heels over head, sprawling across the floor in surprise, blood leaking from her nose and lip. She quickly shook off the surprise of the attack and rolled to the side in time to catch just the edge of his metal boot across her midriff as he attempted to stomp on her.

"Slippery little elf," he cursed at her, shifting his weight and throwing his other leg forward to kick her.

The short kick was not unexpected, and Riana managed to curl her shins up in front of the attack to deflect the force of the blow. She quickly struck her own legs out as he pulled his back, locking her ankles behind his planted heel and then rolling herself over, scissoring his pinned leg between hers.

Malice hit the ground with a heavy clatter and was unable to gather his wits in time to do anything about her heel descending on his exposed head. His nose exploded, washing his vision with red even as Riana rolled over backward and hopped back to her feet.

"I'll cut you to ribbons!" he screamed at her as he climbed back to his feet.

"It doesn't have to be this way Malice," she remarked, wiping at the trickle of blood from her nose and setting herself back into a fighting stance.

"I'll tell you how it has to be," he howled, flexing his fingers.

"Ree!" Jumah shouted as Malice's sword vanished from under his foot.

Riana took a step forward, slamming her open palms into Malice's armored chest with enough force that it sounded for all the world as if his breastplate cracked open.

Malice staggered back, toppling over under her attack. His hands closed around empty air as his sword appeared inches from where his hands had been, then clattered to the ground again. He hit the ground hard and slid several feet, but it wasn't enough distance to get him clear of her as she leapt into the air, extending a foot, and dropping toward his head.

At the last second he shouted out, "Enough!"

Riana shifted her weight, landing on her other foot, with the extended one less than an inch from his throat. She raised an inquiring, purple eyebrow at him.

"No more..." he waved his hands at her in supplication.

"Do you concede?" She pressed the ball of her foot into his throat a little bit more.

He paused for a long moment, staring at her with venom in his eyes, to which she responded by pushing a little harder with her foot. Finally, he gasped in a raspy breath and managed to say, "I concede."

"Fine," she nodded, pulling her foot away and bending down to offer him a hand up.

Malice rubbed at his throat and glared at her angrily, batting her hand away and shuffling to his feet under his own power. "This isn't over. I won't rest until I've got the artifacts."

"I'm very sorry to hear that," Riana frowned. "But I suppose I'll just have to deal with that the next time you come around."

"You think this is some sort of joke little girl?" his raspy tone turned to a shout as he raised a hand to point a threatening finger at her.

"No Malice. You're the joke," Katrina cut in with a mischievous grin on her face. She stuck her tongue out at him with child-like amusement as he growled at her. Unperturbed, she carried on with her taunting, "You come in here, after we do all the heavy lifting, and expect to just take us apart and get the goods for your own nefarious schemes. Well, we're better than that, and now you know it. So get out of here!"

Riana shook her head at her sister's child-like response, then looked back toward Malice and raised an eyebrow, ears perking up, "Go Malice. We'll have another chance at this later."

The man growled like a caged animal, but turned to walk away from them, back toward his own group. Holding his right hand out, his sword vanished form the ground, appearing in his hand again as he walked. "Fine. We'll go."

Riana nodded and turned toward the dais, wrapping her fingers around the metal choker. She saw the sudden movement out of the corner of her eye, a large, black shape, spinning around, and a long, skinny object lancing away from it like a javelin.

Instantly, she knew what had happened. Her heart raced, blood slamming through her veins in a sudden torrent. She turned on her heels, tattoo glowing and eyes flashing, but the spell was too late. The inky black blade slipped past her attempt to stop it, lancing directly for Katrina's heart like an arrow.

She took a step toward her sister, the world around her slowing to a crawl as the sword flew toward its mark. She saw Jumah start to move, but even he wasn't in time to stop it. The sword's tip was less than a foot from her when Exodus blinked out of existence, appearing a fraction of a second later, directly between Katrina and the deadly attack.

The sword buried itself in his body with a sickening, wet sound and the room seemed to snap back into real time with a thunderous explosion of sound and activity. Jumah caught him as his legs gave out, lowering him gently to the ground. Katrina shrieked and collapsed on him, wrapping her arms around him and sobbing as she hugged him to her breast.

Riana turned to Malice, her violet eyes glowing with power and emotion, ears cocked straight back and lips curled in anger, "You bastard!" A corona of energy sprung to life around her. Arcs of electricity swirling about her like a tornado as she stepped toward him, a huge ball of crackling, black energy forming in her right hand.

Malice smiled sweetly at her, his sword appearing in his hand again. "Next time, youngling." The dark blue gem on the hilt of his sword glowed brightly and the entire group vanished from sight a mere breath before Riana's sphere of annihilation passed through the spot where Malice had been standing.

-43-

"What do you mean you can't do anything?!" Katrina's hysterical scream echoed through the immense stone chamber.

"My deepest apologies Katrina. The blade has pierced his heart and its magic somehow prevents my spells from mending the damage," Desse's eyes were watery with tears as she worked frantically to make some kind of spell stick to the dying man.

Katrina seemed torn between trying to hold Exodus to her and clawing out Desse's eyes. Tears streamed down her face and her voice cracked badly as she desperately tried to get a handle on the situation. "Why? Why is this happening?!" she sobbed, finally deciding that holding Exodus was the more important of her tasks. She clutched him to her body, resting her cheek on his bald head and crying.

"I'm so sorry Exodus. I should have…"

"No," he interrupted her with a gasping, barely discernible word. His hand slowly lifted off the ground and covered hers. His grip was weak and losing strength fast.

Desse continued to cast spells frantically as the rest of the group looked on in various combinations of shock, horror, and anger. Her brow was covered in sweat and her face was taking on an unhealthy pallor as she cast spell after spell, trying to keep the man alive, but nothing seemed to take.

"...no other way... I'd rather..." He coughed violently, spitting up a thick gob of blood before finally settling down into Katrina's embrace again and forcing a calm smile back to his face.

"Don't go..." Katrina whispered to him. She could no longer see him clearly for the tears filling her eyes, but she refused to close them as he might slip away while she blinked and then she'd never get to see him again. He continued to smile up at her as his left hand disappeared into his robe and slowly drew out his grimoire, ancient and powerful runes were embossed all across the leather-bound tome, which looked pristine and new, despite its years of adventures. He slid the book over his wounded chest and slowly moved Katrina's hand to rest atop the book, still clenching his weakening hand to hers. "You know... I always... loved you."

"Don't go Exodus. I don't want you to leave me," she sobbed.

"It's time... Take... Take my grimoire... keep it... use it..."

Katrina shook her head, almost violently, tears raining down on his face as he smiled serenely up at her. "No. Not like this..."

"Take care of her..." His eyes drifted around the rest of the group.

Riana nodded solemnly, pulling her sister tightly up against her.

"We will," Jumah replied. "It was an honor to have known you."

"And to have fought at your side," Xembak added in a quiet tone.

"You weren't too bad... for a human finger-wiggler," Firiel even managed to sound a little broken up as she knelt beside him and rested a hand on his thigh. "We'll watch them both for you," she added.

Desse's chanting stopped and she panted, "There is nothing more I can do. My magic is exhausted and nothing will affect the wound. I am sorry Exodus."

He simply nodded to her, then looked back up to Katrina. "Keep it. Use it. I'll always love you. Always be with you..."

Their eyes locked, and his hand clenched around hers as his body convulsed. A flash of brilliant light flashed through the room, gone again as quickly as it had come, leaving them all to wonder if they'd seen it at all. When the light faded, his body lay lifeless on the ground, head still cradled in Katrina's arms and eyes closed serenely.

She clutched his body to her and cried until long after the tears had dried up. Riana sat next to her, sharing her tears and holding her while they mourned.

-44-

The ceiling of Vincent's bedroom came into focus with the speed of a rubber band snapping back to its relaxed state. It even came along with the same brief distortion one might see if that same rubber band was clear, and one were looking through it as it relaxed.

Riana lay there for a few moments, letting her senses come back to her. It had been one day, Kalijor time, since Exodus had been killed by Malice's treacherous attack. It had taken a while for the group to gather their wits and regroup. When they finally did, they used a portal ring to get back to Rathalon. From there, they carried his body straight through the Cohai portal where they met Master Gornin, who answered the door so quickly that it might have given a person the impression that he'd been expecting them all along.

He'd ushered them through the halls and into a room where Katrina was given everything she needed to properly prepare his body for the customary cremation ceremony. Riana, Jumah, Desse, Xembak, and even Firiel had been shown to a large rock garden in the grounds outside the keep where they set about building a pyre of wood on which to set his body.

With two days until the fire would be lit, and Katrina, as the closest thing Exodus had to family in Kalijor, performing the three-day ritual that was used to send mages off into the afterlife, Riana and Jumah had decided to take a bit of a break and see what was going on in the real world.

She had finally clasped the metal choker around her neck just before logging out and, as such, had not done anything to try and discover what powers it may hold. Although, she did get a chance to see Gornin's disapproving look just before she had winked out of the world.

"Hey you," Vincent's soft tenor called from the doorway.

Riana shifted her eyes from the ceiling to the door where Vincent stood, leaning into the frame with his palms pressed against it. The look on his face was a solemn one.

"Hey," she replied, reaching across her body with her left hand to pull the ODN cable out of the port in her right wrist. She watched the little port quickly disappear beneath a layer of smooth skin, the vibrant blue elven rune tattooed there reforming along with the flesh, then returned her eyes to Vincent.

He was wearing a pair of comfortable pants and a simple t-shirt. His long, blonde hair was pulled into that same pony-tail and his bright, blue eyes told her that he would do whatever she needed him to.

"Why do you still game from the couch when I'm here?" She rubbed her eyes with the back of a hand, ears twitching slightly. She shifted her feet off the edge of the bed, sitting up and stretching her arms.

"It just doesn't seem… gentlemanly I guess," he finally managed after a moment's consideration.

She stood up and crossed the room to him, leaning against the inside of the door frame so that their faces ended up mere inches apart. "You are a prince among men Mister Torres," she smiled at him.

"Yeah, probably not so princely as you might imagine. But it's still a nice sentiment." He smiled. "Can I get you anything?"

"Would it be strange if I asked you to just hold me for a while?" she felt guilty asking, but recent events had left her feeling a little needy.

"Of course," he responded with ease, shifting his weight away from the door frame and quickly encircling her waist with an arm.

He pulled her into a tender embrace and just stood there in the doorway with her for half an hour.

"We should probably get something to eat," she managed to get out after a while. Her cheek was pressed into his shoulder, arms wrapped around him, and fingers tracing little circles on his back.

"We're out of groceries. Unless you want rehydrated noodles," he frowned.

"Let's go out then. We've still got about six hours until the ceremony."

"Are you feeling up to it?"

She thought about it for a moment, then nodded. Even if she wasn't, they'd been plugged in for a long while now, and their bodies needed sustenance. "I'll manage. Besides, I think being out in public with some living, breathing people, could help a bit."

He nodded his agreement, then released her after a short squeeze of affection. "Okay. You get first crack at the shower. I'm going to make a few calls real quick, get caught up on business."

"Okay," she smiled at him, then stole a quick kiss before turning toward the bathroom.

The steaming water of the shower felt amazing against her skin. It was far hotter than any normal person could even hope to handle and it caused her skin to ripple in an amazing display of red and white patterns as the scalding water turned her naked body bright red and the nanites in her blood just as quickly repaired the damage. There was something about that slight tingle of almost-pain that she experienced that made her feel so much more alive. It probably had to do with the fact that it was the closest thing she could normally feel to physical pain, since those same nanites so rapidly shut down the information relays that caused her brain to register the pain that her body felt.

She hated to think that she might actually be some sort of masochist, but with a fabricated body such as hers, she found that she sometimes needed those sensations to balance out how sensitive she was to everything else. She could feel a person's pulse through layers of clothing, or even thin armor, her sense of touch was so sensitive, but if she managed to prick her finger, that same sense of touch would just stop working. Any feelings of physical pain just never made it to her brain, only the sense that she needed to change the situation to stop herself being damaged remained. The pressure of a survival instinct had somehow taken the place of that simplest of sensations that had helped the human race survive fifty-thousand years of evolution.

As she turned her face directly into the path of the scalding water and let the rippling wave of almost-pain light up her forehead and cheeks, thoughts rolled through her mind about Malice and what he had done. How easily he had taken her in and convinced her that he was being altruistic. The thought that she might become embittered to the world scared her even more than the potential of any masochistic leanings she may be experiencing.

How could she have been so easily taken in? Was she that desperate to find good in everyone? The control panel in the shower beeped at her, shaking her out of her thoughts. A brief inspection of the offending swatch of wall revealed that she was about to use up Vincent's water quota for the day. With a grunt of irritation, she waived the back of her right hand over the panel and keyed in a purchase order for another hundred units of water on the holographic interface, then tried as hard as she could to get back to her train of thought, but something else suddenly occurred to her, and within seconds she was out of the shower. She left a river of water in her wake as she bounded across the bedroom and planted herself, stark naked, at the computer terminal.

She keyed in a few commands on the floating holographic interface, then waited for a response like a kid waiting at at the edge of the counter for a cake to be cut.

At last, the terminal beeped at her, flashing a response.

APRIL> Hello Riana.

She grinned, as she pulled up the keyboard and typed her response.

RSThorindal> Hey APRIL. How are you and Daray doing?

APRIL> She is adjusting to circumstances. The running seems to help.

RSThorindal> That's good. Anything I can do?

APRIL> Not at the moment. Although there is a situation developing in Tranquility that may require some assistance later. It remains to be seen what will happen, however. You said you needed some assistance?

RSThorindal> Alright, let me know if I can help out. Yes, I was wondering if you had a few minutes to do a hack for me. It's a private security feed in På-rymi. A little gym on the corner of 381st and Clinton. I'm looking for video record of a particular individual.

APRIL> Time-frame?

RSThorindal> This would be about seven days ago. I was there with Vincent, mid-day.

APRIL> Subject?

RSThorindal> Gregory Shantal.

APRIL> I have located the network in question, beginning entry.

"Riana? Are you alright?" Vincent stepped into the room and his eyes followed the wet trail across the room to her naked body, perched on the edge of the chair in front of the terminal. He quickly averted his eyes, looking back toward the bathroom, "You left the water on?"

Riana looked over her shoulder at him and smirked. "You know, it isn't as if you've never seen me naked."

He turned a wonderful shade of crimson. Very close to the color her skin had been under the scalding water. "That's not the point. Why did you leave the water on?"

"I'm sorry, I had a flash of insight and spaced it out on my way to the terminal," she waved his complaint away.

"I've got to be close to my limit. I'd better get in there," he pulled his shirt off and looked over at her. "If you're done that is."

She looked up at him again and smiled, "Yeah, have at it."

He nodded to her, without looking at her again, then disappeared into the steamy bathroom. A moment later he swore rather colorfully, then shouted, "Holy hell woman! You were actually standing in this water?"

She chuckled at him but didn't get a chance to respond before the display floating in front of her changed.

APRIL> I have breached their security. Fairly complicated systems for a gym. I have located you and Vincent Torres on video, sparring in one of the gym's rings.

RSThorindal> Any sign of Shantal?

APRIL> One moment, searching feeds from all cameras… I see no sign of him.

RSThorindal> Are you sure?

APRIL> I am certain of it. My apologies Riana. I would like to have been of more assistance in the matter.

RSThorindal> It's okay APRIL. Thanks for trying. I better let you get back to Daray.

APRIL> She is in the shower, exploring her new body. I do not appear to be of much use in that regard.

RSThorindal> …… I'm not really sure how to respond to that.

APRIL> One moment. I have discovered something anomalous.

RSThorindal> What's up?

APRIL> There is one person on all of these feeds that does not appear in any records that I am able to find and access. He does not match the description of Gregory Shantal that you filed within the Solidarity Online computer network after your encounter with him at Aegis Online. There is however, a resemblance to the individual we recently encountered in Neo-Tokyo, whom you identified as Gregory Shantal.

A picture of a thin person with a head of thick, unkempt, blue-grey hair and a massive scar, at least an inch wide, running across their lower jaw and neck appeared on the display. Riana moved the image off the chat display and over to the right. Suspending it in mid-air and enlarging the image with a flick of her fingers through the air.

She eyed the image critically, turning it this way and that to examine the person from every angle. Quickly deciding that not only was it the same person they had encountered at The Ether-Bean, but they looked more like Gregory Shantal than the person they had recently fought there. Then there was the strange scar. She didn't really know the man, but she felt sure that he would have had a wound like that repaired at his earliest convenience.

It appeared fairly certain that this person was Gregory Shantal. Or at least, what was left of him.

RSThorindal> Can you send me whatever you've found on him?

APRIL> I am sending it to your terminal now. I am afraid that it consists of just the video feeds I used to construct that image.

RSThorindal> Well, it's something at least.

APRIL> Indeed. However, I am in the process of searching video feeds for the surrounding area to determine where he came from and went to.

RSThorindal> How long do you think it will take?

APRIL> It should not take longer than an hour. There is a lot of footage to look at, but having a complete three-dimensional image to source from will help immensely.

RSThorindal> Thank you APRIL, this means a lot to me. If you or Daray ever need anything, please don't hesitate to ask.

APRIL> I will tell Daray as much. Although she is fiercely independent, so it may take a significant need before she takes advantage.

RSThorindal> Understood. But you can always call me.

APRIL> Understood. I will send you my results in one hour.

RSThorindal> Thanks again!

--End of line--

She turned to look toward the bathroom, and found Vincent looking back out at her. He quickly turned his attention away, blushing from the towel around his waist all the way to the roots of his hair.

It took Riana a moment to realize that she was still naked and that this was the reason for his behavior.

"You're being silly," she admonished him as she stepped into a body-suit. He'd refused to come back into the room until she was wearing at least some underwear, but the body-suit seemed to help him all the more.

"Maybe, but we aren't married, and we don't live together," he called from the bathroom where he was pulling his own clothes on.

"Yet we are intimate. You haven't seen anything in the last hour that you haven't seen, at much closer range, a dozen times before."

"Riana, it should be enough that it makes me uncomfortable," he poked his head out of the bathroom to check that she was wearing something, then emerged, fully clothed, and began dragging a brush through his hair as they spoke.

"Is my body flawed in some way?" she asked as she yanked up the pull on the front of her body-suit, sealing herself into the skintight garment, then reaching for a couple looser, more stylish garments to pull on over it. She'd selected a short-cropped top with long sleeves, and a pleated skirt that would hang to mid-thigh. The colors were that same opalescent black that her favorite duster was made of. She loved the way they looked to be any one of a dozen different, metallic colors, depending entirely upon the amount, angle, and type of light hitting them.

"Your body is absolutely perfect Riana."

"Then why does seeing me naked bother you so much?"

"It doesn't bother me at all."

"I'm confused Vincent. You like my body, you say it pleases you to look at it, and yet, allowing you to see it makes you uncomfortable. Are you uncomfortable while we are copulating?"

"No!" He almost shouted his protest, then seemed to remember where he was and lowered his tone, "I find you to be an extraordinary lover Riana. Eager to learn, and eager to please."

"Then what is the problem?" She slid up the pull on the back of her skirt, the seam disappearing entirely as the fabric knitted itself together. Then she sat on the edge of the bed and began working on pulling her boots on and buckling them up.

"Look, it's just not gentlemanly to be ogling a woman when your not... with her..." he blushed again as he spoke, his stance was uncertain and defensive.

"So you like me. You like to look at me," she began ticking points off on her fingers, "you think I'm a good lover, we have professed our mutual feelings of love for one another, and yet you are uncomfortable looking at my body unless we are in the midst of copulation."

She gave him a hard, accusing look that got him blushing even deeper. "I guess that's about the sum of it."

She shook her head and returned to buckling her boots with a sigh of resignation. "Human customs are very confusing to me."

"Tell me about it," he mumbled, then added, "if it helps any, I'm sure other folks feel differently about this sort of thing than I do."

"You mean other people are alright with looking at their naked companions at times other than when they are engaged in, or about to engage in, sexual activity?" She stood up, straightened her outfit, and picked up her mono-wire sword from the bed, attaching it to her belt.

"It's not really like that Ree. I enjoy looking at you very much." He set the brush down and looked at her hip, where the sword stood out like a festering wound. "Do you really intend to wear that on top of that outfit like that?"

She looked down at the cylinder, then back up at him, nodding solemnly, "Yes. And that confuses me all the more. If you like looking at me so much, why do you refuse to look at me?" Moving out of the room and heading for the front door, she said, "I'd like to try that Thai restaurant that you mentioned last week if that's okay?"

"Of course. I haven't been there yet, but I've heard it's really good," he responded as they left the apartment and headed for the lift that would take them down to the promenade between his building and the three others that made up the complex. "And I guess it just doesn't feel right to be ogling your body when you aren't in the midst of actively showing it off. It feels like taking advantage."

They stepped into the lift and she looked over at him as she hooked a hand through his arm and leaned into his body, "Honey, if I'm walking around naked, I'm actively engaged in trying to get your attention."

They were on the ground floor before the conversation could go any further, stepping off the lift into the crowded promenade and making their way toward the appropriate exit from the courtyard. "I just don't want you to ever feel as if I've taken advantage of your naiveté. You're still technically new to all of this, and I don't want to mess anything up for you."

She squeezed his arm and grinned at him again as they moved off into the city proper, headed for their meal. "You really are a prince among men, aren't you?"

-45-

Dinner was amazing, and their conversation drifted, finally, away from Vincent's chivalry, and onto more serious matters. They now had less than four hours, real time, until Exodus's funeral at Cohai, and their dialogue inevitably drifted toward the events leading up to his assassination.

"So the thing swallowed me, and everything went dark for a minute, and the next thing I know I'm in Master Jonin's quarters on the Tyconderoga..."

Vincent gave her a look that screamed out his doubt. "So... You had some kind of vision of your martial arts instructor..."

"No," she corrected, "I was actually there. I had tea with him."

"You think you were actually transported from the game, to the real world, physically..." He tried very hard to keep the disbelief out of his tone, but it was difficult, at best.

"I know it sounds incredible, Vin, but it's true. Only it wasn't like I was transported from the game to his place, it was more like my physical body was transported there and my mind shifted from the game, back to my body."

"I think the other scenario sounds more believable." He frowned, picking at the remains of his meal with his chop sticks.

"I was wearing the same clothes as I was at your place. And the only tattoos I had were the two on my wrists. Which also mysteriously appeared on my body by the way…"

"I don't doubt you Ree. I'm just having a hard time working out the physics of such a thing."

"Master Jonin said that it could best be described as magic, if that helps any."

"It might, if we were in Kalijor. There's no such thing as magic in the real world Ree."

"I see magic every day, Vin. This whole world is magic to me. The twentieth century author, Arthur C. Clark once said, 'Any sufficiently advanced technology is indistinguishable from magic.' I think that applies fairly regularly to my day-to-day life."

"Touche," he smiled. "I remain unconvinced of the magic bit though. So what happened after that?"

"When I got back into Kalijor, I used a lightning spell to catalyze the Leviathan's stomach acid into hydrogen, then protected myself and used a fireball to detonate the gas. The explosion propelled me out like a cannon ball, and you caught me. Which was pretty amazing by the way, how did you know?"

Vincent listened intently, then smiled at her explanation. "You talk about magic out here, and then tell me how you used science to defeat an ancient monster in there. I think you may have a wire crossed somewhere, but it seems to be working for you." He took a sip of his tea, setting his chop sticks down on his plate and smiling wider. "As for how I knew… I'm not sure really. I just had a feeling that you would be fine, and that you would need a bit of an assist to get clear."

"Well, thank you. I can't tell you how much it means to me to have you there catching me when I fall."

"It was my extreme pleasure."

She was about to respond when her wrist computer beeped at her. She waved her hand over the device, calling up the display, then pushed the floating interface out over the table so she could get a better look at it.

APRIL> I finished my analysis.

"Who's that?" Vincent asked.

"It's APRIL," She motioned for him to join her if he wanted to, and he scooted around to a closer chair so he could better see the display.

RSThorindal> Thanks APRIL. Did you find anything worth noting?

APRIL> I am uncertain. I managed to follow the individual in question from a small hanger on the exterior of På-rymi. He made three stops before the gym. One in a bar near the hanger, one at a small motel that is on the Conglomerate list of suspected black market locations, and one at a private residence. After he left the gym, which was approximately thirteen seconds before you came out after him, he went up the street, procured a private transport, and went straight back to the hanger.

RSThorindal> Were you able to uncover any transactions he made before he got to the gym?

APRIL> Unfortunately not. It is likely that he used hard currency for any exchanges he made.

RSThorindal> What about the hanger? Any ship moored there would have to be registered with the port authority.

APRIL> That is correct. Port records indicate that the hanger was authorized for the private supply vessel The End, registered to Tor Rayean.

"Tor!" Vincent exclaimed, his entire demeanor changing to one of agitation. "That guy is a real piece of work. I ended up having to dump Daray on his boat when I had to take care of an emergency on Ceres. Tell APRIL I'm sorry about that, would you please?"

RSThorindal> Vincent is here, he says he is sorry for leaving you two with Tor.

APRIL> His de-hurtful retraction is unnecessary. Daray handled the situation well enough. Station records indicate that The End disembarked moments after the stranger entered the hanger.

RSThorindal> Alright. Can you get me the addresses please?

APRIL> I have already sent them to your terminal.

RSThorindal> Thank you APRIL.

APRIL> It is my pleasure to be of assistance.

Once the conversation was clear, Riana waved away the chat screen and pulled up the addresses that APRIL had sent, along with the video footage she had uncovered.

She scrubbed through the video footage several different times, looking at the person in question's mannerisms and body language. She replayed certain segments several times, particularly when the person was interacting with anyone else.

"So, what's going on here Ree?" Vincent had stepped away, and returned with two cups of steaming coffee. He handed her one as he sipped at the other and waited for her to respond.

"I think this is him," she replied as she accepted the cup and gulped at it. The steaming liquid was half gone before she set the cup down.

"Wasn't that hot?"

She blinked at him, looked at the cup for a minute, then returned her attention back to the terminal and resumed paging through information. "I guess so."

He shook his head and continued, "So you think this person is Shantal, even though there are serious differences in appearance?"

"Appearances can be changed," was her simple reply.

"Right, but that extremely?"

She looked up at him again and cocked her head to the side, "You are asking this of a person born in a video game and migrated to an artificially constructed body. Not to mention the fact that we both know where Daray came from."

"Fair enough. But I think you know what I'm talking about."

"He's still himself. The way he moves, and the way he interacts with people. It's him."

"Alright. Let's say it is him. What's the point? Why do we care? He's off the station now, so whatever he was doing is done, and he's gone, right?"

"We don't know that until we follow his footsteps." She took another pull off the coffee cup and looked up at him again, "This is really good, are these those beans you were telling me about the other day? The ones form that dirt-farmer's shop?"

"Dirt farmer?"

"Yeah, you said he used actual dirt, not hydroponic racks."

He stared at her. Shaking his head slightly. "The things you say Riana, I swear, sometimes I wonder how you get along out here."

"What did I say?"

"He's a farmer Riana. Just a farmer. He grows things in the ground, so he's a farmer."

"So what do you call people who grow things in hydroponic racks?"

He stopped and stared at her, blinking a few times, then shaking his head in defeat, "They're called farmers as well."

"That would have been my guess," she nodded, taking another drink and setting the empty cup down. "I've got the addresses and info APRIL sent me. If we move quickly, we should have plenty of time to check them out and then get back here in time for the funeral."

"Are you familiar with the ancient proverb that says a person embarking on a mission of revenge should first remember to dig two graves. One for their enemy, and one for themselves?"

"Heard that one. I'm just trying to do a little recon work Vin. I'm not asking you to get involved. Besides, I really just want to ask him a couple questions." She stood up and waived her hand over the table's terminal to pay for their meal, then looked at Vincent, trying to hide her fervent hope that he would come with her again.

He stood up and pulled his jacket on, shaking his head the entire time. "I suspect I might live to regret this, but I'm with you Ree. I just have one question though…"

"What's that?" she asked as she threw her arms around his neck and kissed his forehead, a smile forming across her lips at his acceptance.

"What if, when you catch him, he refuses to answer your questions?"

"Then I suspect I'll have to switch over to plan B," she grinned.

"Do I want to know what plan B is?"

"Oh I think you know all about plan B."

"I thought I might," he sighed. "Well, never let it be said that hanging out with you is ever dull."

-46-

Her Majesty's Matron was quite the dive. Which was unusual for a business located in one of the mega-cities of the Earth Ring Station. Normally the dim lights, slashed seat cushions, and sawdust-covered floors were the sorts of things reserved for establishments in the shipyards of the rings, or even Venus Station.

Riana slipped through the door, garnering a leer from the heavyset, leather-clad thug sitting on a stool a foot inside. His look quickly changed to one of disgust as Vincent entered on her heels. Together, they moved to the bar, where a quick glance at the ill-maintained stools convinced them both to remain standing.

The bartender was a tall, skinny man, with dark hair, a forked tongue, and a slightly blue hue to his perfectly smooth, somewhat shiny skin. He smiled at Riana and cast Vincent a dismissive glance as he performed the stereotypical glass cleaning with a soft white rag. "Can I help you lot?"

"We're looking for someone," Riana replied.

"Aren't we all?" He eyed her up and down, this time much more appraising in the sweep of his eyes.

"I'm looking for someone in particular," she forged ahead. Presenting her left wrist, she taped her computer and called up the three-dimensional image APRIL had created of the scarred face. She set it to slowly spinning with a flick of her fingers and presented the image for the man to view.

He looked at it for a moment, then shook his head, quickly returning to the polishing of his perfectly-clean glass. "Never met-em."

"Do you have any other bartenders? Maybe one of the others has seen him?"

"Does this look the sort of place that can afford more'n one barkeep?" he grinned back at her.

"So, he's never been in here?" she grimaced.

"I just said he hasn't, love. And I'm fair sure I'd remember a face like that."

"Why are you lying to me," she asked, just as some music began blaring over the acoustic panels embedded in the ceiling.

"What was that?" he shouted over the din.

Riana was about to reach over the bar to grab hold of the irksome man when Vincent's hand on her wrist spun her toward the door.

She narrowed her eyes at him, but he merely jerked his head toward the door and mouthed the word 'please'.

She glared at the blue bartender, then gave Vincent a hard stare, before stepping around him and moving back toward the door.

Almost the instant she walked away, Vincent leaned over the bar and began speaking in hushed tones with the bartender. Even Riana's artificial hearing couldn't make out their conversation over the noise of the music.

She had no problem making out the words of the doorman as she approached, however, turning around to watch Vincent with her hands's folded across her chest and a grumpy look on her face.

"What's the matter baby? Not able to keep up with the boys? If you'd like a real man to take care of you, all you have to do is ask." His scarred, pock-marked face was partially obscured by the giant, toothy grin spread across it.

She barely even looked at him as she replied, "You're not my type. And I seriously doubt you could take care of even the barest of my needs."

Vincent was now making a few gestures, one of which seemed to be indicating her, followed by a vigorous shaking of his head.

She was so focused on trying to make out what they were saying, that she didn't hear the doorman's reply, until his hand clasped her shoulder, instantly changing her focus entirely to him.

"...said, what makes you think I couldn't take care of you?"

She looked over her shoulder at him, then reached up and plucked his hand off her arm by gently, but firmly, pinching his middle finger between her index finer and thumb. "Please, don't touch me again," she said, disregarding his demand for explanation. "I don't want to hurt anyone."

"And just what the hell do you think you are going to be doing to me?" he rumbled, puffing his chest out and pulling his shoulders back.

She grinned at him, finally turning to face the man. "That's pretty good! I like the way you got about ten percent larger there. You know, where I come from, there is a species of fish that balloons out to make itself larger like that. Of course it only does that when it feels threatened or intimidated. Which I am sure is simply not the case here. You're probably just having an allergic reaction or something. If you take a couple antihistamines and drink a large glass of water, the swelling should go down in an hour or so."

"What the? Why you little, purple-haired, pointy-eared..."

"I see you're hitting all of my best features. You're very glib!" she smirked at him, then made to turn back toward Vincent. She turned about a quarter of the way before his hand was on her shoulder again.

"Nobody talks to me like that! You're going to get it little girl!" As he pulled on her shoulder, to make her turn and face him, he was completely unprepared for the speed and precision of her reaction. But then, most normal people reacted about one tenth as quickly as she did, and were one tenth as strong to boot.

She quickly moved one hand up to the appendage he'd placed on her shoulder. With a twist of her body at the hips and a roll of the hand gripping his, she had him off her in less than a second. In the next second, she took a step to one side, bringing his arm with her, and adding a second hand to her control as she bent his hand up toward his inner wrist and continued to twist it slightly. She concentrated quite hard on ensuring he felt the maximum possible pain and discomfort, without actually suffering any permanent damage or disability. It wasn't as easy as it might have looked. There are eight bones in the human wrist, and the wrong amount of pressure, applied in just the wrong way, at the wrong time, could utterly destroy any one, or even all of those bones.

She moved around behind him, his captured hand twisted around in a chicken wing configuration and his bent hand still held firmly. Only one of her hands held the bouncer's limbs captive as she moved her other hand to his opposite shoulder and walked him forward toward the bar. He quickly complied, moving to escape the pain she was causing.

Finally, his hips pressed into the bar and she easily folded the rest of him forward, pressing his chest into the pitted metal surface. At that point it was all over except for the witty comment, so she raked through the quotes she'd heard during the various action films Willhelmina had made her sit through. Settling on one that fit, she dramatically leaned forward, looking into his scared eyes, and tweaked his wrist a bit to make sure she had his complete attention. "Was it good for you baby? Or did you want to go another round?"

"N...no... I'm... okay," he stammered, having stopped fighting back.

With a final tweak and a push that had his face in a small container of some sort of pickled meat, Riana stepped back from the man and resumed looking at Vincent, who just seemed to be turning his attention from her, back to the barkeep.

They spoke for another minute, as the doorman collected himself and tried his hardest to regain his composure as he moved back to stand at his post by the exit.

At last, Vincent smiled to the blue man, shook his hand, stood up straight, and moved over to meet her. "Okay, let's go."

"So what was all of that?" she asked as they moved down the street.

"That was everything going according to plan. Thank you for playing your part perfectly by the way." He smiled, "Now tell me something. Why are you so insistent about tracking down Shantal?"

"So he has seen him?" She brushed away the question, turning to look at him with raised eyebrows.

"Yes, he has, Now please tell me this isn't a revenge thing, Riana."

"What did he say?" she was beginning to sound a little upset, her ears were drooping lower, moving toward that straight back look that was indicative of anger.

Vincent stopped and gave her a hard stare, arms folded across his chest. "Seriously Riana. What is going on here? I love you, and I will do damn near anything for you, or in support of you, but if you are after this guy just to make yourself feel better about a fight, then I won't have anything to do with it."

"Just, please, tell me what he said," she glared at him as she spoke.

He leaned casually against the wall of a building and gave her a look of his own. "I don't want to get childish about this Ree, but I'm not participating any further until you level with me."

"Tell me Vincent," she bellowed. A few pedestrians stopped to stare, but most of them just gave them a wider berth as they passed by, eyes averted.

"Not until you level the field," he shook his head and tried to look nonchalant.

She moved so fast he couldn't even see it happening. Her right hand raised up from her side, where it had been pressed against her hip, and lashed out with blinding speed. Closing into a fist at the last second, the blow tore a fist-sized hole in the metal wall of the building, less than an inch from Vincent's head. "Tell me!"

"No!" He shook his head, looked at her forearm, still so close that he could feel the heat of her body across the gap. "I wont help you go after the man for your own wounded pride." The look of sadness on his face was crippling as he pushed himself off the wall, leaning close to her, he shook his head again before turning and walking away from her, saying nothing more.

The entire street had stopped by then and all eyes had turned toward the mad, building-destroying woman and the crazy-man who had the stones to anger her. He hadn't made it ten steps when she extracted her hand from the wall, watching the damage it had done to her fist and forearm disappear. The blood dried up and the armor weave that was part of her skin rapidly vanished as the cuts and scrapes caused by the torn metal of the wall, closed themselves.

"He knew," she said, barely a whisper as she stared at her arm, thoughts of humanity and how it was truly defined rolled through her head. Vincent stopped and turned to look at her, saying nothing, but giving her the chance to explain.

"When Malice attacked Kat in Rathalon. He beat her within an inch of her life before he dragged her off to that oubliette to rot. While it was happening, I was in a room with Shantal and his goons, and he knew what was happening in Kalijor, described it to me in detail."

"So you think he and Malice are in collusion," he took a step toward her.

She nodded, still watching her arm as the nanites even went so far as to repair the torn sleeve of her bodysuit. She was about as far from being human as a maintenance robot.

"It could have just been a joint operation. Plans made, and intentions described in detail..." He took another step toward her. Seeing the shift in emotions playing across her face, had completely changed his attitude, but he still needed to make sure she understood his seriousness in the matter of revenge.

"No, it was more than that. It was like a live update. They're either connected somehow or..." her voice trailed off.

"Or there's a third party running communications between them," he finished, taking another step and reaching out to touch the hand she'd been watching so intently. She jumped, but managed to hold still enough that his hand stayed on hers. "You know none of this matters to me right?"

Somehow, she knew he wasn't talking about Malice and Gregory Shantal. "I know you say that..."

"And you also know that I don't say things I don't mean," he used his other hand to lift her chin so he could see her eyes and smiled.

"I know that. I just..." She turned her head to look at the hole in the wall and sighed. "I have to wonder how long it won't matter. I'm not exactly a stable person."

"At least you're aware of that fact. Which makes you a cut above the rest of us. I love you Riana Thorindal. I always will."

She turned back toward him and put on her best, embarrassed smirk. "I love you too."

"So," he smiled, "the thinking is thus. Gregory Shantal and Malice are, at the very least, on speaking terms. It is likely that they each know, at least to some extent, what the other is doing, and if the connection isn't constant, then we know it can be made real-time."

"Right," she changed gears right along with him.

"So it stands to reason, that if we can get Shantal to spill about the link they share, that we can get some insight into how Malice is getting his information about us, as well as find out what the traitorous bastard's plan is."

She nodded again as Vincent gripped her hand and turned to resume walking down the street as if the incident had never taken place.

"And, if we can trace it back even further than that, we might be able to find out who's holding both their leashes," he mused.

By then, she was grinning again. It was certainly nice to have someone who was able to follow her thought patterns. It made conversations so much easier, and also served to validate her own reasoning. "That's exactly right."

"And you've known this for how long without telling someone about it? Why exactly?" his tone was sarcastic again.

"Well you know how I like to hog all the credit when all is said and done," she stuck her tongue out at him, shifting her arms around to encircle one of his and hugging herself to him in child-like fashion.

"Right. So on that note, the bartender confirmed that the guy in the image was there, and agrees that he looked a lot like Gregory Shantal on a very bad hair day. He said the man came in, moved directly across the bar to talk to a regular that 'knows how to get things'." He smirked before continuing, "Those two spoke for less than five minutes, and then the Shantal look-alike took off again."

"Did you get the name of the other guy?"

"Said he goes by Symon. He's in there all the time and is the local front-man for the black market."

"Which clinches the thought that the next address on the list is more than a cheap hotel."

"Right. But only if you have the right access codes and passwords to get past the guard dogs. Information which your escapades at the front of the bar were instrumental in freeing from our own friend, the bartender."

Riana grinned at him, saying, "So baby, you want to go to a hotel with me?"

Vincent simply rolled his eyes at her in response, shifting into a near run to keep up with her.

-47-

The hotel, or motel rather, was suspicious from the outset. Any establishment named La Morte, which Riana's countless hours absorbing ancient Earth texts told her was French for 'the dead', would be the sort of place most people would mark into the 'avoid at all costs' category. Added to the highly suspect name, was the fact that the low, two story, metal building was in an extremely poor state of repair. The corrosion-resistant material was horribly corroded, the small parking lot was filled with refuse and debris of all kinds, and the general, mangy appearance of the people loitering outside the doors to the individual rooms gave the overall impression that this was an establishment that catered to a much less discerning clientele than even a cheap hotel might like to claim.

"Nice place," Vincent commented as they took in the overall state of things from the street.

"Not really," Riana responded in a flat tone.

"Do you remember me explaining to you about sarcasm, and how people will sometimes say exactly the opposite of what they actually feel, when it is obvious how they really feel?"

"I do. Was this one of those times?" She looked over at him, trying to gauge his response.

"It was," he confirmed.

"Oh."

"You know, there is no absence of sarcasm in Kalijor. I'm often surprised by some of the more basic things that you just don't get."

She wrinkled her nose at someone walking by them, the smell of filth clinging to them in a cloud that would announce their presence a dozen yards away. "Maybe people just aren't as clever as they think they are," she suggested, then pointed to the main office of the motel. "We've been watching this place for the batter part of an hour and all of the activity that isn't centered around a rentable room, is in the office. That must be where we want to go."

"Want, being a relative term," he groused. "I really ~want~ to be at home, sitting on the couch with you in my arms, watching a vid, or a fire simulation, or wandering through the central park."

"There will be time for all of those things later. For now, we need to uncover the link between Shantal and Malice, and see if it leads back to someone else when we tug on it." She started moving toward the office, leaving him to catch up with her.

"I know. But still, someone as literal as you tend to be might appreciate the difference between want, and ~want~. That's all I'm saying." He stepped up beside her as they neared the door. Inside was a small lobby with a few ratty, old seats that looked slightly less comfortable than a bed of nails, and some equally offensive individuals standing and sitting about. Most of them gave no overt signs of watching the pair as they entered, although a trained eye would certainly pick up on the dozens of subtle movements indicating that they were under very close scrutiny, even before they stepped through the doors.

More so, the group was silently communicating about the new arrivals. While conversations never really stopped, there was a series of looks, eye and hand movements, and innocent, yet significant motions and gestures that spoke volumes. Riana knew they had checked them both out, and shared notes with one another by the time they'd stepped up to the front desk, less than fifteen feet from the door.

"Singles are seventy-five a night, or ten an hour," the rather gruff man behind the counter announced as they stopped. The man was skinny, but muscled, much like a habitual runner, although his overall look was otherwise very rough. He wore what looked like a genuine leather jacket, with an ample collection of studs, spikes, and chains. His body was obviously tattooed heavily, with partial images visible at his wrists, neck and chest.

Riana looked sideways at Vincent, raising an eyebrow, and an ear, questioningly. She almost asked him about hourly rates, but seemed to think better of it and return her attention to the man.

"Symon sent us over," Vincent replied. "He said the vending machine on the main floor had some killer house-brand soda in it."

The man's demeanor changed slightly, a twinge of his intimidating demeanor seemed to drain away as he responded, "It's pretty good, but the refrigeration unit's tanked on us, and the reader died a year ago."

Vincent nodded his understanding then added thoughtfully, "I'm sure there's an ice machine around. And I was told the thing would take tokens of some kind."

Suddenly, the entire room seemed to deflate a little, the ambient tension melting away as the thugs all relaxed. "He's right about that. Here you go," he produced a small, round, metal disk with the face of some bearded man on one side and an old temple of some kind on the other, handing it to Vincent. "The machine's just down the hall there."

They followed his pointing finger through another door and into a hallway, then moved down it until they found an ancient looking vending machine in a small alcove. It was old enough that it still had a coin slot, and physical buttons that actually moved when they were pressed, as opposed to touch panels or a holographic interface.

"I guess this is us," Vincent mused, inspecting the machine.

"So it would seem." Riana's ears twitched slightly, and she cocked her head to one side.

"What's up?"

"I'm hearing four people in a large, metal room of some kind. There's a lot of shelving, or tables, or something, breaking up the sounds. And they're all armed. A couple rifles, something smaller hanging from a shoulder..." Her ears twitched again and she closed her eyes for a moment. "Yeah, some kind of sub machine-gun. The fourth has something small and light. Could be an energy weapon."

"That's a handy talent," Vincent grinned as he reached out to drop the little disk into the slot. It fell through the machine's inner workings with a few metallic plinks, finally dropping into some kind of metal hopper that sounded as if it had a few dozen more of the tokens in it.

"It's all about paying attention to the little details," she shrugged, watching him work the machine with interest. She'd never seen anything quite like it before.

"Yeah, I'm sure the super-human hearing doesn't help much either eh?" he grinned as he pressed the button for the plain cola, then waited a few seconds and pressed it again.

After a second, the whole machine slid back into the recess in the wall, revealing a door in one wall of the recess, they stepped in where the machine had been, opened the door, and stepped through into a small ante-chamber. The door closed behind them and they could hear the machine moving back into place. Once it stopped, the inner door opened to reveal a large, mostly empty space, with metal walls, and a series of racks and tables lined up in several rows. They could immediately see three people, two of them standing within ten feet of the door and staring at the pair, rifles in hand. In the middle of the room stood another person with a small sub machine-gun dangling under one arm.

"Come on in," one of the rifle-bearers said, putting a half smile across his face. "What can we get for you?"

"Information," Vincent replied.

"That'd be Joe," the man responded, jerking his thumb over his shoulder toward the back of the room.

Moving in the indicated direction, the pair walked past tables and shelves loaded with weapons, explosives, computers, data crystals, old fashioned optical discs, real books, and a hundred other kinds of objects. The one thing they all had in common, was that they were, at one point or another, deemed to be illegal by the Conglomerate.

Riana marveled at some of the artifacts they passed. Things she had only seen in ancient videos, or read about in the Tyconderoga's rather extensive library. Her finger traced a gentle line across a copy of Alice in Wonderland, the cover faded and worn, but still quite visible.

"That's ten platinum," a woman's voice announced. Riana snatched her finger back and looked toward the voice, ears laying back. What confronted her was not what she expected. A young woman wearing a suit of reactive armor, similar to Riana's normal mission-wear, had a good-sized energy rifle slung over her shoulder. Her sandy hair was cut in a short, serviceable coif, and she had a serious, but not unwelcoming look about her features.

"Joe?" Vincent asked.

"You got'er," she replied with a shallow smile.

"We're looking for someone, and we understand they came in here a few days ago," Vincent responded. He then motioned toward Riana, who raised her arm and called up the three-dimensional image on her wrist computer. A slow wave of her other hand set the image to slowly spinning.

Joe looked at the image, then back up at the pair, appraising them from head to toe by moving nothing but her eyes. "What do you want to know about this person?"

"What he bought, anything he said while he was here, and if you know where he went when he left here," Riana said, narrowing her eyes at the other woman.

"I'm afraid that betraying a customer's trust is something that's just not on the menu here," she replied.

"We believe this person has connections that are directly responsible for the death of a close friend," Vincent tried.

"Doesn't matter chief. I won't betray anything about you two when someone comes calling later and I'm not about to betray him either. If we get a reputation for ratting people out, no matter what the circumstances happen to be, we'll be outta business, or dead. You have my sympathy for the loss of your friend, but I can't help you."

Riana took a challenging step forward, and Vincent's hand shot out instantly, the flat of his hand pressing against her stomach. Joe responded as well, lifting the business end of her rifle and aiming it squarely at Riana's chest.

"Riana, don't," Vincent hissed.

"Yeah Riana, don't," Joe responded through clenched teeth. A few clicks and movements from around the room confirmed that the other three attendants were joining Joe in the pointing of their weapons at Riana and Vincent.

"I can make you tell me," Riana eyed Joe.

"I'm sorry, but you can't," Joe narrowed her eyes.

"Come on Ree, let's go check the next address," Vincent kept his hand on her, his blue eyes imploring her to walk away.

Riana and Joe locked eyes for a long moment before Riana broke off the contact, then swept her eyes around the room, taking in the entire scene. Finally she nodded to Vincent, offered Joe a forced smile, and produced ten, tiny bars of platinum from her pocket, handing them to Joe, who accepted the bars with a skeptical look.

Picking the book up from the table, Riana showed it to Joe, then cradled it in her left hand and strode toward the door, Vincent trotting a bit to catch up.

"Thank you, come again," one of the guards near the door smiled as they moved past.

"That was pretty close," Vincent commented as the door closed behind them, locking them in the little room behind the broken vending machine as it was retracted into the wall to permit their exit.

"No. That was far from close," Riana replied. "What comes next... Now that will be close."

"What are you talking about Ree?" A worried look came over his face as she pressed the little book into his hands.

"Would you hold this please? I'll be right back." She pulled the mono-wire sword off her belt and activated it, the barely-visible strand of metal wire extending from the tip of the weapon, suspended rigid within the magnetic field.

"Riana, I don't think that..." he began to protest, but it was too late. A flick of her wrist saw the solid edge of the sliding door cut from jamb to floor. The cut was so quick, and so quiet, that it was possible the people in the other room hadn't even noticed it.

She quickly retracted the blade, reattached the weapon to her belt and gave the door a solid kick that knocked the panel into the next room with a solid boom.

-48-

Riana leapt through the doorway, instantly raising a hail of weapon fire from the occupants of the room, and causing Vincent to press himself against the wall of the tiny entryway in order to avoid any stray blasts coming towards the door. Riana hit the floor in a tight roll, causing them to overshoot her in their initial volley. Their fire exploded against the outer walls of the large room, which appeared to have been hardened against just such an eventuality.

Rolling back to her feet, Riana spun to the side, avoiding another hail of gunfire as she moved in closer to one of the two guards next to the door. Placing herself well inside his stance, the man couldn't bring his weapon to bear against her, which allowed her to trap the rifle between her arm and body. Shifting to the side and lifting her arm, she flipped him head over heels into a display table, and then ducked to avoid a salvo from the other guard.

She inspected his rifle as he lay on the table, back arched the wrong way as it tried to conform to the shape of the various objects piled atop it. It was a standard ten millimeter assault rifle with a couple illegal mods. She pulled back the charging handle, then disengaged the magazine and looked at the caseless rounds stacked inside. Armor piercing.

Shaking her head, Riana rolled to the side then ducked under a table as the the middle guard, the one with the sub machine-gun under his arm, peeked up the aisle she'd just been in. Slipping out from under the table, she stood up, and hurled the loaded magazine at the remaining door guard's forehead. The object struck him in the forehead, short edge first, and sent him spinning off his feet.

"Drop it!" the middle guard shouted at her, leveling his weapon on the back of her head. Riana held the empty rifle out in one hand and slowly began to bend as if to set it down. As she crouched, she dove into another foreword roll toward a table, flinging the empty rifle backward as she moved.

The weapon struck the man's gun, throwing off his aim and peppering her armored jacket rather than the back of her exposed head. The impact of the bullets added momentum to her roll, causing her to overshoot and end up crouched down in the aisle that lead to the exit. This left her well in view of Joe and her energy rifle, which made a high-pitched whine as it cycled up and a short electrical 'kawoosh' as it discharged a long, narrow lance of blue-white death.

Riana hopped upward, her cybernetic strength lifting her nearly to the ceiling, avoiding the blast, which left a smoking pit in the floor where she had just been. As she returned to the ground, she picked up a small appliance of some kind from the table near her and flung it in the direction of the man with the sub-machine gun, even as she rolled off the table heading toward him.

The small kitchen appliance slammed into the man, wrenching the weapon from his hands and launching him over backward with a grunt of pain. Joe's energy rifle whined again as it charged up for another blast, and without thinking, Riana snatched a handgun off the table near her and spun around to face Joe, pointing the weapon at her shoulder.

"Tell me what he bought, and where he went, or I'll stop throwing blunt objects and start blasting," Riana threatened.

Joe eyed her for a moment, then a slow smile crept across her face. "Go ahead. Blast away. Let's see who comes out on top."

Riana's ears twitched as she heard the faint sound of Joe's finger tightening on the trigger. Reacting totally by reflex, Riana twisted to the side, aiming carefully as she moved and squeezing the trigger of her purloined pistol. The sharp crack of the pistol firing could be heard over the quiet sizzle of the plasma discharge. Joe grunted and spun to the side, her rifle dropping to the floor. Riana felt the heat of the plasma blast searing the skin of her shoulders as it arced past her, burning through her jacket.

"You shot me!" Joe complained, clutching her wounded shoulder to staunch the flow of blood.

"I warned you!" Riana shot back, standing up straight and narrowing her eyes at the woman, ears cocked back in annoyance. "You ruined my new jacket."

Riana stalked around the display, closing quickly on her opponent. Snatching the rifle from her, she tossed it carelessly over her shoulder and then stood Joe up roughly, bracing her against the wall and pulling her hand away to look at Joe's wound.

After inspecting it for several moments, she shrugged, and plunged her pinky finger into the wound track, eliciting a howl of pain from Joe, who was unable to back away from her. "You crazy bitch! What's wrong with you?!"

"Shut up a second, I'm trying to find the bullet," Riana frowned at her.

"There isn't one Ree," Vincent said, approaching from the door. He stopped next to them and took the handgun from Riana, turning it over and showing her the empty magazine compartment in the handle, "There weren't any bullets in it."

"The hell there weren't!" Joe protested as Riana removed her finger from the wound, wiping the blood off on Joe's shoulder.

"Okay, that's pretty strange," Riana admitted, inspecting the empty weapon. "Maybe there was a round in the chamber."

"Yeah. Maybe," Vincent looked more than a little doubtful.

Joe started to slide across the wall while Vincent and Riana spoke, but Riana reached out an arm, without even looking her direction and placed a firm hand on her shoulder, stopping her instantly. "I had to try, right?"

"Did you?" Riana looked back up at her.

"Maybe not," Joe frowned. "I'm not going to get out of this am I?"

"Not likely," Riana shook her head. "But you should know that I don't want to harm you permanently. All I want is information about Gregory Shantal. He's been causing us a lot of trouble, and we think whoever's paying him to do it has much larger plans. Plans that we can't allow to go through, especially if they are going to keep killing our friends."

"And how are their plans any different than yours?" Joe narrowed her eyes, "As far as I'm concerned, as long as I keep selling stuff, it doesn't matter who's in charge."

Riana growled at her, then fished a tiny canister out of her jacket pocket, pressing a control on the side that caused a small nozzle to pop out of one end. Joe's eyes grew several sizes larger as she realized what the device was.

"Oh, lord. Those things suck," she groaned.

Riana simply shrugged as she unceremoniously jammed the nozzle into the bullet wound and pressed the actuator again.

Joe grunted, gritting her teeth in pain as a thick, flesh-colored, pasty foam oozed out around the nozzle. Pulling the device back out, Riana smoothed the patch out over the wound and then discarded the little device in a near-by waste receptacle. "I'm not going to argue with you. I'm certainly not going to beg you. And I won't threaten you either," she said.

"You really need to work on your bargaining technique." Joe frowned, trying hard not to look at the protein patch in her shoulder. "This is normally where the threats start being bandied about."

"I know, but I'm not about threats. How about this instead. I'll promise never to come back here again, if you help me catch the bastards that killed my friend, and beat, then kidnapped my sister."

Joe's face turned serious then, and she finally just shook her head once, adding, "Alright. What do you want to know?"

-49-

"So, do you have any information on this Doctor Ferrin?" Vincent asked as they moved toward the doctor's residence.

"Never heard of him before," Riana answered.

The building was in sight now. It was much taller than the buildings around the outer edge of the city, and classical in its design. Being mostly shimmering glass, it reflected the starry sky from the massive dome that covered the city.

As they moved up to the lobby doors, they were met by a cyborg, who gleamed just as brightly as the building's exterior. He was easily ten feet tall and armored as if he was expecting to take on a column of military combat robots. His face was very mechanical, with a barely-human set of features that looked more skeletal than anything, and eyes that glowed a bright, piercing orange as he folded his impressive arms across his chest. The look he gave them had no real emotion in it, but Riana felt sure it was intended to be a grimace of some kind.

"This building is closed to the public," his voice boomed. It sounded perfectly human, although amplified and very bass.

"We're here to see Doctor Ferrin. It's really important," Riana tried, her ears dropping down.

"Do you have an appointment," he bellowed.

She looked at Vincent, who shrugged noncommittally, then turned back toward the cyborg and shook her head, "No, we don't, but the matter is extremely serious and involves the death of a very close friend."

"No appointment. No entry," the cyborg grumbled, doing his best to look upset and menacing with his limited facial expressiveness.

"There's nothing I can do to convince you? We just need to see him for a moment, and you can escort us if you want. We don't intend any trouble." She put on her best pleading face, but her frustration level was quickly rising.

The cyborg shook his head, and said nothing more, simply staring at them like some sort of high-tech gargoyle, protecting the building from some evil spirits.

"There has to be another way to get hold of him," Vincent spoke quietly as he set a gentle hand on her shoulder. The singed flesh beneath the gaping wound in her clothing had already healed, visible now as a patch of strangely exposed flesh on her back.

"He's not here any more," the cyborg suddenly spoke up again.

"What?" Riana turned to look at him, ears perking up.

"Doctor Ferrin. He's no longer here." The cyborg uncrossed his arms from his chest and tilted his head to one side, as if he were trying to soften his look somehow. It came off completely wrong, making him look almost comical instead.

"He's gone for the day? Is there another place we might catch up with him? Or a number we could reach him at," Riana asked, hope welling up in her heart.

"You misunderstand ma'am. Doctor Ferrin is no longer here, as in, no longer on the mortal plain. He died in his office a few months back. Something about a computer accident."

"He's dead?"

"Yes ma'am. Now, if you'll excuse me…" He made to turn and walk away, but Riana reached out a hand to touch the transparent material between them and called out again.

"Wait!"

The cyborg stopped and looked over his shoulder at her, the long, thin, blade-like antenna that had been folded down across his back twitched to life and rose up over his head, little cameras popping out of the tips and focusing on her in ways she was certain had nothing to do with visible spectrums of light. "Yes?"

"Thank you for the information. Do you... know where he lived? Or where he was interred?"

"Riana what..." Vincent began to ask, but the cyborg cut him off with his reply.

"Funny thing that. The only reason I really remember any of this, is because just after he died, his home was ransacked, and his body was stolen."

"Stolen?" Vincent raised his eyebrows, suddenly much more interested in the conversation.

"Yeah. There was a piece of video footage, most of the rest of it was corrupted somehow. I'll never forget it though, big guy like Doctor Ferring being carried off, up a sheer wall, by a little slip of a girl."

"Up a sheer wall?" Vincent and Riana spoke in unison, turning to look at one another. That certainly sounded like someone they both knew.

"Yeah, somehow she broke into the building, got up into his office, broke out a reinforced window with some kind of energy weapon, and then carried off his body, up the side of the building, where she, and the doctor's body, vanished before security could get to the roof. All of the building's security footage was corrupted by some kind of virus, so the only footage we got of any of this was from a public security camera across the street there." He pointed to the building across the street.

"Was this a little blond girl? Maybe five feet tall?" Riana asked, holding her hand out at exactly Daray's height, which was less than five feet, to illustrate.

"Yeah, that sounds about right. You know her?"

They both gave him a hard stare, but Riana understood the concept of give and take, so she decided to tell the truth. "Yes, I think so."

"Can you give me any information? There's a reward..."

"I'm sorry, I can't. If it's her, she's a close friend," Riana shook her head.

"But," Vincent added, "if it is her, then you can rest assured that the doctor is in excellent hands and has been handled with the utmost respect."

The three of them stared back and forth for a few minutes before the cyborg finally nodded and responded, "Fair enough. You two have a good evening." He turned and walked away into the lobby.

"If Daray went to all that trouble for his body, then she will know something about why Shantal was after him," Vincent commented as they moved away from the building.

"Calling her now," Riana replied. She brought up the holographic interface on her wrist computer and flicked through a few menus before she found a picture of Daray and pressed the call button.

The screen hung there for a few moments before Daray's face appeared, floating above Riana's wrist and looking from one of them to the other with a cheerful smirk. "Hey Ree! Vin. What's up?"

"Hi Daray," Vincent waved, stepping in closer to Riana so they could both be seen at once. "How's your world?"

She shrugged and took a bite of something off a pair of chop sticks, swallowing quickly before she responded, "Not bad. Sorry I'm eating, hyper metabolism and all. I'm staking out an Aegis Online facility on Venus Station, so I haven't got much time. What's up guys?"

"We're tracking down Gregory Shantal and APRIL helped us use local security cameras to reconstruct his path here on the ring station. It seems he stopped by the office, and likely the home, of a Doctor Ferrin," Riana explained.

Daray's face grew serious, then moved as if she were setting down her chop sticks and looked back at them as Riana added, "We spoke to a guard at his office, who explained about how you broke in and stole his body after he died mysteriously, then rifled through some of his things."

"Are you investigating or something?" Daray looked a little worried.

Riana shook her head, ears splaying out a bit as she looked quickly at Vincent, then back to Daray again. "No. Not really. We trust that you had good reason for whatever you did Daray. We were just hoping you could shed some light on why Shantal would be looking for him."

Daray's face changed instantly, picking up her utensils again and taking another bite of something. She chewed it thoughtfully for a moment, her eyes looking up and to the side as if listening to something, then swallowed and turned her attention back to the pair. "APRIL says that Doctor Ferrin was one of the foremost authorities on artificial intelligence. He wrote her program, and several of the key AI systems that govern Kalijor."

"Why would Gregory Shantal and Malice want to get hold of someone like that?" Riana looked at Vincent for an answer, but he simply shrugged. "What could they possibly hope to gain?"

Daray looked off into space again for a moment, then refocused on them, shaking her head, "APRIL says she's not sure, but that there are definitely links between Kalijor and the real world. Banking, information transfer and storage, communications… She says that if they were trying to tap into any of those systems, or dozens of others, that they would need to get hold of the source code in Doctor Ferrin's archives."

"Okay," Riana grimaced, any one of those systems could cause major troubles all over the solar system if they were tampered with. "Now is when you tell us that you took possession of his archives when you took care of your business over here…"

Daray shook her head negatively, scrunching her face up into a cute, but disappointed look. "No can-do guys. We looked for it in his office, and at home, but couldn't find anything at all. Sorry."

"Does APRIL know of any other locations that he might archive his work? We really need to find out what they were after, and whether or not they found it."

Daray thought for a moment then shook her head again. "No, and we haven't had time to look for it as yet. Xavier's got us running around non-stop lately. She says that Doctor Ferrin worked closely with Doctor Hakiro Yamato, a computer sciences guy in Tranquility, as well as a Doctor Emil Frederick, geneticist, and Doctor Wayne Nelson, Cybernetics. She says most of them were involved pretty heavily in your construction, as well as mine."

Riana's face went pale and her ears sagged at the mention of Wayne Nelson, the little goblin of a man that was a constant thorn in her side whenever she was aboard the Tyconderoga. Aside from Doctor Yamato, whom she'd only met briefly on her first official mission for Solidarity Online, he was the only one on the list that she actually knew. "I need to get back to the Tyconderoga," she breathed.

"I'll let you go then, I need to get busy on this smash-and-grab anyway. Maybe I'll see you two around soon," Daray smiled.

"Sure thing. Thanks Daray." Vincent smiled.

"Yeah, sorry it couldn't be more. And listen, if you get a lead on Doctor Ferrin's archives, could you give us a call? APRIL says she'd like to have a look at her source code and she thinks it's most likely there."

"We will," Riana replied. "Thanks again you two, we'll talk to you soon." She waved off the comm channel and looked up at Vincent. "I hate that little man," she said, referring to Wayne with a shiver.

"I know," he wrapped an arm around her shoulders and pulled her into him as they began to move toward his home.

"I need to go back and talk to him," Riana's voice betrayed her reluctance.

"I know."

"I don't want to go."

"I know," Vincent acknowledged.

"Will you come with me?" She looked at him hopefully.

"If you want me to. We should take separate ships though, Xavier will probably load me up, and I could use the payday."

"That's fine. I just don't want to be stuck in a room with that tiny little ego-monger all by myself. And you can keep me form twisting his maniacal little head off," Riana said, encouraged.

"I know," he replied again, hugging her to him as they walked. "Let's go get packed…"

-50-

By the time the Neophyte Serendipity was cleared for a hanger on the Tyconderoga, Riana had been there nearly twenty minutes. The Kestrel was faster, by far, than the Serendipity, so Vincent was not surprised to see Riana waiting for him when he opened the outer hatch. What did surprise him, was the pained look on her face. She looked as if she'd been crying for an hour, except for the fact that her eyes, and face, were bone dry.

"Riana? What's the matter?" He quickly stepped down from the ship and took her in his arms, hugging her to him as she sobbed her tearless sobs.

"He's dead Vin. They actually killed him," she squeezed him more than was really comfortable, but managed not to hurt him as she buried her face against his chest.

"Killed who Ree? What's going on?"

She looked up, locking her violet eyes on his crystal blue. "Jax. He died while connected to Kalijor…"

Vincent's eyes went wide as the news hit him in the face like a solid fist. "But isn't Jax…"

"Exodus's player," Riana confirmed. "When Malice killed Exodus, somehow it translated back through the system and killed Jax here." She returned her face to his chest and squeezed him a little tighter.

-51-

In Kalijor, the passing of a friend is never treated as a time to mourn. That isn't to say that mourning does not happen, as it most certainly does. But family and friends mourn in private, before the wake and funeral ceremony take place. The three days that Katrina spent in private with Exodus's body, cleaning and preparing him for the ceremony, was her time of mourning.

Of course, she wasn't really expected to be happy and joyous when the ceremony began, but she understood the reasons, and purpose of the celebration, and so she took part, doing her best to be engaged in the activities.

The Cohai observatory was filled to overflowing with people on the morning of the funeral. They gathered around the pyre, with Exodus's body neatly arranged atop it, and shared stories of their experiences with the man. They all talked, and celebrated his life as family, friends, and loved ones.

There was food, and drink, and long hours of conversation that carried on into the night, and the night after that. At dusk on the third day, Katrina lit the pyre with a word, and a wave of her hand. She stood there next to Riana, their arms supporting one another, Jumah standing on the other side of Riana, and Desse and Xembak on Katrina's other side. Firiel even managed to look quietly respectful, standing alone, arms across her chest, quietly celebrating the passing of a respected warrior.

After his body was consumed by the flames and the gathered mages set off a spectacular display of spells that lit up the sky above the Uraval Mountains for miles in every direction, Riana and Jumah took Katrina, Desse, Xembak, and Firiel aside and huddled around a smaller fire to share their news.

"When we tracked Shantal's movements back to a few specific individuals, we rushed back to the Tyconderoga to speak to Doctor Nelson about his connection to all of this. That's when we found out what happened," Riana looked at Katrina with a serious expression. "I'm so sorry Kat."

"Sorry? For what?" Katrina's face took on the pallor of someone expecting to be slapped, hard.

"I checked the logs three times to be sure," Riana continued. Katrina's expression didn't improve. "The very instant that Malice killed Exodus, Jax died in his game pod of a massive embolism."

Katrina just stared at her, eyes glassed over and ears twitching slightly as if she were waiting for the punchline.

"What are you saying Riana?" Desse arched an eyebrow even as she rested a calming hand on Katrina's shoulder and squeezed gently to try and comfort her.

"Whatever is going on here, Malice and Gregory Shantal are in it together. We think their reins are being held by someone pretty high up the corporate chain and somehow they've found a way to assassinate people in the real world, by killing their avatars in Kalijor," Riana replied.

"So to demonstrate their new power, they killed my man, in two worlds?" Katrina's voice cracked and her eyes began to pour rivers of tears as her ears dropped so low that their tips nearly dragged on her shoulders.

Riana moved next to her sister and enfolded her in her arms. "I am so sorry Kat. I promise you that we're going to get to the bottom of this. We're going to find out who did this, and why, and then we're going to make them answer for what they've done."

She cast her eyes around the tight circle of friends and comrades, receiving confident nods and affirmations from each of them in turn. Katrina sniffed and managed to put on a smile of thanks for her friends and their willingness to help. As she sat up again, Exodus's spell book slipped free of the inner pocket of her robes.

Fumbling to catch the tome before it hit the ground, she suddenly leapt to her feet as the book rose up into the air and floated in front of her as if it were resting on a podium in a lecture hall. "What the hell?"

The whole group followed suit as Exodus's voice issued forth from the floating book, "Then it is agreed. Together until the end. Thank you all for your support."

Katrina gaped at the book for several long moments before squeaking out, "Exodus? Is that you?"

"Yes Kat. I'm sorry this was the best I could manage on short notice, and now it's all that's left of me. But it should be enough to be of assistance."

Reaching out slowly to touch the enchanted book, as if testing it to insure that it was really there and not some figment of her imagination, she finally just nodded, opening her hand and spreading her fingers out over the cover of the book. "Together then," she cast her gaze around the group.

Each of them reached out and added their hand to the pile atop the book. "Until the end," they chorused in the darkness, the light of the fire dancing across their features and the air thrumming with the energy of the unknown, uncertain future.